Other Books by Chase MacLeod

<u>Ascension Series</u>

Phoenix One

Skeleton Planet (coming soon)

HEMORRHAGES

A HORROR NOVEL

BY

CHASE MACLEOD

A Martian Mallard
Press, LLC Publication

Cheyenne, WY

Published in the United States by Martian Mallard Press LLC and distributed by IngramSpark.

Martian Mallard Press LLC

Cheyenne, Wyoming

Hardback ISBN 978-1-7339469-2-6

Paperback ISBN 978-1-7339469-4-0

eBook ISBN 978-1-7339469-3-3

Cover Art By: Chase MacLeod

Internal Artwork By: Chase MacLeod

HEMORRHAGES

Prologue

The building looked familiar. It was as if everything was shrouded in darkness, a murky haze hanging in the air. His heart felt as though it were trying to escape his chest. He could hear nothing but the sound of blood rushing in his ears. Nothing made sense. In his hand, there was a black pistol, and he gripped it tightly. He could smell burnt gunpowder.

Had he shot someone?

Something pulled him forward, toward the building. He moved in a half-crouch, pressing himself against the wall. It was oddly quiet. He thought this should put him at ease, but it did not. The silence terrified him.

He crept along the wall. He was getting close. To what, he did not know. He only knew that it was of the utmost importance to get there.

A scraping, crunching noise came from above him. He was being stalked. He stopped moving, hoping that whatever hunted him would move on.

It didn't.

Something dropped down toward him. Something with luminous red eyes.

And very, very sharp teeth.

Chapter 1

Carson Tanner woke up with a start, the nightmare clinging to him. Another night, another nightmare. He hoped it would fade as the day wore on, but most of his nightmares never did. Not since his father died.

His wife, Kate, slept soundly beside him. He quietly crawled out of bed to avoid waking her, shedding his T-shirt and sweatpants before pulling on his Air Force uniform. He slipped on his boots and made sure they were tied tightly.

Once dressed, Carson left the bedroom of his modest sized home and headed downstairs. His thirteen-year-old daughter, Irene, was sitting on the couch in her pajamas watching cartoons. Chris, Carson's nine-year-old son, was pouring himself a bowl of cereal.

"Good morning, Daddy," Irene said as she saw him come down the stairs.

"Morning, kiddo," Carson replied. "You need to get ready for school."

"I'm ready," Chris called from the dining room.

"I know, buddy," Carson said. "Thank you."

"I'm just trying to wake up," Irene said as she stretched dramatically, a mischievous smile on her face.

"Go get dressed, please," Carson responded, refusing to take the bait. She was being playful in her way, and he knew it. Irene yawned and nodded before heading upstairs to her room.

"Do you have work today?" Chris asked.

Carson chuckled. He was fully dressed in his uniform and the question seemed silly to him. "Yeah bud."

"Aww," Chris pouted. The sad look on his son's face pulled at Carson's heart. He'd much rather stay home with his kids.

For a moment Carson considered grabbing something quick to eat before heading off to work but changed his mind. *You know what?* Carson thought to himself. *Not today. I never get to have breakfast with my kids and I'm going to today.* Most days he would rush out the front door, often without eating, but this morning he opted instead to spend some time with his kids. He knew they would be teenagers before he could blink—Irene was already thirteen, and they would probably want little to do with their lame dad. He wanted to relish the time he had until then.

Irene came back downstairs a few minutes later, dressed in a strange combination of shorts and a long-sleeved shirt. Carson knew better than to question it. Irene was eccentric in her own way, and she never seemed to get bullied for it. Times had certainly changed.

Carson poured himself a bowl of cereal and sat at the table.

"Daddy, can we play *Super Mario 3D World* when you get home?" Chris asked. Irene looked at Carson expectantly.

Carson hesitated. He would love to play games with his kids, but there was usually a fair amount of housework to do after he got home, in addition to helping them with their homework. Then he would have to make dinner. Schooldays were usually a bust.

"Depends on how long you guys take with your homework," he answered after a moment. Irene started to grumble when she sat down.

"Homework always takes forever," she complained.

"You know the rules, kiddo."

"Yeah, yeah. No screentime until homework is done," Irene recited. "What if I only play a couple of rounds and *then* I do homework?"

Carson shook his head. "You know mom would pitch a fit if I let you do that. Sorry kiddo."

"Homework is stupid," Irene mumbled.

"I can get my homework done really fast," Chris said, hopefully.

"True," Carson answered, and then looked at Irene. "But it wouldn't be fair to your sister if we started without her."

"But-"

"You know it wouldn't be," Carson interjected.

Chris started pouting again. He looked at Irene. "Okay, but you gotta do your homework fast, Irene."

Irene leaned forward in her seat and opened her mouth, ready to fire back, but Carson cut off her retort.

"Hey, buddy. She tries. Rushing her won't help. You just have to be patient."

Irene sat back in her seat and closed her mouth, but not before sticking out her tongue at Chris.

"Hey! Don't stick out your tongue!" Chris yelled at Irene.

"Alright you guys, no fighting."

"But-" Chris began.

"I mean it," Carson said, though a small smile stayed on his face. "Behave you two."

After five minutes he had finished eating, gave both of his children a tight hug, and wished them a good day before heading out the front door.

A short drive later, Carson pulled into the parking lot of a nondescript building during a cool Northern California spring. His shift was scheduled to begin at seven thirty, though the clock on the truck radio read seven forty. It wasn't a good look for a Staff Sergeant in the United States Air Force to show up late. He may have been the most senior ranking person in his shop, but that didn't excuse tardiness.

He wanted to hold himself to a higher standard. He had high expectations but felt he could never meet them. Would he ever be more than a desk jockey? What about the kids? Would they look up to him as they got older and see him the way he used to look at his dad? Carson wanted them to. He wanted to matter. He didn't want to be another nameless face to fade into oblivion with the passage of time.

He didn't want to go out the way his dad did, sad and alone with the feeling that nobody cared and nothing he did mattered to anyone. It wasn't true. Carson had cared. His dad had mattered to *him*. No matter what, though, Carson had never been able to make his father see that.

Carson caught himself dwelling on his grief and shortcomings. He'd been told that it was dangerous to do that, but several therapists. Instead, he should try to sit in the moment, in the present.

Carson stepped out of his truck. The weather was nice and cool, though he knew that the temperature would rise as the day wore on. Carson was not a fan of the heat, but there was little he could do about it, other than keep the AC going. Fortunately, the derelict building had functioning air conditioning, usually.

The work center was located behind a heavy metal door sealed with a cipher lock and a keypad. Outside the door was a small wooden shelf where his coworkers stored their cell phones. Carson figured it must be torture for the younger airmen to go eight hours without having their phones close at hand, but he was never personally bothered by it. He had grown up before cell phones had become popular and he had never felt tethered to one.

Carson slipped his cell phone into one of the many slots, punched in the pin code on the keypad and opened the heavy door. Senior Airman Andrew Benson looked up from his monitor, his desk in direct view of the doorway, and gave Carson a brief hello. As Carson closed the door behind him, he expected to hear a comment from his fellow NCO, Sergeant Paul Booker. Instead, he didn't hear a word. *Odd*, Carson thought. *Booker* always *has something to say.* He poked his head into the office occupied by his four resident airmen, including Benson. In the back corner of the room sat Airman First Class Gabriel Hernandez, though the seat was currently empty. Carson knew that Hernandez was on shift because the young man's camouflage hat was on his desk. *No doubt at the bathroom.* Off to Carson's left sat A1C Alda Velazquez and A1C Arturo Trejo.

Both airmen offered a quick greeting and Carson responded in kind. It was another slow morning from the look of it. Velazquez and Trejo resumed their conversation, and Carson wondered—not for the first time—if something was going on between the two. Trejo and Velazquez had grown close in the three months since she'd arrived. They were close in age and seemed to share many of the same interests. Carson had already said his piece about workplace dating, but as long as it didn't impact work, he wouldn't concern himself with their personal lives. He only hoped that it wouldn't cause problems down the road.

Carson stepped into the small office he shared with Sergeant Booker and noticed that his friend did not so much as look up when he entered. Their desks were tightly crammed in the small room, leaving very little space to move. Carson plopped his hat casually on his desk and picked up his coffee mug, allowing Booker ample time to make his usual sarcastic remark. Still, nothing came. Carson began to worry about his friend.

Oh well. There would be time to deal with whatever was going on *after* he poured himself a cup of coffee.

Carson walked toward the end of the short hall of the work center and fished a disposable pod of coffee out of an unmarked cardboard box. The coffeemaker was one of those Keurig coffee makers, and Carson liked to supply his own pods of coffee so that he never had to worry about running out. Once again, as it had become a daily occurrence, the coffeemaker was unplugged, and Carson had to wait for the water to heat up after plugging it back in.

What's going on with Booker? Carson thought. Something about the man's silence was unnerving.

Paul Booker was easily seven inches taller than Carson, though that did not say much since Carson was only five inches over five feet tall. Booker took exercise seriously, and it showed on his large frame. He and Carson were both in their early thirties, with Carson being only slightly older.

The light on the coffee machine changed from red to blue, indicating that it was ready to brew. Carson opened a pair of packets of natural sweetener and dumped them into his mug before sliding the mug under the spout. He popped in the coffee pod, shut the lid and pressed the button to start brewing. He heard the machine whirr as he walked back to the office where his airmen sat.

They had a miniature refrigerator in the office with them, and Carson had supplied several varieties of non-dairy creamer for everyone to use. Three out of four of the airmen enjoyed coffee as much as he did, and he knew they appreciated the gesture. They even went so far as to replace one of the containers if they used the last of it.

"What's up with Booker?" Carson asked quietly as he bent over and grabbed a container of creamer.

"What do you mean?" Benson asked. "He seems fine to me."

Trejo glanced over. "He *is* being a bit quieter than usual this morning."

"Yeah, that," Carson replied. "He say anything when he came in?"

The airmen shook their heads. "That's so weird," Carson said as he shut the refrigerator and headed back to the coffee machine. As he grabbed his mug, he heard the heavy office door open. Hernandez was back.

Carson got along with almost everyone in the office, but Hernandez was an exception. Something about him was just…off. He asked odd questions and always seemed to be analyzing everyone around him. It made Carson, who was already perpetually self-conscious, uncomfortable. That, and the way Hernandez conducted himself. It was almost like the young man was a robot. He showed little-to-no emotion and often made comments that made Carson wonder if he felt empathy, or anything at all. He wouldn't say so, but Carson wondered if maybe Hernandez was a sociopath. Then again, he wasn't a psychologist, so what did he know?

After preparing his coffee, Carson shut off the coffee machine and threw away the used pod before heading back toward the refrigerator. He tried to quickly put away the creamer and duck into his own office before Hernandez could say anything, but he was not fast enough.

"Morning, sir," Hernandez said. He wore a smile, but his eyes seemed to be searching Carson's expression for something. "Nice haircut."

Carson arched an eyebrow and then ran his hand over his head. He liked to shave his head rather than go to the barber every two weeks to get a haircut so he would stay within military grooming regulations. He had forgotten that he had shaved it again the evening prior.

"Oh, yeah. Thanks," Carson said. "It was starting to get a little longer than I like."

Hernandez's brows furrowed, yet the smile did not leave his face. It was an odd expression. "I can tell you're the kind of person who likes to keep things simple."

Carson was not sure how to respond. "It's cheaper than going to the barber," he said after a moment.

It was true. Since joining the military, Carson figured he had saved over three hundred dollars, at least, by shaving his head. Honestly, he preferred the look. He also sported a thick mustache that he kept within military regulations, which Carson figured made him look more his age. Everyone else in his work center was clean shaven. Other people might have thought it was strange, but it was his personal preference, and he did not care if other people liked it. It was the one of the few times that Carson did not regard others' opinions.

"Right," Hernandez said, the expression unchanging. "Makes sense. Not everyone can pull off the bald look, but it seems to work for you."

"Thank you," Carson said slowly and then left the room before Hernandez could continue. Talking to Hernandez always felt like an exam and he often felt that the younger man looked down on him, not just literally.

As he sat down, Carson looked over at Booker. The man was staring intently at his computer monitor and had yet to speak a single word since Carson arrived.

"What's going on?" Carson asked. "What's wrong with you? You look like someone shit on your desk."

"Hey, Carson," he said, a ghost of a smile forming on his lips.

"Dude, what's up?" Carson asked, the mirth gone from his voice.

"Bro, have you seen the news?'

"No, why? Is it Korea? They getting froggy again?'

"No, man," he said as he stared at his computer monitor. "That shit hasn't popped off yet. Maybe never will, now."

Carson couldn't understand why he sounded so distracted. This was good news for him. "So then, what's wrong? You look like you're trying to climb through your monitor."

"Y-you need to see for yourself."

Carson stood up from behind his desk and walked around behind Booker's so he could see what his friend was seeing. On the front page of the website, in large bold letters, it read:

UNEXPLAINED CREATURES SPOTTED IN THE MIDDLE OF DOWNTOWN SACRAMENTO.

Okay, unexplained creatures. So what?

Carson continued to read further down and had to sift through the usual slog of bad writing to get to the meat of the story. He had seen many articles about "strange sightings," and he was ready to dismiss this as another one, but this one was on a major news outlet rather than on social media. That alone lent the story more credibility—though not much.

The story, put simply, was about an older woman who had been visiting the pharmacy when she saw *something* dash behind the building. At first, she said she thought it was a dog or something, but there was something odd about how it moved. It moved, as she described, "like a large insect or rodent."

It just sounded like the usual crap Carson had read before. So why was it being taken so seriously? It turned out that she wasn't the first person to report seeing something strange over the past few days. Other sightings, spread out across the county, have been reported. The descriptions varied, but the basic premise was the same. None of them had gotten a good look at it, whatever it was. It wasn't until house pets started turning up dead that people started to worry.

There were, of course, many theories flying around. A wild animal, perhaps? Moving in as we continued to expand outward? That was a popular one. Other people said it was a hoax or possibly an act of terrorism. This made Carson laugh because of the sheer absurdity of it. Terrorism? Really?

The article did not end at the woman's testimonial, though. Someone else, an employee of the pharmacy, saw it too when he was walking into the back entrance. It was his description that caught Carson's eye.

The testimonial said it looked like a massive grasshopper with tiger stripes, except it had large legs in front as well as in back. Carson thought the man imagined things, as had the authorities, but a drug test had shown that he was clean. It wasn't a hallucination. He said it moved faster than anything that awkward looking had any right to move, and it scared him senseless. He only caught a glimpse of it, but this was the first clear description that anyone had been able to provide.

The story made Carson uneasy. This guy described a monster, not an animal. Carson had always been a rather paranoid person with a very active imagination, so of course, his mind began to wander. Science experiment? Aliens? What was it?

He tried to dismiss the article and focus on his work for the day as he sat back behind his own desk. When he logged on, he saw the stories were all over social media as well, particularly Facebook. He only really used the site to communicate with his wife during the day since his cell reception was horrendous, and she would call his work number otherwise. It was less disruptive to use social media for that.

Posts flooded his news feed about mysterious sightings. He just couldn't get away from it! He minimized the window and instead turned his focus on the day's tasks.

Lunchtime came around, and Carson wasted no time leaving the office to go home for lunch, eager to get away from the ceaseless conversations about cryptids and hoaxes. He went home for lunch almost every day, which put his leased truck near the annual limit. He blasted the rock station as he drove home and it worked to distract him, at least a little bit. Traffic was unusually light for the time of day, and this struck him as a bit odd. Had he missed something?

As he drove along the road, he passed a field with cows grazing lazily. He could swear there were more cows on the base than people.

Carson pulled into the driveway in front of his house and sat in the truck for a moment. He could say he was waiting for the song to end—and maybe he had been, partially—but the news article kept running through his head. What the hell was going on? Had his wife heard anything? She hadn't said anything while Carson was at work, but his internet connection was often spotty at the office. He hadn't received any emails from her that day, either.

He got out of his truck and walked into the house, half expecting to see his diminutive wife, Kate Connelly, on the couch watching a movie or playing a game. Something to pass the time while the kids were at school and Carson was at work, opting to wait until they were home so that *everyone* would be involved in the housework. She never did it when nobody was home.

Today she was standing in the dining room, staring out into the backyard. Carson sighed and shook his head as he took in his surroundings. The house, as usual, was in disarray. He knew that after work he would be expected to clean up and get everything back in order. He'd passed it off as depression at first.

"Hi," Carson said as he shut the door behind. She didn't move. Carson doubted she heard him, so he said hello again.

"Oh, hi," she said, turning to face him. The first thing Carson noticed was that she was unusually pale. "Home for lunch?"

"Yeah," he said as he walked into the dining room and took off his uniform jacket. Carson draped it over the back of his chair at the dining table and then walked over to where she was standing. "Are you alright?"

"I saw something behind the yard. The dogs started freaking out," she said. "What's going on? I keep seeing things on Facebook about 'sightings.'"

"I don't know," Carson answered as walked to look out into the backyard, wishing he could say something else. "I have no idea. People are talking about an alien invasion or something, but I haven't heard anything about it at work. Not officially. People are talking about it at work, too, but I didn't see anything from leadership about it. We didn't have a briefing or anything. I think people are just paranoid."

"Do you think the kids are safe at school? What if it's not a hoax?"

"If it were a big deal the school would call," he reasoned. Yet, a nagging feeling began to creep up on him, breeding doubt. What if the school had tried to call? Carson checked his phone for a voicemail but did not have a notification for one. "I don't want them to panic or anything. It was probably just a dog that got loose."

Instead of opting to pick up their kids from school, much to Kate's dismay, Carson headed back to work after he finished a quick lunch, but his mind would not stop wandering during his fifteen-minute commute. What if, for once, the hype was true? What if something *was* happening that couldn't be readily explained?

A large part of Carson hoped that it was just a hoax perpetuated by the media to cause panic or bring fame to the people who saw the "creatures." There was a part of him—a part he suspected had always been hiding within his psyche—that hoped the stories were true. Was life really that mundane? Was his life so boring that he *wanted* the myths and mysteries to become real? Carson imagined he was not the only person who had felt this way, though.

How many people hoped that the stories of Bigfoot and the Loch Ness Monster were true? Booker was one of them. Carson had heard him obsess over weird creatures and conspiracy theories. He wouldn't be surprised if most people *wanted* these things to be real. *Maybe I do, too, come to think of it.*

The thoughts disturbed him as he drove along silently down the road. Carson had decided not to turn on the stereo this time, which often happened when he became tense or irritable. Instead, he allowed his mind to wander and ideas to form. Crazy theories and wild fantasies began cropping up, some not altogether unpleasant while others were downright terrifying. He wondered silently if they were amid an alien invasion, but why wouldn't the military be mobilizing if that were the case? They—meaning the generals and politicians—likely didn't believe the wild stories themselves. Why waste money on a hoax? Carson imagined that the people in charge would wait until it was too late to decide to act, in which case they would have to protect themselves and to hell with everyone else. It, unfortunately, sounded far too plausible.

He arrived back at work a little later than he had intended, but there wasn't anyone in the office that would care much. That was just the nature of his job—a lax workplace that only became stressful a few times a year. As long as they did their jobs their hours did not matter much.

When he walked into the office, everyone was still staring at their computer monitors, transfixed by whatever they were reading or watching. Carson didn't want think too much about it as he walked into his shared office with Paul Booker, but his colleague was staring at his monitor as well. *Now they're* all *doing it.*

It was Paul's silence and the expression on his face that worried Carson. Paul was not a quiet person. He had a kind of jubilant energy that was infectious, despite how busy things were or how stressed he may be. This change in demeanor was Carson's first indication that something might be *very* wrong. In fact, everyone was acting odd.

"Dude, Booker, what's wrong?" he asked, not for the first time that day. "You're acting a bit strange."

"There have been more stories coming in," he said without looking up. "More sightings. The part that worries me is they're not all the same, but similar. It's like people are seeing different kinds of monsters now. There's even been a death that people are claiming was caused by one of those *things.*"

"Really?" was all Carson could muster in response. This development only served to increase his paranoia, which some people would say was a bit high to begin with. But could it be real?

"Some guy was found mauled in an alley," Booker continued. "Cops are saying it was some kind of animal, but people all over the internet are saying the creatures that people have been seeing had done it. Everyone is really freaking out."

"Mass hysteria?" Carson said simply as if that was a viable conclusion. "I bet there's something else going on that they don't want us to know about. I mean, it wouldn't be the first time."

"Maybe," Paul muttered, but he sounded about as convinced as Carson felt. "I'm not sure this time, though."

"Don't tell me you actually *believe* these people, man."

"Why not? It's not like it's a small group of people claiming to have seen things."

Carson sat at his desk. How could he respond? What could he say? Booker had a point.

"Has leadership said anything?" Carson asked, though he doubted they had.

"I don't know," Booker said. "Outlook has been up and down all day. I haven't gotten any new emails in the last hour or so."

"Let me check mine," Carson said as he logged back into his computer. "It's been working okay for me, mostly."

He punched in his password and waited as the computer logged him in. The computers they had to work with were agonizingly slow, as was the network they were connected to. He had grown up when the internet was just taking off, and people were starting to have personal computers. Of course, at that time, everything was incredibly slow. The computers he had at work would have seemed like they were hopped up on cocaine compared to the old ones Carson had as a kid, but he had gotten used to the improvements in technology. He liked it when his computer booted up in under a minute.

His email took a moment to update the inbox, and Carson saw that there were about eleven new emails. Most of them were the usual crap, mostly junk, but there was an email from his flight commander that caught his attention.

ALCON

We have been made aware of an influx of disturbing information. As of now, there is no evidence that said information is factual or correct. Media outlets are being continuously monitored by all agencies to ensure that information is being disseminated properly after extensive fact-checking. You are directed to continue standard operations at this time. Any changes will be released as soon as available.

v/r

Lt Col James Whitehorn

Carson sat back in his seat after reading the email, then called Paul over to read it himself. He just sighed and shook his head.

"Fucking figures," he mumbled before heading back to his desk. "They aren't gonna tell us anything until shit actually hits the fan."

"Maybe he's right, and nothing will come of this," Carson offered. "I'm sure he'd tell us if something was *actually* happening. He's cool like that."

"Maybe," Booker said, but Carson knew he didn't believe it.

He didn't really believe it himself.

Chapter 2

The rest of the day Carson tried to focus on work, though there wasn't much to do at the time. He just tried to avoid social media for a while and all the panic that was flooding his news feed. It was becoming so pervasive that he pulled up a book he had been reading on the computer, Stephen King's *IT*, and let himself get wrapped up in the story. For someone who tends to be a bit paranoid, it would seem odd that he would gravitate toward the macabre. He had always been that way, though.

Reading always had a way of distracting Carson. He found that after about a half hour he was so immersed in the novel that he had temporarily forgotten all about the sightings and the news articles. Reading about killer clowns was distracting enough. At least he hadn't chosen to read *The Mist*.

Before he left Booker called him over. "Dude, check this shit out."

Carson closed his browser and exited out of his email before walking over to Booker's desk. "More sightings?"

Booker moved back in his seat so Carson could see the monitor. He watched a video from someone's cell phone of a man running down a street. The shot followed the man for a moment and then panned back toward an intersection from where Carson assumed the man had come from. Seconds passed, then a bizarre creature loped into view and dashed down the street after the man. Carson squinted as he looked at the video, noting the odd appearance of the creature and the way it moved. Something seemed off about it.

"Looks like someone tried to make a CGI creature, and failed," Carson said. "It looked…wrong. The movement was off. Dude, I think this whole thing is a big, fat hoax. To me, that video just proves it."

"I don't know, man. Looked real enough."

"About as real as a low-budget film," Carson retorted. "At least it isn't a man in a rubber suit."

Booker shook his head and laughed. "Maybe. Gotta give them some credit, though. Pretty impressive for a cell phone."

"People can do some interesting shit with technology these days," Carson said. "I'm heading out. See you tomorrow."

"See ya tomorrow. Maybe I'll whip up a little 'creature-feature' on my phone too."

Carson shook his head and chuckled as he shut off his computer, grabbed his hat and walked out of the door. Carson was still ruminating on the book he had been reading as he walked out to his truck, mixed with the odd video Booker showed him. He wanted to dismiss it, but he remembered that

Kate said she had seen something similar out their back window. Once again, he felt his anxiety creeping up on him.

Carson had a habit of fearing the worst. It used to bother people, but it also forced him be more prepared than average. He had purchased a rather expensive 72-hour emergency bag for four people several months before, almost as if he was clairvoyant.

He also had procured two firearms, though his wife was more than a little uncomfortable with the things. It had taken him months to convince her to let him buy the pistol, then another several months to buy the rifle. In Carson's room, locked away and out of reach, were his Beretta 9mm pistol and an AR-15 that he had fitted with a cheap scope.

He was glad that he had made some preparations in advance, but as Carson drove home, he began to think about everything else he could possibly need if shit really hit the fan. The bug-out bag was a good start, as was having some form of protection, but he knew that he would need more food and water. If things went as bad as his active imagination was leading him to believe, he would need far more than 72-hours' worth of supplies. He also knew that a couple of boxes of ammunition for each firearm may not be enough.

In addition to the things Carson already had, he knew he would need spare gasoline to continue to fuel his truck (Kate's car was a bit better on gas, but his truck could easily fit twice as much, which he thought was a bit more important) as well as blankets, clothes (warm and cold weather), and medical supplies. Carson found himself wishing he had been more the paranoid survivalist type, but he had tried to be practical and frugal. It wasn't like the military was making him rich.

As Carson made a mental list, he contemplated stopping at the Base Exchange to pick up some more supplies. Hell, he knew he could find *some* of what he figured he needed, but he instead opted to continue on home.

Carson pulled into the driveway beside Kate's Toyota Camry and got out, his mind still buzzing. The block was as quiet as always, though the school had just let out, so kids would be walking home soon. The car in the driveway told him his wife had already picked their kids up from school. He found he felt a great deal of relief just thinking about that. It was one concern he no longer had to worry about.

As he walked through the door, he heard a children's cartoon playing on the television. Chris sat on the floor less than a foot away from the television, his eyes glued to the flashing colors on the screen.

"Hey, buddy," Carson said. Chris took a moment to respond, his reaction delayed.

"Hi daddy!" Chris said excitedly as he jumped up and ran toward the door. He wrapped his little arms around Carson's waist in a tight hug. Carson reached down and tousled Chris's messy blonde hair.

"How was school?"

"It was fine," Chris replied. That was the typical response every day. Just fine. No elaboration. No complaints. It was fine. Carson didn't expect a nine-year-old to start in with the canned responses, but Chris had always seemed a bit older than he actually was.

"Just fine? Nothing… interesting? No weird rumors or anything?"

Chris cocked his head as he looked at Carson. "Rumors? Um…not really."

"Where's your sister?" Carson asked after Chris let go.

"I dunno," Chris answered absently. "Upstairs maybe."

"Irene!" Carson called up the stairway situated directly across from the front door. "Whatcha doin'?"

He heard Irene several seconds before she popped out from around the corner at the top of the stairs. The kid was less that sixty pounds, but the way she walked made her sound like she was over *one hundred* and sixty. "Oh, hi daddy."

She came bounding down the stairs—it sounded like she was about to go *through* them—and gave him a sideways hug.

"How was school, kiddo?" Carson asked. He already anticipated her answer and could have replied for her.

"It was okay," Irene answered in typical teenage fashion. Thirteen and already in the throes of teenage angst.

Carson just chuckled and shook his head. A typical reply for a typical teenager. He found it more amusing than anything. "Okay kiddo. You guys have homework?"

"No," Chris and Irene answered together. Carson suspected that they probably did—what school didn't give out homework? —but he chose not to press the issue. If they did, and chose to ignore it, then their grades would reflect it. He would address it then.

Kate walked around the corner into the living room at that moment, a dish rag in her hands. Had she been doing the dishes?

Carson walked over to meet her and, while giving her a hug, glance over at the kitchen. Plates and bowls sat on the kitchen counter, still dirty from the previous evening's dinner. No, she hadn't been washing dishes, Carson realized. She was just using the rag to dry her hands.

Damn. He had wanted, for once, to relax after work before starting dinner. But, yet again, that was not to be.

"How was work?" Kate asked. She still looked a bit pale, and a faint tremor creeped into her voice.

Carson wanted to answer with what Booker had been seeing, and the overall anxiety that everyone in the office had begun to feel, but he knew doing so would make Kate start to panic. And when Kate panicked, she got short-tempered.

Instead, Carson took a page out of Chris and Irene's book, simply answering "It was fine."

At that moment, Bella and Doll, their two dogs—labrador mixes as far as they could tell—came bounding out of the kitchen and raced through the living room. Doll, the younger of the two, began jumping up at Carson. She pawed at his chest and whined with excitement. Bella, on the other hand, couldn't give two shits that Carson was home. She darted past him and trotted up the stairs.

"I swear your dog hates me," Carson sighed.

"Well, you're always mean to her," Kate replied.

"What? I'm not…I've never…" Carson sputtered. "She doesn't listen to me unless I raise my voice. I'm not mean. She just ignores me if I don't."

Truth be told, Carson didn't really like Bella much. She was grouchy and stubborn. She also seemed to have a skin condition that grossed him out. He knew none of it was Bella's

fault—he hadn't had time to train her, and Kate hadn't tried—
but it had worn on him over time. And he stopped trying to wash
Bella. He'd have more luck bathing Gabby, their three-year-old
gray tabby—Gabby the Tabby ha ha—than Bella. Kate couldn't,
and wouldn't, bathe her dog either. Then again, Bella probably
outweighed Kate by a few pounds.

"*I* don't have to yell at her," Kate retorted.

Carson sighed, feeling defeated. She wasn't going to
budge on this. It had been a common snipe at him, regardless of
how he acted toward the dog. "I don't know, then."

The evening passed uneventfully. Carson washed the dishes and
prepared dinner while Kate and their kids sat in the living room
in front of the TV playing on the Wii U, something Carson
wished he could do. He wanted to be the fun one. Instead he was
doing all the housework while they hung out together.

When dinner was ready, they all ate in relative silence—Kate
was fixated on her cell phone—and then Carson set about putting
away the leftovers while the kids went upstairs to get ready for
bed.

"Do you think you could take over for a bit?" Carson
asked Kate. "I'd like to tuck them in to bed."

"You already started on the dishes."

"I know," Carson responded. "But I don't usually get to tuck them in or read to them. I thought it would be nice to do that tonight."

"I'm tired and my back hurts," Kate countered. "I don't think I can stand over the sink long enough to finish the dishes."

"I just thought it would be nice," Carson muttered sadly.

The routine wore on Carson. He had let it go for a while, especially after they had first moved in, but he had started getting angry about it. The longer workdays, when they did occur, made it even more difficult to cope. Maybe it *wouldn't* be so bad if the sightings were real.

Don't even think *like that!* Carson chastised himself. Yet another part of him seemed to whisper in excitement. *If they were, then Kate wouldn't be the problem anymore.* Carson ground his teeth as his stomach soured, guilt hitting him immediately after the thought. No, it was wrong to think like that. He was just angry, that's all.

Getting the kids to bed was delightfully simple, at least. When he finally walked into the bedroom, he saw that Kate had already changed and had got comfortable under the covers. Without a word, Carson changed into his pajamas—sweats and a T-shirt, really—and brushed his teeth. He slipped under the covers when he was finished and, moments later, fell asleep.

Chapter 3

He stood in a field, the wind gusting around him. The sky was growing dark and with it, he knew, the terrors would come. He looked down and saw that Chris and Irene were clutching firmly to his waist, terror filling their eyes. What had them so scared? He wasn't sure, but it felt like the most logical thing in the world.

Other people were milling aimlessly. Expressions were blank on everyone's faces. Only Chris and Irene seemed scared. And so was he. Something bad had chased them, and they had barely gotten away. What it had been, Carson didn't know. He didn't understand why he was standing in the middle of a field, either. He recognized the place, though.

It was the field between the base housing and the elementary school. He looked around and, despite knowing where he was, he couldn't seem to locate their house.

A rustling sound came from somewhere overhead. He glanced up and saw a grocery bag—one of those plastic white ones that Wal-Mart used—darting around in the wind. Something about it felt wrong. It felt incredibly dangerous. Almost... sinister even.

Suddenly, the grocery bag changed direction and moved opposite the wind. Before his eyes, the bag started to change form. It still had the plastic texture and remained translucent, but it had wings, and the bottom portion lengthened into a tail. The thing flapped though the sky and darted straight toward them.

Chris and Irene screamed. Carson stood frozen in place, as though paralyzed. The other people didn't notice at all. They didn't notice anything was amiss and the screams fell on deaf ears, until the thing darted down and wrapped itself around a woman's face. She jerked and began clawing at the thing clinging to her. Screams erupted all around him and the people ran in all directions.

Carson still couldn't move. He couldn't do anything but watch. He looked up as he heard another rustling sound. Up above, another plastic bag was floating in the wind. Then it stopped and angled toward him.

It dove straight at his face.

Carson gasped as he awoke in a pool of sweat, desperate to draw in breath. The nightmares were getting worse. Was it stress? Exhaustion? Anger, maybe? He hated it in any case. Carson felt as though he hadn't slept at all. His body was sore, and his neck was stiff.

He rolled his shoulders as he slowly sat up in bed. Kate continued sleeping next to him, oblivious to his sudden awakening. She looked comfortable and completely content. It made him angry. She got to sleep soundly while he had was, it seemed, perpetually exhausted. And why shouldn't she? It wasn't as though she had much to do during the day to cause her stress.

Rather than ruminate on his irritation, Carson dragged himself to bed and focused on getting ready for another day. Thankfully, it was Friday. He had a weekend to look forward to. Well, not really. His weekend was probably already spoken for. Kate, undoubtedly, had the weekend all planned out. And Carson? Well, he just had to go with it. If he resisted, then Kate would get pissed and take it out on the entire household. Carson would rather suffer than let his kids face that kind of treatment.

After a quick shave, Carson made his way downstairs, calling out to Chris and Irene to wake up as he went. He opened the crates that Bella and Doll were sleeping in—they were destructive and would destroy the house if they roamed free— and let them out into the backyard. The day was going to be another mild one.

A cool breeze wafted through the opening and drifted over him. For a moment, Carson was content. He could smell the grass coated in morning dew and the scent of spring flowers was already in the air. Maybe today would be a good day. Carson hoped so. He could use one.

Unlike the day before, Carson skipped breakfast and instead brewed a cup of coffee in a travel mug. He quickly hugged Chris and Irene, wishing them a good day, and left the house.

The drive to work was quiet and peaceful. Some vehicles were on the road already, which was to be expected. Most of the drivers were probably servicemen on their way to morning PT. Carson was glad that, as the lead NCO, he could decide when his shop would do PT. He had opted for a self-paced, individual approach after work. If the others didn't exercise, it would show when they did their annual fitness test. They were all adults and Carson didn't think he needed to hold their hands. He knew that Airman Trejo and Airman Vasquez, along with Sergeant Booker, would have no issue staying in shape. They all seemed to enjoy exercise.

He pulled into the parking lot ten minutes before the shift started and allowed himself to relax for a few minutes. He sat in his truck and laid his head back against the headrest. The radio was playing, but Carson wasn't paying attention to what song was on. With his eyes closed, Carson focused on his own breathing. He was, for the moment, at peace.

Then a voice came over the radio. The speaker spoke in a shaky voice. He sounded rattled. When Carson tuned in to what was being said, he understood why. The sightings occurred again. This wasn't a passing hoax, then.

Booker was fixated on his computer screen all day while Carson was at work. Needless to say, nothing at all got accomplished. The only topic of conversation was the bizarre sightings and along with that came a myriad of theories. Science experiment? The apocalypse? Was it manmade? So many questions and no answers. By the end of the workday, Carson was sick of hearing about it.

It was either a very elaborate hoax, which was becoming increasingly unlikely, or people were getting worked up about something that could easily be explained. In a week it would no doubt have a boring, mundane answer.

Carson wanted to not care about the hysteria. He wanted to think it was nothing. And maybe he could have, had the cows been acting normal.

Today, they weren't. The cows were bunched up in a protective circle. Carson had never seen that kind of behavior in them before. Not in the time that he'd been stationed on the base.

He slowed the truck as he began to pass them. Their large eyes were wider than normal, and their tails flicked in agitation. Perplexed, Carson continued to watch. He was so fixated on their behavior that he almost didn't see something dash across the road in front of him.

Something with black and yellow stripes. Something very, very fast.

His heart pounded as he immediately hit the accelerator. No way was that real. His mind *had* to be playing tricks on him. All the obsession over the supposed invasion must have gotten to him, right? He wanted to believe that, but the way the cows immediately charged past him on their side of the fence dispelled that hope.

Clutching the steering wheel tightly, Carson forced himself to drive the speed limit on his way home. He was impatient to get inside, hug his kids, and go on believing things were fine.

But, when he pulled into the driveway behind Kate's car, he couldn't shake the feeling things were not, in fact, fine.

The house was empty. His kids, Irene and Chris, weren't downstairs playing in the living room, nor was his wife. Were they upstairs? He didn't think the kids were outside because they usually had the garage door open. It was possible, though. They liked to play on a rudimentary swing that had been installed in a tree behind the house before the older kids got there.

Carson stood in the entryway for a moment trying to hear something, anything, that would indicate he wasn't alone in the house. His two dogs, Bella and Doll, were out in the backyard. He could see them through the window in the dining room. Carson wasn't completely alone in the house, but he could tell he was the only *human* there.

Had his wife walked to pick up the kids? It was certainly possible, given the decent weather. For some reason that he couldn't describe at the time, he found himself panicking once again. Carson struggled with anxiety and depression, so it was not too unusual for him to panic more than the average person, but he had reason to be concerned. The sightings had shaken him.

"Honey, I'm home," he called upstairs. He waited a moment for a reply, but nothing but silence greeted him. "You guys here?"

He walked upstairs and, after glancing into both of his kids' rooms, walked into his bedroom. Carson honestly expected to find Kate sitting on the bed, but she wasn't. She and the kids weren't home yet. Should he try to meet them at school? They'd probably get home just as he pulled out of the doorway. Once again, he found himself struck with indecision.

Carson decided he would just change out of his uniform and into regular clothes. He figured they would be walking through the door any minute and he wanted to be changed already. He threw off his uniform, tossed it in a pile on the floor by his bed, and pulled on a pair of jeans and a T-shirt with a Disturbed band logo on it. It was comfortable, and they were one of his favorite bands, so he wasn't ashamed in the least of wearing a shirt with their logo on it. He leaned down to pull on a pair of black running shoes but changed his mind and put on a pair of steel-toed boots.

Carson had gotten fully changed, and the rest of his family *still* hadn't gotten home. By this point, he began to panic. Had something happened? The thought literally made him sick to my stomach.

"Fuck," he muttered. "Damn it, where are you guys?"

He sat down on the bed heavily and grabbed his cell phone. He thought about calling Kate's cell, but reception was almost non-existent on base. She wouldn't know he called until she came through the door and the cell phone connected automatically to the wireless internet. Still, it was worth a shot.

He pulled out his phone and dialed her number. It went straight to voicemail. He tried several more times, thinking that maybe her cell would pick up some reception as she moved around.

Still nothing.

Carson jumped up and went over to peer out the window. He wanted to grab his pistol and look for them but doing so would be highly illegal. If he was being paranoid, the consequences wouldn't be worth it. But he *had* seen something not too far away. If it was the things on the news, then they were extremely dangerous.

On the other hand, if his concerns were accurate, he would wish he had the gun. He resolved to make the decision if he saw something, anything, that would indicate danger. He looked out over the front yard and at the field across the street. So far, he had not seen a thing.

He was about to turn away when he caught sight of something moving behind one of the houses. Carson stared, hoping it would come back into view. A full minute passed before he saw it again. His breath caught in his throat when he saw the creature from the video Booker had shown him stalking across the field. He blinked several times, expecting the image to vanish, but it was still there.

"Well, shit," Carson gasped and then rushed to the bedroom closet where he stored his pistol in a combination safe.

It wasn't exactly legal to carry a weapon on base, though it was legal for him to own them and store them at home, but he was willing to take the risk. It could really bite him in the ass if he got caught, but the school wasn't far, and he could conceal it under his jacket. He had gotten his concealed carry license while in Texas, so he had a holster for his pistol that fit inside his waistband. A full-sized pistol wasn't comfortable to carry concealed on his small frame, but he hadn't had the opportunity to purchase a smaller pistol.

The weight of the pistol in his hand offered a small measure of comfort. Carson slid it in the holster and affixed it to his belt. It bulged a bit, but a jacket would hide it easily. He shut the safe and walked out of the room, the Beretta heavy on his hip. He walked down the stairs, grabbed a jacket from the entry closet and walked outside, his heart hammering in his chest.

He considered calling security forces to, at a minimum, report what he saw. But, when he tried, the call wouldn't go through.

Shit, I can't wait on someone to answer the goddamn phone.

Carson then decided to make another call.

The phone rang several times before the voice on the other end spoke up.

"Hey man, what's up?" Booker said.

Carson took a breath to try control the panic he knew would be evident in his voice. "Hey, Booker. You remember that video you showed me earlier?"

"The one you called a hoax? Speaking of, I almost forgot that I was going to try to make one myself," Booker answered.

"I don't think it was a hoax."

"You don't? The same guy who thought it was video editing and a rubber suit changed his mind? Why?" Booker's usually jovial tone started to disappear.

"I think I saw one earlier on the way home," Carson began. "Going after some cows. I didn't get a good look though."

"I wouldn't think that would have been enough to convince you."

"Then I looked out my back window when I got home. This time, I definitely saw it."

"You fucking with me man?" Booker sounded like he expected Carson to say something like "psyche" or "gotcha." It was understandable. They often joked with each other like that.

"I wish I was," Carson answered, his tone leaving no room for doubt. "No, I absolutely saw one. It looked just like the one on the video."

"Oh shit."

"Listen," Carson began. "I have to go check the school. Kate and the kids aren't home yet and I'm getting really worried after seeing that thing. These *things* are on base and I don't think it would be a good idea to come anywhere near here until Command gets it figured out. Keep Ally and your boys safe. Unless you hear anything from our leadership, anyway."

"Man, the First Sergeant will lose his lid if we don't come in to work tomorrow."

"If these things swarm the base, we'll be the least of his worries. I'm just saying I have a real bad feeling about this. I can't make you stay home from work, but I strongly encourage you to."

They both knew what that phrase typically meant. It meant that there was only the illusion of an option, when in reality it was a thinly veiled order.

"Listen man," Booker started. *"I can't promise that I won't try to get on base later, but I'll make sure to keep my eyes open for any kind of message from Command. And, if I see one on my way in the morning, I will turn right the hell around."*

Carson squeezed the bridge of his nose with his thumb and forefinger. After a moment, he sighed. "Fine. But if you hear *anything* please let me know. And call the Airmen. They need to know, too. If I hear anything, I'll be sure to let you know."

"Okay buddy. I will. Take care of yourself Tanner."

"You too, Booker." Carson hung up and turned to leave the house.

Once again, Carson half expected to see Kate and the kids walking up to the front door. He would have to explain the pistol when he went to put it back in the safe, but that would be fine. It would be preferrable. Unfortunately, he couldn't see them anywhere near the property. Without hesitation, he shut the door, locked it, and walked toward the school.

A light wind blew as Carson walked around the corner of his house and headed across the large field behind his backyard. He clutched at his jacket so it would not allow the wind to reveal the pistol he was carrying. He wanted to zip up the jacket, but what if he needed the gun in a hurry? Carson worried that he was acting a bit unrealistically. It took a moment to convince himself that he should err on the side of caution rather than let his paranoia get the best of me. Carson worked the zipper as he walked across the grass.

It was unusually quiet, even for his neighborhood, and that should have been a major indicator that something was amiss. If he had been out for a leisurely stroll, he probably would have picked up on it sooner. Carson was determined to get to the school and find out just what the hell was taking his wife and kids so long to get home. He wasn't angry with them. Quite the contrary. He was getting more and more anxious as the day wore on.

There were houses on either side of the field, their fenced-in backyards clearly visible. Carson still hadn't seen any kids walking home from school. There should have been groups of children walking home, but he saw nobody. A part of him figured that it was probably a good thing that he didn't see anyone since he was carrying a firearm illegally through a residential neighborhood.

Carson could have walked along the road and crossed at the bend, but he figured cutting through the fields would be faster. He was in a hurry.

The elementary school wasn't far from where he lived. Driving to the school would have been much faster, but Carson did not want to miss Kate and the kids if they were on their way home. He continued to glance around as he walked, trying his best not to look nervous. He doubted that he was succeeding, but nobody was around to see him. The field rose in a slight elevation as he got closer to the school. Carson could see the playground and some of the classrooms at the back. Still, he saw nobody around.

He was on the verge of a full-blown panic attack when he finally caught sight of life. A child, no older than his nine-year-old son, was peering out one of the classroom windows. It was hard to tell from a distance, but Carson thought the kid looked absolutely petrified.

What the hell was going on?

He quickened his pace and saw the kid, a young girl with a boyish haircut, staring at him with wide eyes. Carson tried his best to look as non-threatening as possible. What was the kid so frightened of? As if in answer he heard movement off to his left. He turned his head toward the sound and saw, nearly a football field's distance away, the creature.

The description of the grasshopper-like legs wasn't far off. This thing's rear and forelimbs did bear a striking resemblance to those of a grasshopper, though the thing was easily the size of a full-grown dog. The other detail Carson immediately noticed was its color. It looked like a large bumblebee, but the coloring was in a pattern like tiger stripes. Bright yellow and black stripes covered the length of the creature. From a distance, it was a little hard to make out the details of its head, but he was able to notice the glowing red eyes.

Immediately, a similar image flashed through his mind. The thing in his nightmare. But how?

The thing didn't notice him right away, but it seemed to sense that he was looking at it. It snapped its head to look directly at him and began bounding toward Carson in a way that seemed to defy logic. The creature's physiology should have made it nearly impossible to move at any great speed, but the beast launched forward with otherworldly speed and grace. His heart immediately felt as though it was going to seize up. He froze as it advanced, incapable of moving or looking away as the thing barreled toward him.

It wasn't until he got a clear good look at the thing's head that Carson was finally able to move again. It had canine-like jaws that opened horizontally rather than vertically filled with needle-like teeth. An unearthly warbling howl burst from the thing's throat as it hurtled toward him.

Carson turned immediately and ran toward the school, his adrenaline already pumping, and his heart was threatening to explode out of his chest. He heard the creature gaining behind him, and his eyes began to water as he began thinking he would never see my family again.

As he ran Carson fought with the zipper of his jacket, fumbling with fingers that suddenly seemed much too large. After a split second of fighting with it, he decided to just hike up his jacket and reach for his pistol.

It seemed like the universe was against him at that moment. His pistol wouldn't slide free of the holster, which would have been a decent safety measure in any other circumstance. Now, Carson found himself cursing the manufacturer of the holster as he yanked on the grip of the pistol. The creature sounded as though it was right behind him by the time he pulled the gun free. Carson hazarded a glance over his shoulder and nearly pissed himself as a creature that even his worst nightmares couldn't produce was nearly right on top of him.

On instinct, he spun and tried to fire. The fucking safety was still on! The movement caused Carson to fall backward and, as he landed, he heard a crunch. For a moment he thought he had broken a bone, though no pain came. He then realized that his cell phone had been in his rear pocket, something he had never done. He didn't have time to confirm his suspicions, as the beast leaped over him and tumbled in the dirt.

Carson flipped the safety off, rolled over on to his stomach, and tried to fire again. This time he heard the satisfying report of the pistol as it sent a hollow point round toward the creature. The bullet struck one of the creature's limbs, and he saw the leg shear at the joint. He didn't hesitate as he fired more shots. The creature jerked with each impact but didn't go down.

He knew nine-millimeter rounds are not the most powerful ammunition available but come on! It only seemed to piss the thing off, though.

The creature hissed and, unbelievably, sprang at Carson again. He rolled to dodge the thing, but he had reacted a second too slow. A burning pain flashed down his side as its claws tore into his flesh. Carson yelled out in pain.

The creature had landed, turned, and was preparing to launch itself at him again. Carson emptied several more rounds into the thing as it sailed toward him.

The weight of the monster slammed into his chest and knocked him flat on his back. The oxygen was forced painfully from his lungs. Carson felt his chest hitching as he tried to draw breath.

If the damned creature wasn't dead, he would be an easy meal.

He looked behind him and saw the thing lying in a heap. It wasn't moving so he assumed it was at least incapacitated. He hoped it was dead but wasn't willing to press his luck.

Carson wasted no time as he crawled to his feet, his lungs *still* refusing to draw in a breath. He got a better look at the monster that had attacked him and would have pissed himself again if he had anything left in his bladder. It was easily the most terrifying thing he had ever seen. Those canine-like jaws looked like the entire skulls of a wolf attached by muscle to the creature's head. Tentacles writhed above its hellish mandibles and a pair of dog-like tongues lolled out beneath. The eyes, of which there were four, still maintained their red glow.

He holstered his pistol, the magazine nearly empty. As he was holstering the weapon, his hand brushed his side and he sucked in a breath as the mere touch sent pain flaring though the area. He opened his jacket and inspected himself. The jacket had been torn and it appeared that the tip of the creature's claw had made it through to carve a shallow burrow in his side. The wound was painful, sure, but it was superficial. He could put a bandage on it later, *after* soaking it in antiseptic.

He sucked in ragged breaths as he pulled his phone out of his pocket. As he had suspected, the screen was smashed. He grumbled while he shoved the useless device back in his pocket and struggled to jog toward the school, eager to get as far away from the monster as possible.

For a moment, Carson expected Security Forces to be waiting for him with their guns drawn. There weren't any, but he knew it would only be a matter of time now. *Someone* would have heard the gunshots.

When he got to the school grounds, he could see nobody outside. They were likely taking refuge in the classrooms. Carson knew where each of his kids' classes was, but which one would they be hiding in? Would they even be in one? What if they were in the cafeteria or the main office? He figured he would just have to start with the closest one and work his way toward the office.

Chapter 4

The school grounds were vacant. No children milled about. No teachers walked their students to the parking lot where the parents would be waiting to pick them up. It was as empty as if it were a weekend. Carson would have been surprised if he had not just fought for his life against a creature that had no right to exist. Now he hoped the teachers had kept their students inside the classrooms. That would have definitely been safer than letting them roam.

As he passed the first small building, he saw children staring out the windows at him. Carson suddenly felt as if he were in a fishbowl. He made sure his firearm was out of sight, suddenly feeling guilty about carrying it onto a school campus. He did not regret having it on him, as it had saved his life, but he was still tethered to the rules and was keenly aware that he was in direct violation of several laws. Felonies at that.

Carson quickly passed another of the outlying buildings until he neared the center of the campus. The cafeteria and the main office were to his left, and a large open quad was to his immediate right, flanked on three sides by more buildings. His son's class was on the far side of the quad, at the other end of the building.

He heard sirens off in the distance. *Here they come*, he thought. Carson felt a pit in his stomach begin to form as he anticipated a confrontation with base security. How could he explain the gun and why he was blatantly breaking the law?

There would be no easy way out of it. He could try to show them the corpse of the monster he had shot, but they would have to give him the time of day to speak, first. He would be arrested immediately, and his family would be in danger if more of those grasshopper-monsters showed up. Realistically, they had more to contend with. He doubted his little "infraction" would matter if they ran into the creatures, but Carson could not bank on that eventuality. Even more likely they would see him as an immediate problem and try to apprehend him rather than chase a creature that, by his description, would sound like the ravings of a madman.

Carson hurried through the open quad space and nearly sprinted toward his son's classroom. He barely knew Chris's teacher, having only met the woman twice throughout the school year. Carson hoped that Kate, Chris, and Irene were all there. It would at least make his admittance into the classroom easier.

He walked up to the door and peered through the glass. Inside he saw children huddled toward the back of the room with the lights off. Carson spotted Kate with Chris once his eyes adjusted to the gloom. He watched as his wife said something to an older woman, Chris's teacher, and pointed his way. The woman nodded, and Kate hurried across the classroom and opened the door.

"Where's Irene?" she asked before Carson could say anything.

"She's not with you?" he replied, panic creeping into his voice.

Kate shook her head, her eyes wide. "I came to pick up Chris, and then the school went into lockdown. I haven't been able to leave the room!" She glanced over his shoulder and then pulled him into the classroom before shutting the door. That was when she saw blood leaking through his shirt.

"Holy shit! Carson, what happened?"

"Those things people were seeing," he began as he touched the wound. "They're real! It's all real!"

"What? Really?!"

Carson glanced down at the scratch on his side. "Oh yeah. I-I don't believe it myself, but it is. We need to get Irene and get out of here. We're sitting ducks in here."

"They locked the school down."

Carson shook his head. "That's all well and good, but we're too spread out. We need to get somewhere that is better reinforced."

Kate hung her head and sighed. "What if those things show up?"

Carson lifted his jacket and showed her the pistol on his hip. "I fought one off. That's what gave me my new body decoration."

When her eyes fell on the butt of the pistol, her expression hardened. Even with what was going on, it seemed to piss Kate off that he was carrying a gun.

"Just be careful, and go get Irene," Kate said sharply.

Carson opened his mouth to respond, but the sirens nearby cut him off. He just nodded and took off toward Irene's classroom. There was an irrational part of him that was furious that Irene was not with Kate and Chris. She usually met at the front of the school. Had she gone there instead? If so, it probably meant that Irene was in the school office or the cafeteria.

Oh, the cafeteria. It had no windows and only two large metal doors. When he found Irene, he could lead everyone there. It would be safer. Carson's heart hitched in his chest as the blaring sirens cut off.

Security Forces had arrived at the school.

He felt a mixture of relief and anxiety. They would be much better armed, but they would also immediately stop him since the school was on lockdown, and some idiot had fired off a weapon. He'd have to get everyone inside the cafeteria first and then contend with them.

So, today appeared to be a day for running. He skidded up to the building near the front of the school and peered into the window of Irene's classroom. Even in the gloom, he could see the room was empty.

"Shit," Carson hissed. He felt himself lock up as indecision paralyzed him. Should he risk going to the main office? The cafeteria was closer, but only by a hundred feet or so. He could check there, but Security Forces would have him penned in, and if Irene was not there he would not be able to leave to find her. He had to choose correctly the first time, as there would not be a second chance.

The thudding of boots on concrete snapped Carson out of his paralysis and sent him into motion. Rather than sprint he slowly made his way back toward the side of the building farthest from the parking lot. The sound of boots had not come his way, and he figured he would let them move away before heading past Irene's class toward the cafeteria.

Carson decided to check on the cafeteria since it was likely that any teacher on duty at the rotunda—their fancy name for the curb where the parents picked up their kids—would have ushered the students there in the event of a lockdown.

He crouched as he moved along the wall, ducking below the windows. As he neared the corner of the building he saw two patrol cars parked out front with their lights still flashing. Nobody stood near the cars or on guard near the office.

From where he stood Carson could see the small staircase that led up from the parking lot to the main office building and cafeteria. It was easily fifty yards from his location. He could sprint the distance in under three seconds when he was younger. It would likely take a bit longer now and Carson knew he would be heard if he tried. Sneaking there seemed like a better option, but it would take far longer and leave him exposed for longer than he felt was safe. Perhaps calmly walking could work? He shook his head at the notion. At this point, anyone walking around calmly would be extremely suspicious. He would just have to sneak as quickly as possible. The idea alone made his ankle hurt even worse.

Carson took a deep breath and then began to move toward the cafeteria in a crouch. He gritted his teeth against the pain as he shuffled along the building until he reached the edge and could see the open quad area once again.

The cafeteria lay directly ahead, but the short distance was visible from several angles. If he did not reach the cafeteria before one of the Security Officers rounded a corner on their return he would be spotted in an instant. He was already visible as it was. Carson gulped, whispered a plea to make him unseen, and then set off in a hunched-over jog.

He heard the approach of several footsteps just as he hit the top step. Rather than slow down Carson sped up and slid to a stop in front of the cafeteria doors. The double doors were usually open, even after school let out, but he was not surprised that they were both closed. He pulled on one of the handles and, as he expected, found it was locked. He knocked rapidly and bounced up and down as he waited for someone, anyone, to answer. The footsteps grew louder as the officers neared his location. Carson's heart slammed painfully in his chest as he waited anxiously. Any longer and he would have to bail.

The door opened a crack, and he saw a dark-haired woman he recognized from the front office peer through the opening, Mrs. Dupont. "You're Irene's father. Sir, we are on lockdown. She's safe."

"I need to pick up my daughter," Carson said quickly, barely letting her finish speaking. "Please. I need to know she's okay."

"Didn't the office call you?" Mrs. Dupont asked incredulously. "The school is on lockdown!"

"Phone's broken," he snapped. "Please, just let me in! I need to find her. Please!"

Mrs. Dupont started to close the door, but Carson stuck his foot in the opening, preventing the door from shutting. He pulled the door open and forced his way inside, nearly knocking her to the ground. She shouted out at him to stop, and Carson felt a pang of guilt as he stepped past her. "I'm sorry," he said repeatedly as his eyes darted around the large room, desperately searching for his little girl.

"Daddy?" she called as she stood up. Carson saw her toward the center of the room.

"Oh, thank goodness!" Carson cried as he hurried over to her. Irene met him nearly halfway, burying her face in his chest.

"I'm scared. What's going on?" she asked, her voice muffled.

"I don't know, sweetie," Carson said as he held her tight. "Mommy is with Chris in his class. They're safe."

He looked over at the door as he heard it open. The woman he knocked over was talking loudly to a man dressed in uniform carrying an M-4.

Security Forces had arrived, and Mrs. Dupont was pointing straight at him.

Shit.

Chapter 5

The officer stared straight at Carson and gripped the rifle in his hands tight. Carson moved Irene behind him, shielding her.

"Freeze!" the man called; the rifle aimed at Carson's chest. "You had better present some identification, now. No sudden moves."

Carson nodded and slowly reached his right hand toward his rear pocket where he had stuffed his wallet. He was glad he had the foresight to at least make sure his wallet was on him. He held out his left hand so the officer would not perceive him as a threat. Without looking, Carson found his military identification and pulled it out of the wallet. He held it up and stayed as still as possible as the man approached.

"Sergeant," the man said. "The whole area is on lockdown. You can't go barging in here. Do you have a kid who goes to this school?"

"Yes, sir," Carson said. He could read the man's name tag on the front of his vest. It read Swanson. Above it, Carson saw the rank insignia for a Senior Airman. "My daughter Irene, and my son, Chris." He led Irene out from behind him.

"Where's your son?"

"In his classroom with my wife."

Airman Swanson stared incredulously at Carson. "We got reports of gunshots. Do you know anything about that?"

Carson considered lying about the gun. It would save him from immediate trouble but would only make matters worse later when—not if—he got caught. His vision blurred as his anxiety forced his heart rate to climb. "Officer, that was me. I was attacked on my way to the school." He showed Swanson his wound.

"Are you telling me you discharged a firearm in a residential neighborhood?"

"Listen to me, officer," Carson began. "Something is very fucking wrong. What attacked me wasn't natural. Some… creature attacked me on my way here. I can even show you once we get everyone together in the cafeteria. It'll be safer there."

"Staff Sergeant Carson Tanner, I need you to come with me," Swanson said, his rifle trained on Carson. "I don't know what you're talking about, but you are under arrest."

"For fuck's sake airman, please! You must understand that I would *never* fire my weapon if I didn't absolutely have to! And believe me, I really had to."

Swanson moved to apprehend Carson when his radio went off. "Unit two, come in!"

"This is Senior Airman Swanson," he replied. "Over."

"Get over to the back of the school!" the voice over the radio said in a panicked voice. "You need to see this!"

Swanson waited a moment and then spoke into his radio. "Negative. I have a suspect in custody responsible for the reports of gunfire in this vicinity. Over."

"Get your ass over here, Swanson!" the voice barked. Swanson looked torn as he glanced over at Carson.

"Shit," he hissed. "Sergeant Tanner, stay put. Do. Not. Move."

Carson nodded, though he had no intention of staying where he was. Swanson hurried out of the cafeteria and Carson allowed a sigh to escape his lips.

"Are you in trouble, daddy?" Irene asked.

"It's okay, honey," Carson said. "It's just a misunderstanding. They have other things to worry about. We just need to get your mom and your brother and get home."

Irene saw the blood on Carson's jacket as it soaked through. "You're hurt! Oh my god! You're bleeding!"

He glanced down at the blood. "I'm alright. It's not as bad as it looks." In truth, he was starting to get dizzy. "Let's go, sweetie. We'll take care of it at home."

Irene clutched tightly onto Carson's arm as he led her toward the cafeteria door. He noticed she was trying to avoid touching the blood as they walked. Mrs. Dupont blocked his way as he approached.

"Sir, you can't leave," she said. "You heard the officer."

"Ma'am, with all due respect," Carson said through gritted teeth as he tried to ignore the burning pain in his side. "I don't care what he said. I'm gathering everyone in the cafeteria. Which is where you should be going. Security Forces can deal with me there. Now please get out of the way."

She scowled and crossed her arms. "I can't let you go."

"Get the fuck out of the way," Carson snarled, immediately feeling horrible for his aggressive response. "Now. And get to the damned cafeteria with the rest of your students." She looked like she wanted to argue, but something in his eyes made her reconsider. She had the other students to worry about, after all.

Carson moved briskly past the woman, leading Irene out of the cafeteria. He quickly looked around, scanning the school grounds for signs of the monster grasshoppers, but saw nothing. He pulled Irene along as he hurried through the quad back toward Chris's classroom. Irene shrieked when the sound of gunfire erupted near the rear of the school. It sounded like someone had set off fireworks.

Carson didn't stop. He made sure to keep from sprinting so Irene could keep up, though at this point she probably could have outpaced him. His legs had begun to feel like they were made of lead.

He knocked on the door as they reached the classroom, and Kate was quick to open it. Carson guessed that she had been waiting anxiously by the door since he had left. She helped him lead Irene inside and barely shut the door before Carson collapsed to the floor.

"Shit," Carson muttered. He looked at his thoroughly soaked jacket. "That's probably not good."

Kate crouched next to him and placed her hands on each side of his face. "Don't you pass out on me."

Carson nodded. He looked over at Chris's teacher. What was her name? Miss Harewhit? For some reason, he could not quite remember. His head was getting foggy. "Ma'am, do you have any sponges, towels, and duct tape. Or band-aids?"

"I think I might have something like that in the craft supplies," she replied. "What for?"

"I need to stop the bleeding," Carson managed. The effort to speak took quite a bit out of him. She nodded and hurried over to a cabinet in the corner of the classroom.

"Sponges? Duct tape?" Kate asked dubiously.

"I don't really have a first-aid kit at my disposal, so that stuff will have to do for now," he groaned. "I really should clean it. It wasn't deep." He looked over at Irene and saw the terrified expression on her face. "Irene, sweetie, please distract your brother. I'll be okay. Mommy is going to help me. Can you do that, kiddo?"

Irene nodded, tears rolling down her cheeks. To her credit, she didn't argue or complain. She just walked over to Chris and asked him to show her where his desk was. Carson could see that Chris was terrified as well, but he went along with her. It made Carson smile.

Chris's teacher brought over several sponges and a large towel. "We don't have duct tape, but we do have quite a bit of yarn."

Carson grabbed the proffered supplies, including a large ball of yarn, and nodded his thanks. "You wouldn't happen to have one of those bottles of hand sanitizer that we sent on the first day, would you?" Miss Harewhit quickly went to her desk and pulled a bottle from a drawer. Once she gave it to him, he handed Kate the items and began fumbling with the zipper of his jacket. She noticed him struggling and gently moved his hands away so she could unzip the heavy jacket. Carson laid his head back and rolled his shoulders backward as Kate tried to pull the jacket free. He grunted in pain and had to stop for a moment to catch his breath, then nodded and they tried again. After what felt like forever, they managed to get the jacket off. He looked down at the wound and exhaled.

"Tis only a flesh wound," he joked. Kate managed a weak smile. Thankfully, the wound wasn't deep, but he it was looking a bit gross.

"Don't… don't worry about my shirt. Put some hand sanitizer on the sponges and just start pressing them against it and tie the yarn around them, one at… a time," Carson instructed. He would do it himself if he could, but his head was getting increasingly fuzzy. "Then wrap the towel around me and tie that off, too… if you can."

Kate worked hesitantly, and in moments she had done her best to cover the wound. It looked weak and wouldn't hold for long, but it was the best they could do, and she knew it.

"There," she said. "But it isn't going to work very well. You need a doctor."

"I don't know if a doctor is going to know what is in that cut," Carson argued.

"You *need* a doctor, dammit!" Kate snapped. "Stop trying to be a hero."

"Okay, okay," he conceded. "Does your phone have any reception?"

Kate checked her phone and nodded. "I have a couple of bars."

Carson nodded and laid back against the wall, his face pale. "Good. Call them and then we need to get out of here. I saw the cafeteria and already told Irene's teacher to get everyone there."

Kate ignored him as she dialed out for an ambulance. Carson watched through heavy-lidded eyes as she stood with her phone to her ear. After a moment she hung up and tried again. Kate went through this cycle several times before finally hanging up.

"No answer?" Carson asked.

"It just keeps ringing," she said, her shoulders slumping.

"Help me up," Carson said. "We need to get moving."

Kate scowled at him. "There is no way you will make it more than ten feet without passing out. I'll keep calling."

Carson wanted to argue but he felt incredibly light-headed. She was right. If he stood up, he would black out. However, sitting in an elementary school classroom while monsters prowled in search of food was not an ideal position. His mind reeled as he struggled to come up with an idea. After a moment, an unappealing idea formed.

He could wait until one of the Security officers returned. By now they would have no doubt encountered the freakish creature and he would no longer be a concern. It was not the best idea in the world, but it would have to do.

Carson glanced down at the makeshift bandage on his ribs. He was not sure, but he suspected that the bleeding had begun to slow. Against his better judgement he pulled the towel away and moved the tied-off sponges away from the wound. He was relieved to find that the wounds were shallow. Apparently, his jacket had managed to keep the freakish creature's claws from digging in too deep. Satisfied that the wound would hopefully be sterilized, he put the sponges back into place, tightened the strings, and rewrapped the towel. Carson took a breath and stood up.

His head immediately swam, and his vision went blank.

***

Carson found himself trailing behind a man wearing a black uniform and equipped with gear commonly found on SWAT officers, but the armor did not have the SWAT writing on the back like he expected. Immediately Carson questioned who the stranger was, but his attention shifted to his environment. They were in a building that looked like it had once been an administrative office, but it was empty. The walls around him seemed wrong. The white stucco walls were bulging in multiple areas as if the walls had a bad case of acne. The bulges looked like massive white-head pimples that were pulsing gently. Even more disturbing was the overwhelming sensation of déjà vu. He could not explain why, but the entire sequence seemed vividly familiar, though he knew that this had never happened.

As he followed the stranger, he realized his wife and children were with him. The new development filled him with dread. This place felt evil, and the presence of his family sent his protective instincts into overdrive. He wanted to turn and force them out of the building, but he could not move except for slowly following the uniformed stranger. The building vibrated slightly and the nodules on the walls seemed to pulse faster. Carson could barely see around the man in front of him, but he caught a glimpse of something fleshy and large looming down the hall. Before his escort had a chance to open fire one of the pulsating nodules shot out like the tongue of a frog and struck the man in the neck, hitting the only patch of exposed skin. Immediately the man clutched at his neck and tried to scream, but the sound came out as a gurgle.

Carson stood in horror as he watched the man drop to his knees and appeared to collapse in on himself. The exposed skin of the man's neck dissolved before his eyes and Carson realized that whatever the things on the wall were had caused the man to dissolve from the inside out. Terror made his heart slam against his ribs as he tried to retreat. Down the hall, finally unobstructed, Carson saw the fleshy mass that approached. Eyes blinked across the amorphous mass as tendrils darted out and latched onto the walls, propelling the beast toward him. He screamed as the monster rushed straight toward him.

***

Carson jolted upright, gasping for breath. He blinked and ran his hands over his torso, fully expecting to find his body disintegrating. He struggled to understand what had just happened. Had he passed out? But it had felt so damned *real*! He looked around and relaxed as he realized that he was still in the unlit classroom, Kate at his side.

Carson had become accustomed to nightmares in recent months. Usually, they would revolve around his father, which was painfully distressing as he had not fully accepted the reality that his father was gone, a victim of suicide. The event had pushed him into a deep depression and until the recent events he was contemplating ending his own life, but never fully acted on it. In any case, the nightmares would eventually end, and his grief would start anew when he awoke, but this nightmare was very different.

"Easy," he heard her say as she wrapped her arms around his shoulders. It took a moment for Carson to control his breathing enough to form a response.

"What happened? I remember trying to stand up and then I had the most intense nightmare. Did I pass out?"

Kate rubbed his shoulders as he shook. His nerves were frazzled. "It's okay. Yeah, I think you passed out. You sort of just…froze, and then you fell over. It freaked us out and Irene ran to the nurse's office."

"Irene left? Where is she?!" Carson tried to stand. He felt hands on his arm pulling him back.

"Sir, relax," he heard an unfamiliar female voice say. "Irene is right here. She's safe. You, on the other hand, have lost a lot of blood. It's a good thing she came and got me."

Carson looked over at the speaker and noticed the woman, easily in her early fifties, was gathering up the bloody sponges that had been pressed against his ribs. He looked down at the wound and saw clean white bandages wrapped around his midsection.

"You were out for a bit," Kate said. "Mrs. Dalton patched you up while you were unconscious."

He looked around and saw Irene standing next to the school nurse, tears in her eyes.

"Oh sweetie," Carson said as he reached for his little girl. "I'm so proud of you. That was really brave of you."

Irene buried her face in Carson's chest as she began to sob uncontrollably. He rubbed her back as he held her, despite the pressure on his ribs making the wound burn.

"Shhh," he said as he held her. "I'm okay."

"I was so scared, daddy," Irene said, her voice muffled as she kept her face against him. "Please don't do that again."

"It's okay, honey, I promise," Carson said as tears started to well up in his eyes. "I'm okay. You did good."

Finally, Irene looked up at him, her face puffy and red. She nodded. "You're welcome daddy."

"Sir, you probably should go to the hospital to get stitches. The wound isn't deep, but it is looks like it might be infected."

Carson looked at the middle-aged woman. "I don't know if going to the hospital is exactly feasible right now. I'm pretty sure Security Forces are going to arrest me before I can."

Mrs. Dalton, seemed to consider this for a moment. "Probably, but they'll take you to a doctor first. Why do you have a gun on school campus?"

He was about to respond when he was interrupted by a series of pops. He recognized the sound as an M-4 firing on the burst setting. *Fuck,* he thought. *They found more of those bug-things.* Irene's eyes bulged as she heard the noises and Carson felt Kate's grip on his shoulders tighten. Chris scrambled over to them and latched onto Carson's leg.

"Because of whatever Security Forces are shooting at right now," Carson said quietly. Mrs. Dalton's eyes seemed to bulge just as Irene's had. "What's out there is not like anything I have ever seen and it's how I got these." He gestured at the bandages.

"What are they?" the nurse asked.

"Hell if I know," Carson answered honestly. "Looked like some kind of mutant grasshopper, except it was the size of a Golden Retriever."

The nurse gave him a quizzical look. "You lost more blood than I thought."

"I'm serious. Those things aren't natural, and this isn't the first time they've appeared. I don't know if you have been watching the news, but those monstrosities have been seen all over the country. Apparently, they're here on base, too."

Irene looked terrified and Chris seemed to be panicking as well. They were both clinging on to Carson so tightly his wound felt like it was on fire. "Easy you guys."

Kate stood up and looked out the window. "One of the Security guys is coming this way."

Chapter 6

The officer banged on the door of the classroom. Carson wanted desperately to ignore it, but he knew something was wrong and it would only make his current predicament worse.

Kate glanced at him. Apparently, she was not keen on letting the man into the classroom either. Carson nodded and she immediately opened the door. The man burst into the room and slammed the door shut, barricading it with his body. He was out of breath and looked terrified.

Carson noted that the man was the same officer who had tried to apprehend him earlier. He figured by now the issue of his illegal possession of a firearm was the least of Senior Airman Swanson's concerns.

"You saw it, didn't you?" Carson asked. Swanson did not seem to hear him at first. He just kept glancing out the window over his shoulder.

"Hey, Airman!" Finally, Swanson's eyes met Carson's. "You saw them."

Swanson nodded, though the bewildered look in his eyes told Carson that the man did not fully believe what he had seen. "What the hell are those things?"

"I told you, they aren't natural," Carson answered, shaking his head. "I have no idea what they are."

Swanson looked out the window again and immediately dove to the floor. He had his finger to his lips as he pressed his back against the door. He quickly checked the magazine of his rifle and appeared to deflate. "Shit! I'm out of ammo."

Carson watched the young man as he began checking the front pockets of his vest. He grabbed another magazine and promptly dropped it on the floor as his hands shook. Carson wanted to try to calm the man but did not dare move. The barrel of Swanson's M-4 was pointed straight at him.

"Airman Swanson," Carson said quietly. "You need to calm down. There are kids in here and you're scaring the hell out of them."

This seemed to get Swanson's attention. "I'm sorry, Sergeant, but you have no idea what I just saw."

"Freaky grasshopper mutant the size of a dog? Looks like a movie monster?" Carson responded, unable to refrain from sarcasm. "Yeah, I think I do."

"Listen to me, *Sergeant*," Swanson said, his tone hostile as he addressed Carson. "You didn't just see three of those goddamned things jump your partner and tear his fucking limbs off!"

Almost every kid in the classroom shrieked at Swanson's words. Carson saw several kids burst into tears and cling to one another. Fantastic. Now the kids are panicking.

"Look at what you did," Carson snapped. "We were quiet until you ran your mouth. These kids were already scared but now they're losing their minds. If you intended to give away our position then you succeeded, dumbass."

"Don't you start with me!" Swanson hollered. "I wouldn't even *be* here if it weren't for you!"

"Probably a good thing you are, don't you think?" Carson retorted. "At least now I'm not the only person who encountered those things. You still want to arrest me? Or do you want to help me get these kids out of here and to safety?"

Swanson looked like he wanted to continue his tirade but thought better of it. He shook his head, snatched up the fallen magazine, and slammed it into place as the spent magazine was ejected from the rifle.

"These kids won't all fit in the squad cars. I need to call for backup, but in the meantime, we need to make sure those *things* don't get in here. I'll deal with you later, Sergeant."

"We need to get into a better defensible location," Carson snapped back. "How do you propose we do that? I have maybe two rounds left in my pistol and no spare mags. Looks to me like you're the only person who stands between those freaks and the kids in this room. So, pick yourself up and keep it together. See if you can contact command and let them know, if they don't already."

Swanson cursed under his breath, though Carson heard him clearly enough. He was not sure what the man was thinking but he doubted it boded well for him. Carson regrettably half-expected the officer to ditch them and run for safety. He couldn't say he would have blamed Swanson if he did.

"Like I said, I don't have many rounds left," Carson began. "I can't provide any measure of backup unless you have a spare pistol mag or two. My pistol is a nine mil, just like the ones you guys get issued with. Otherwise, we're fucked."

"Shit," Swanson hissed. Swanson ran a hand over his face. Carson could see that the man was frustrated. "I have only a couple of mags on me besides the one that's in my sidearm. Those *freaks* take a lot to put down. Unfortunately, my rifle is pretty much empty. My partner had a couple of mags on him, along with his rifle."

Swanson pulled a full magazine from the pouch near his holster and tossed it to Carson. Carson reached out to catch the magazine and felt an intense burning in his side. The magazine clattered to the floor. Carson scooped it up with shaking hands, examined the magazine and then ejected the nearly empty one from his pistol. His vision blurred slightly as he slapped the full magazine in the well. He knew he still had a round in the chamber, so he didn't bother pulling the slide back.

"How far away from here is he?" Carson asked hesitantly. "I know you don't want to go back there, but if it's close, we can get to your partner, grab what we need, and get back."

"No fucking way!" Swanson barked. "There is no way in hell I am going back there!"

"Airman Swanson, you have a better idea?"

"Yeah, how about I just-?" Swanson glanced around the classroom and chose not to finish his sentence. "Damn it! No, I don't. Listen, Sergeant, I don't know you and I don't trust you, but I know you have at least *some* training with firearms and the two of us working together gives these kids the best chance of getting out of here. But make no mistake, you fall behind, and I will leave your ass. Got it?"

Carson scowled and wanted to say something scathing but resisted. Instead, he just nodded. "Whatever you say, boss."

Kate took the opportunity to chime in. "Don't tell me you're thinking about going back out there!"

Carson sighed. "We need to. Airman Swanson needs to restock on ammunition, and we need to radio for help."

Kate glared at him, her hands on her hips. "Then let him go get it. You don't need to go, too."

"I'm not going to let him go by himself," Carson countered.

"You just want an excuse to play the hero," Kate muttered under her breath.

"If he gets attacked out there, then we're on our own," Carson replied, hoping to make Kate see reason. "It'll be safer if I watch his back."

"Whatever," Kate snapped and then turned away to walk back toward Chris and Irene, indicating that the conversation was over. Carson just sighed and joined Airman Swanson by the door.

Swanson peered out of the window and took a moment to survey the area. Satisfied that nothing was creeping right outside the door he slowly opened the classroom door and stepped out. Carson crept beside him, peering around the man and scanned the area. His heart thudded in his chest at the prospect of encountering another of those creatures, but he reminded himself that his family was counting on him to get them away safely.

Swanson turned to his left and began heading toward the parking lot in front of the school

"Where are you going?" Carson questioned as quietly as possible while still being heard.

"I need to radio for backup," Swanson snapped back. "This shitshow is already out of hand. I have a man down and a school full of children. There is no way in hell that the two of us will be able to get them all out safely."

Carson scowled but nodded. "Fine."

Swanson slowly advanced, pistol up and ready. Carson followed suit, careful to avoid sweeping the man with the barrel of his own pistol. He stayed low, despite the pain in his side. They moved forward at an agonizingly slow pace, but Carson understood the necessity. The last thing they wanted was to wander into a pack of the monstrous beasts.

The pair neared the corner of one of the classrooms, which Carson recognized as the kindergarten classrooms near the front of the school. Swanson pressed himself against the side of the building and carefully peered around the corner. Carson did the same, staying as close to the man as possible. He saw Swanson's shoulders droop and his head sag.

"Son of a bitch," Swanson swore.

"What is it?" Carson asked, fearful that Swanson may have spotted a swarm of the creatures or something equally terrible.

"The car," Swanson replied quietly.

Carson looked over Swanson's shoulder and saw what had deflated the man. The squad car was trashed. Massive gouges covered the engine compartment, and the windshield was smashed in. Smoke billowed from the engine. It appeared as though something massive had unloaded every ounce of rage on the vehicle. The side of the car was crumpled as though it had been T-boned by dump truck.

"Any chance the radio still works?"

Swanson exhaled a deep sigh and shook his head. "Without power from the battery it would be about as useful as a brick." He pointed at the front of the squad car. Battery acid, from what Carson could tell, appeared to be leaking onto the ground underneath and mingling with other fluids.

"Shit," Carson spat. "What now? What about your radio on your vest?"

Swanson pulled the receiver of his radio off his vest and held it up for Carson to see. The cable had been severed and the handheld receiver looked smashed. He had survived his first encounter with the monsters, but his radio hadn't.

"Is there a chance your partner's radio is intact?'

Swanson looked over at him, pain in his eyes. "I don't know. Probably not. I-I don't think I can go back to his body."

Carson nodded. "I understand, but we don't have another choice now. Those kids need us."

Swanson leaned his back against the wall and looked skyward. He was shaking.

"Come on, Airman," Carson said, his tone a bit more forceful than he intended. "You need to pull yourself together. Hundreds of children are counting on you to get them out of here."

Swanson glared at him and opened his mouth as if to scream at him, but slowly closed it and took a deep, shaky breath. "Give me a moment, *Sergeant.*"

It was Carson's turn to glare, but he chose not to respond. Instead, Carson took a moment to peer into the window to the classroom next to him. The room was dark, and it took him a couple of seconds for his eyes to adjust. Thankfully, the classroom was empty.

"Whatever did that to your squad car was a lot bigger than those grasshopper creatures," Carson said quietly. Swanson didn't reply. "What about the phone in the main office?"

"That may work," Swanson said after a moment, his breath shaky. "So long as the office isn't locked. The whole school is on lockdown so I wouldn't bet on it."

"Worth a try."

"Anything is better than sitting around out here," Swanson agreed.

The pair slowly stepped out from the cover of the kindergarten classroom and slowly made their way toward the office. Carson was looking around frantically, afraid that something would jump out at them. For once Carson was comfortable with his overactive anxiety. It kept him alert, and the fogginess he was experiencing before had seemingly vanished. To his relief nothing sprang at them from under cover. The advance toward the office was agonizingly slow despite the short distance.

Swanson held up a closed fist as they reached the office door. Carson stopped obediently and waited as Swanson knocked on the door. Carson could hear movement inside the office and slowly let out a breath when he saw a pair of eyes peering out at them from the window. The eyes disappeared and then the office door slowly opened.

"Ma'am, I'm Senior Airman Diego Swanson," Carson heard Swanson whisper. "I'm with Security Forces. I need to use your phone to call in. My radio isn't working."

Carson waited quietly nearby, his eyes constantly scanning his surroundings. He saw the door to the office open wider as the woman behind it let Swanson inside. Carson wanted to follow, but he knew his appearance—including the blood covering his left side—would likely scare the office administrator. Instead, Carson opted to stay outside. The pain in his side still burned and he had to shake the fog from his head. The wound wasn't fatal. He knew that much. However, he *had* lost a fair amount of blood, and it took a great deal of effort to stay upright.

Diego Swanson came out of the office a moment later, his face red. Carson figured the response Swanson had received was less than he had hoped for.

"My squadron can't spare anyone," Swanson growled. "Apparently the entire base is swarming with those monsters."

Carson's heart sank and he suddenly felt queasy. "So now what?"

"I have orders to secure the location," Swanson said, shaking his head. "If that doesn't work then we will have to get the kids out of here. Leadership suggested utilizing the school busses if needed."

Carson leaned against the wall, afraid that his knees were going to buckle. He had been hoping for more. The news that more of the nightmare creatures were on the base flooded him with dread. "So, we're on our own."

"Yeah," Swanson sighed. "Looks like it." His chin dropped to his chest and his eyes closed. "Fuck!"

"Our best bet, then, is to move everyone into the cafeteria like I suggested," Carson said more calmly than he felt, trying to relax the young man. "It would be a far more defensible location. I-I don't want to suggest this again, but…we need to get your partner's rifle and ammunition. I'm not much use with just a pistol."

Swanson swiveled his head toward Carson, a murderous look on his face. "You want me to go back to my friend's corpse and loot it?"

"I'm sorry about your friend," Carson said slowly, choosing his words carefully. "But I don't think he would want us to defend the school as we are. I'm not fond of the idea, either, but we need any advantage we can get. Fall back on your training and push your emotions aside, Airman Swanson. It's not about you or me. It's about the kids. It's about our duty to protect them."

Swanson stared at his boots and took several large breaths. "You're right, Sergeant. I know you're right. I-I'm just not ready to see him like that."

"I understand," Carson tentatively placed a hand on Swanson's shoulder. He was glad that Swanson didn't shake his hand away. "I don't want to see that either, but we're short on options and low on firepower."

"Dammit," he hissed. "Alright, let's go. We get over there, grab the rifle, the spare magazines and anything else we may need and then we get everyone inside the cafeteria."

Chapter 7

Carson and Swanson crouched under the shadow of the tenant building of the school. Carson was thankful that neither of his children were trapped in one of the classrooms detached from the main building. The short walk from the cafeteria to where they now stood had been nerve-wracking, as they anticipated an ambush at every step.

The gap spanned perhaps one hundred feet, but it had felt like miles as Carson and Swanson crossed it without the comfort of cover. Now that they had reached the outer building, they took a moment to settle their nerves. Carson knew that Swanson was just as terrified, though he suspected a large portion of that fear was reserved for seeing his dead partner.

Carson had never seen a dead body in person. Television didn't count since the corpses were either actors in heavy makeup or a dummy. He knew that seeing a corpse in person would be vastly different and he had to suppress his anxiety.

He noticed that he was on the verge of a panic attack, which he had not had for years. His fingers tingled, as did his face around the nose and mouth. His stomach felt constricted, and his vision was starting to blur. Carson placed a hand against the wall to his right and focused on slowing his breathing. Swanson did not say a word.

It took a full five minutes for Carson to get his nerves under control. Swanson looked shaky, which somehow comforted Carson. Perhaps seeing another person struggling to stay under control just as he had kept him from feeling inept. Carson had to remind himself that he was human, and it was perfectly reasonable to feel fear in his current situation.

Swanson glanced over his shoulder at Carson. "Are you going to be able to do this?"

Carson nodded. "Yeah. You?"

Swanson sighed but did not reply. Instead, he checked around the corner of the building, his rifle at low-ready. Carson saw his body tense for a moment and a breath caught in Carson's chest. The tension in Swanson's body passed after a moment. They were, fortunately, not under attack. He had most likely spotted his partner.

"Let's go, low and slow," Swanson whispered.

Carson stayed within arm's length of him as they moved away from the building at a low crouch. After several steps Carson felt an ache creeping into his lower back. He couldn't understand how people could move in such a way for any length of time.

Oddly, Carson was reminded of a video game that relied on stealth. The characters often traversed large distances in the stance that Carson was currently adopting. *Another inaccuracy of video games and entertainment,* Carson thought to himself. He gave a small shake of his head and pulled himself out of his head and into reality.

Swanson went to one knee as he arrived next to his fallen partner. Carson felt his stomach flip and tumble as the body came into view. He had tried to mentally prepare himself for the sight but had ultimately failed. The shock of reality nearly swept the ground out from beneath his feet. The overwhelming coppery smell of blood, intermingled with bile, made Carson vomit. He turned away and retched into the tall grass. After several seconds he turned back toward Swanson, but the smell and the sight made him retch a second time. Carson felt a hand on his shoulder.

"Take a moment," Swanson said with surprising warmth in his voice. Carson could not answer besides nodding weakly.

Instead of looking at the body Carson looked at the surrounding area. He caught the glint of light off spent bullet casings in the grass. Some of those had probably come from Swanson's rifle. What struck Carson as odd was the lack of blood nearby, other than where the body lay.

From the lack of a blood trail and the close grouping of bullet casings it was highly likely that the man had not had time to run before he was cut down. He did not see many casings in the grass so that probably meant the poor man had barely even had time to fire his rifle. Fortunately, the man had died quickly.

After taking in the information, Carson found it easier to disconnect his emotions from what he was seeing. To him it became a collection of information. He found that he was able to look at the body without vomiting. The smell still turned his stomach, but Carson managed to suppress it. He carefully knelt and lifted the rifle from the ground beside the body. He inspected the weapon, making sure that dirt or blood had not coated the weapon. He saw several spots of blood and decided he would spend time taking the weapon apart and cleaning it later. He had a cleaning kit at his home, should he ever return.

The rifle was attached to the body by a sling. Carson had to shift the weight of the body to free the weapon. He felt his stomach churn momentarily as he touched the corpse with his bare hands. He slid the sling off the body and contemplated removing the sling from the rifle.

Blood had seeped into the nylon and Carson felt that it would never wash out completely. He was squeamish about letting the sling touch any part of his body. He ultimately decided to keep the sling attached but would not use it, as he would have to touch the bloody thing just to remove it. He let the nylon strap hang below the weapon, careful to avoid letting it touch him.

Carson's trepidation ended up being pointless as he had to slide the spare magazines from the blood-soaked tactical vest. He tried in vain to wipe the magazines clean in the grass. After a moment he gave up and stuffed several of the magazines in his jacket pockets and handed the others to Swanson.

"Good thing I used the phone in the office," Swanson whispered as he held up the broken remains of his partner's radio.

"Yeah, but having a working radio would have been convenient," Carson replied as he ejected the magazine from the pistol that was still in its holster on the body. The magazine was completely full and there were more in a pouch next to the holster. Carson handed one over to Swanson and kept the other. He also removed the emergency medical kit from the tactical vest. For a moment Carson considered using the quick-clot bandage in the kit but decided against it. His wound was not deep enough to need it.

"Let's get back to the classroom and start moving everyone into the cafeteria," Carson said.

Swanson looked over at him and opened his mouth to answer, but nothing came out. His eyes went wide as he looked over Carson's shoulder. Carson immediately felt his muscles begin locking up. He heard an unearthly grown somewhere behind him. He had hoped desperately to avoid running into the freakish monstrosities again.

"Down!" Swanson bellowed as he raised his rifle. Carson barely had time to react when he fired. Fortunately,

Carson did not hesitate to drop to the ground. He rolled onto his back as he heard rapid reports from Swanson's rifle. As he looked past his feet, he saw one of the grasshopper-things jerk as the bullets struck it. Carson immediately noted that this creature appeared significantly larger than the one that had attacked him.

It also had wings and another pair of appendages. The thing was nearly the size of a box truck.

Carson gripped his rifle in both hands, his thumb quickly checking the selector on the side. After noting that the safety on the weapon was off, he pulled the trigger. Three quick shots were fired in rapid succession. If Carson had had time, he would have checked the chamber to ensure there was a round in it, but he had been distracted. He was thankful that the weapon had been ready to go.

The beast slowly approached in a jerky manner as it seemingly shrugged off the bullets hitting it. Carson took a second to aim for the glowing red eyes and carefully squeezed the trigger. The rifle bucked mildly in his hands as several more rounds exited the barrel. The creature reared backwards as its left eye exploded.

"The eyes!" Carson yelled. "Go for the eyes!"

Swanson quickly adjusted his aim and carefully fired as he strafed to the right, pulling the thing's attention away from Carson's prone form. Carson noted that Swanson had not switched his rifle to burst fire. He understood and thumbed the selector forward one click, changing the firing mode of his rifle to semi-automatic. He continued to aim at the monster's eyes, firing off several rounds and then adjusting his aim when the freakish maw of the beast opened. His first shot was wide by an inch and glanced off the outside of the creature's jaw. His second and third shots were true. The creature shuddered and then fell in a heap.

"Holy shit," Carson gasped as he crawled to his feet, his eyes staying on the creature. "Do you think that was the thing that tore up your car?"

"Probably," Swanson wheezed. "Bastard was big enough."

"Let's get the hell out of here," Carson said.

"Agreed," Swanson replied.

The pair took off back toward the center of the school at a sprint.

Chapter 8

What had started as an already bizarre day had turned into a full-blown nightmare. Carson could never have predicted that the events of the day would have unfolded as they had. People were often bored of the mundane, the predictability of their narrowly focused worlds, and often would wish for something exciting and new. It was no surprise that myths and fantasy were so popular. Carson, at that moment, would have given anything for a return to his mundane life.

The encounter with the massive creature and his first-hand observation of a dead body shook him. He knew that he could very easily become catatonic if he fixated on it. Humans weren't inherently prepared for such a shock to the system. He already felt some of the tell-tale symptoms, not too unlike from a panic attack, and forced himself to focus on something else entirely: The M-4 rifle in his hands.

The rifle was practically identical to the M-16 he had been required to train on during basic training. He had grown proficient with the operation and maintenance of the rifle in a short time. The M-16 had been a bit clunky in his opinion and the M-4 was a pleasant upgrade, much like his AR-15. The red dot sight was a welcome change from the dismal iron sights of the M-16.

Carson had very nearly received a score of Marksman when he trained on the M-16, until he had to hastily clear a jam near the end of the exercise that caused him to forget which side of the target he had been aiming at. The target had six different sized silhouettes on it to simulate distance and in his haste, he had missed his last three shots.

Carson knew he would have far less trouble with the upgraded sight. It also helped that he wasn't wearing a worn-out gas mask with cheap vison-correcting inserts to stand in for his glasses that did little more than distort his vision. Carson also appreciated that the stock of the M-4 allowed for adjustment, once again like his AR-15, which helped as Carson was below average height. He would have to take the rifle apart completely to clean it when he got the chance, but he knew that he would have little trouble doing so.

As he and Swanson carefully made their way back to the cafeteria Carson examined the ejection port of the rifle. He was glad that there was no sign of dirt or, worse, blood around it. There was a good chance that the interior components had not been compromised. After firing the weapon Carson was relatively confident that it would not misfire, as he had sent a dozen rounds through it without incident. But he would strip it down and check it all the same. There was no sense in taking chances.

Shifting his attention to the details of the rifle helped calm Carson's nerves. He had found that he was capable of what he called "clinical detachment" when he needed to. He had done so after he and Swanson arrived at the corpse of the fallen Airman.

If he focused on information and kept his emotions at bay, he would be able to focus on the current mission. It would be difficult since his family was at significant risk, but his rigorous training would not be wasted. He knew how to focus on a task with laser-like precision, and it was that focus that would keep his loved ones alive.

Carson's attention was pulled away when Swanson spoke. "We need to evacuate the classroom that you were in, first. After everyone is safely inside the cafeteria, we will check the rest of the classrooms."

Carson nodded. "When I was in the cafeteria it looked nearly full. Most of the classrooms are probably empty."

"Probably," Swanson said. "But I won't be satisfied until we're one hundred percent positive. I know you want to stay with your family, Sergeant, but I am going to need your help in clearing the rest of the school. Can you do that?"

"Better to be safe than sorry, Airman Swanson. Yeah, I can do that."

"You sure?"

"Yes," Carson nearly snapped. Swanson's constant challenges to his integrity were starting to get to him.

"Sling your rifle before we go in the classroom," Swanson instructed. "We don't want to spook the children. It will be scary enough seeing you armed."

"Don't worry," Carson assured him, though the idea of letting the blood-soaked sling touch his body made him feel sick. "I had already planned to."

"Good," Swanson replied. "And with everything going to hell in handbasket, just call me Diego."

"Fair enough," Carson responded. "You can call me Carson."

The pair reached the classroom holding Carson's family and as instructed, he looped the sling of the rifle over his shoulder. He felt a squirming sensation across his skin as the blood-soaked nylon touched him. Diego slung his weapon as well and then they opened the door. Carson immediately sought out Irene, Chris, and Kate in the gloom of the classroom. He saw the look of relief cross their features when they saw him. Then Kate's expression changed to concern.

"Is help on the way?" she asked.

Carson hesitated, unsure of how to best answer the question. He decided to be direct. "No, not at the moment. We're on our own for now. Airman Swanson, Diego, is under orders to secure everyone in the cafeteria for the time being.”

Kate did not look pleased. “What? Why the hell not?”

Carson took a deep breath and opened his mouth to reply. Diego beat him to it. “The base is on lockdown. The Security Forces Squadron has its hands full with keeping the base safe. For now, they can’t spare any manpower. Your husband has enough training to help me keep you all safe. But first we need to get you all into the cafeteria.”

Kate scowled while Irene and Chris continued to look terrified. Their expressions were mirrored by the rest of the children in the classroom.

“Are there more monsters?” Chris asked. This made his older sister’s eyes nearly bulge in their sockets. Chris had always been the more observant one.

“I don’t know, buddy,” Carson said gently. “But there aren’t any more near us.”

Irene did not look convinced. Her breathing started to come in short bursts, and she fired off questions in between each inhalation. “What if they come back? What if they try to get us when we leave the room?”

“Then Diego and I will get rid of them before you guys come out,” Carson said, trying to comfort his daughter.

"Your daddy and I already killed a big monster," Diego said with surprising tenderness. "The little ones will be no match for us, okay? We kicked their leader's butt."

Irene nodded and seemed to relax a bit. Carson looked over his shoulder and mouthed the word "thanks." Diego nodded in reply. Carson had to admit that the young man was growing on him. Carson found that he was beginning to trust him. The glimpse past the disciplined exterior helped him relate to Diego. The gentleness with which he handled the frightened children helped improve Carson's opinion of him.

"What I need you all to do is gather your things and form an orderly line," Diego instructed. He looked at the older woman near the rear of the classroom. "Ma'am, can you make sure they do what they're told?"

"Yes, Officer," she replied shakily. Then she switched into teacher-mode and was all business. Carson watched as she checked every child to make sure they had everything they needed and ensured that they stayed calm. Carson admired the ease with which the woman handled the frightened children. He knew she was as terrified as the kids, but she didn't show it.

"Okay, now," Diego continued. "Sergeant Tanner and I will go out first to make sure the coast is clear and then we'll wave our hand. When you see that I want you guys to come out of the class in a neat line and follow us. Don't wander off or stop moving until we get you into the cafeteria, okay?"

Nearly thirty small heads nodded in response. Carson felt his pulse quicken as he prepared to step out of the relative safety of the classroom. He took a deep breath and focused his attention on his mission.

"Remember, wait for us to wave before you follow us," Diego said just before he opened the door. Carson stood right behind him and unslung the rifle from his shoulder, keeping the weapon in a low-ready position, imitating Diego's actions.

Diego carefully opened the door and, leading with his rifle, glanced around before stepping out. Carson followed suit, making sure the barrel of his weapon never swept over Diego's back. Behind them Kate, Chris, and Irene waited. Diego glanced back at Carson and nodded. Carson turned and waved at the classroom. Behind him his family, twenty-five children, and the elderly schoolteacher followed.

"We should go home," Kate whispered to Carson.

He looked over his shoulder at her incredulously. "Home? Getting to the house is way too dangerous right now. We need to get to a defensible position."

"The house is defensible position."

"What about everyone else? The other kids? There's not enough room at the house for everyone."

"We need to keep *our* kids safe," Kate hissed.

Carson stopped and turned back to look at her. "Are you suggesting that we leave the others behind, to face whatever the fuck is attacking? Didn't you hear what Diego said. The whole damn base is on lock-down. There not just here."

"Diego already radioed for help. As long as he stays with everyone, they'll be fine until backup can show up."

"There isn't any backup, Kate," Carson retorted. "Diego is one person. He won't be able to protect them all by himself."

"Oh no, you're right," Kate snapped, rolling her eyes. "We need *you* to protect everyone. Is that it?"

"What? I-," he threw his hands up. "No, that's not it. It's about safety in numbers." With that, he turned back and continued following Diego.

"Sure," Kate muttered. "As long as you get to play the hero."

Chapter 9

They turned right after leaving the classroom. Ahead was a wide pavilion with a recessed area in the center. Ringing the pavilion were buildings, other classrooms. After clearing the corner of the building Carson and Diego turned right again. Less than fifty yards directly ahead of them were the main office and cafeteria. Hugging the wall, Carson and Diego slowly moved forward, their eyes scanning their surroundings.

Carson held his rifle with his right hand and felt the wound on his ribs with his left. He knew the wounds would likely need stitches, though the bandages were doing what was necessary. The bandage put pressure on the wound, slowing the bleeding. Carson would need to change the dressing and hoped there were butterfly bandages in the medical kit he had fixed to his belt. He was conscious of the kit's presence; afraid it would come lose and fall to the ground. Hopefully, the cafeteria had a restroom so he could tend the wound. If not, the kitchen would have to do.

As quietly as possible they escorted the frightened children across the pavilion and made it to the large, heavy doors of the cafeteria without incident.

Irene was working hard to keep her breathing under control while Chris walked quietly. He would probably break down later once they were all safe inside the cafeteria walls.

Diego rapped his knuckles on the door and stood impatiently while someone answered it from the other side. Carson recognized the woman who peered out at them and knew she recognized him as well. It was Mrs. Dupont again. If Diego hadn't been standing in front of him, she would probably have shut the door on them. Fortunately, Diego's presence seemed to pacify the woman a bit.

"Ma'am, we have close to thirty children out here," Diego explained calmly. He had even adjusted his stance to appear less imposing. "I have orders to secure them inside with the rest of the school's population."

Mrs. Dupont merely nodded.

"Do you know if there are any other children unaccounted for?" Diego continued. Carson was content to let the man do the talking.

"I'm not sure," she replied, peering over Diego's shoulders with narrowed eyes. "We were in the middle of afterschool pick-up when we had to lock everything down. Some of the parents might have already picked up their children and went home. Sorry."

Diego nodded, though his expression made his frustration obvious. "I see. Well, I will be searching the classrooms for anyone who may not be in here."

"And him?" she asked, glaring at Carson.

"Sergeant Carson is assisting me, ma'am," Diego responded. Mrs. Dupont did not seem thoroughly satisfied. "He will be with me at all times, I assure you."

Carson wanted to speak. He wanted to clear the air and put the woman at ease, though he knew nothing he said would help. Instead, Carson remained silent, careful to avoid her piercing gaze. The distrust hurt him. He had not meant to frighten the woman, but the safety of his children had been more important than her feelings at the time. Now he just felt like a bully, and it sickened him.

Mrs. Dupont opened the door and allowed Diego to usher the children inside, followed by the elderly schoolteacher and Carson's wife. Diego waited for them to get inside before following. Carson worried for a moment that Mrs. Dupont would shut the door on him and was relieved when she didn't.

"Ma'am, is there a restroom inside?" Carson asked gently. He tried to seem as unthreatening as possible.

"Off to the side, through the main office," she replied after a moment. It seemed to Carson that the woman was hesitant to divulge the trivial information, as if Carson might be planning to do something crazy—like plant a bomb.

He gestured toward the blood-soaked dressing on his side. "I don't want to scare the kids, but I need to tend to my wounds. Is the nurse's office in this building as well?"

"In the office, same as the restroom," was the only reply before Mrs. Dupont turned away from him and resumed checking on the children under her care.

Carson caught up to Diego and quickly informed the young man that he was going to change the dressing on his wound and would be right back. Diego nodded.

The school's office was small. Carson saw three large desks in the small space and noted that the administrative staff were still at their stations. He had been inside the office before, but he had only been near the rear once when he and Kate had enrolled their children. A door stood open and on the wall near the frame stood a sign saying *School Nurse*. He set his rifle against the wall at the behest of the staff and gently knocked on the open door. The woman inside was thin, with dark hair that had begun to gray. She had a gentle expression and didn't seem startled by his presence. Carson felt a small measure of relief, up until the nurse noticed the blood.

"Oh my God!" the nurse, Mrs. Weathers, nearly yelled. "What happened?"

"Animal attack," Carson replied, not entirely lying.

"You need a hospital," she said.

"I can't get to the hospital right now," Carson said, mildly irritated. "The base is on lockdown. I just need to clean the wound and get a proper dressing on it."

The nurse nodded and motioned for him to sit down on the small bench in her office. He felt silly sitting on a bench reserved for a small child but did so anyway. He slowly pulled off his jacket, wincing as the movement pulled the wounds open. Carson had to catch his breath as he set the jacket to the side and slowly pulled his shirt up to reveal the bandage.

"It's soaking through the bandages," Mrs. Weathers noted. "You don't look good."

"Must be the adrenaline," Carson offered. He had to admit that he was feeling incredibly lightheaded again. "Or maybe the things carried some kind of bacteria. I tried to disinfect it as much as I could."

The nurse nodded. She directed him to hold the sponge to his side as she rummaged in her desk. She pulled out a roll of gauze, rubbing alcohol, and some large Band-Aids. "This won't be as good as stitches, but it will at least keep the wound closed and keep anything out of the wound. You'll still need to go to the hospital once the lockdown is lifted."

Carson watched as she grabbed a wad of brown paper towels and pressed them against the wound after removing the saturated bandage. "Hold that there," she instructed. Carson followed her direction and pressed the paper towels painfully against his ribs. Slowly, after dousing a paper towel with rubbing alcohol and applying it to the wound, Mrs. Weathers removed the wrappers from the bandages and stretched them across both sides of the large gashes, pulling the wound closed. She nearly emptied the box of Band-Aids as she finished. She took the bloody paper towels from Carson and deposited them in a waste bin with a red plastic bag poking over the rim. He had seen the same thing in doctor's offices. Mrs. Weathers carefully removed the latex gloves and dropped them in the bin following the paper towels.

Pulling on a clean pair of gloves, the nurse began winding the roll of gauze around Carson's torso. It was tight enough to keep the pressure on the wound but not so tight that it was terribly painful. "That will have to do," she said as she stepped back, examining her work.

"Thank you, ma'am," Carson said as he lowered his shirt over the dressing and began pulling on his jacket. He felt the tug of the bandages against his skin as he shifted. Carson stood up to leave and immediately fell over, his vision going black.

***

A face appeared before Carson, scraggly and gaunt. He immediately could feel that something was off about the man before him. The man moved toward him in jerking, uncoordinated movements. Unkept hair draped over the man's shoulders. Carson felt a surge of panic as the man's face seemed to swell and then the skin parted vertically down the center. The sides of the man's head moved outward and in the center of the ragged wound was a row of pointed, jagged teeth. Near where the man's mouth had been Carson could see an eye peering at him.

The image shifted rapidly and then Carson was staring at a large red line. He was confused as he tried to make sense of the image. Slowly he became aware that the line had appeared in the air before him, as if reality were tearing. The red line widened, and Carson could see movement from within the blood-colored depths. Appendages poked out of the red depths, like the legs of a very large spider.

***

Carson sat up with a start. He noticed that he was on a thinly carpeted floor, the legs of a bench near his face. It took him a moment to get his bearings. He remembered that he had been in the school nurse's office and the next thing he knew he was confronted with nightmarish images. A voice that sounded too far away was trying to get his attention.

"Sir, are you alright?" came a woman's voice.

Carson blinked stupidly at the voice's owner. She repeated the question and Carson slowly nodded.

"Sorry, I...uh, I must have fainted," Carson answered. "I'm okay."

He felt hands under his arms as he tried to get to his feet. His legs felt like jelly. Carson blinked, but the room continued to spin. He must have lost more blood than he had thought. But what was with the bizarre dream?

"I'm not sure if you fainted or not. Your eyes rolled in the back of your head," Mrs. Weathers said with a noticeable tremor. "You're lucky you didn't hit your head when you blacked out. If you fall outside, you could really injure yourself."

"I'll be okay," Carson asserted. "I just need a moment to collect myself. Could I get a glass of water?"

She nodded and filled a small paper cup with water from the tap. She handed it to Carson, and he took it as he sat on the bench, sipping from it slowly.

Once again Carson found himself wondering about the second nightmare — vision? — of the day. Already he was struggling to remember the details and after a moment he began to wonder if he had imagined it. By the time Carson left the nurse's office and rejoined his family he had nearly forgotten the nightmare completely.

113

<h1 style="text-align:center">Chapter 10</h1>

Carson and Diego stood near the doors of the cafeteria, planning how best to check all the classrooms quickly. Diego had suggested starting with the outermost classrooms and working their way inward. Carson contemplated the suggestion. It certainly made sense, but he wasn't comfortable leaving the cafeteria out of sight for too long. No matter how they planned to search the school, they would have no choice but to leave the rest of the kids unprotected for longer than was desirable.

"Maybe we should start with the closest ones first," Carson suggested. "Then move to the outer classes and work back towards the cafeteria."

Diego shook his head. "If there are any kids in the outlying classrooms they'll be at the greatest risk. We know that these kids here are relatively safe. We can't say the same for any stragglers. Those creatures seem to be hanging around the perimeter."

"Yeah, I know," Carson replied, nodding slowly. "But that could change, too. I just want to make sure they stay safe, and I would feel better if I could easily keep watch."

"No matter what we need to get everyone else to safety," Diego retorted, his tone growing harsh. "The cafeteria is safer than anywhere else in the school. Think about the others."

Carson sighed. He knew Diego was right, as much as he hated it. He couldn't help thinking about the damage to the squad car in the parking lot. If the creatures could do *that* to a car, he doubted the doors of the cafeteria would hold for long if the creatures decided to get in.

"Nobody in here is armed except us," Carson said after a moment. "If those creatures try to get in, they'll be sitting ducks." An idea quickly came to him. "I can leave my pistol with my wife. She might hate it, but she knows how to shoot it, somewhat, and knows how to be safe with a firearm."

"I'm not comfortable leaving a civilian armed," Diego scowled as he spoke. "Anything goes wrong and it's on me."

"Actually, it would be on me. Like I said, my wife has some experience," Carson said, trying to keep his voice even. "It would be better than leaving them without any protection."

Diego looked at the ceiling, clearly conflicted. Carson understood. The suggestion was not ideal, but the alternative was a nightmare in the making. Lacking manpower, they would have to trust someone with the children's safety. Carson trusted his wife to handle the task, but Diego clearly was not thoroughly convinced.

"She and I have been to a firing range several times," Carson continued. "She knows how to handle the pistol and how to handle any complications that may arise. She knows how to clear a jam, how to reload, and how to field strip the pistol if absolutely necessary."

Diego continued to scowl, though Carson saw his expression falter. He was getting through to the man. "I don't know," Diego said after a moment.

"Either that, or I stay here while you go out alone," Carson replied, quickly losing his patience. "I'm not leaving those kids unprotected."

The look Diego gave Carson was disconcerting. For a moment he worried that Diego would lose it and shoot him. The poor guy was clearly stressed, and the fear threatened to break him. Diego hung his head and shook it. "Shit, fine. But if *anything* happens it is your ass, Sergeant."

"Yep," Carson retorted. "Let's get this done and get back here as quickly as possible."

Carson strode over to Kate and sat next to her on the cramped bench, kids huddled close together as they tried to understand what was happening. He kept his back to the kids and leaned close to Kate so he could keep his voice low. He carefully pulled the pistol from the holster at his waist and handed it over to her. She stared at him. He could tell that she wanted to refuse it, but it seemed that reality had finally set in.

"Airman Swanson and I are going to make sure there are no other kids stuck in the other classrooms," Carson whispered. "I wasn't going to go unless we left someone here armed. I trust you."

"I've never shot anything living," Kate argued. "All I ever shot were targets."

"I know," Carson replied, his hand on her shoulder. "Think of whatever might be a threat as a target, nothing more. Don't think about it being a living, breathing thing."

"What if I miss?"

Carson pulled two full magazines from his jacket pocket. "Between the ammunition already in the pistol and these, you'll be sure to hit *something*. Don't overthink it. You can do this. Chris and Irene need you. I need you. The kids in this school need you. You *can* do it."

Kate nodded slowly, staring at the full-sized pistol in her small hands. Carson had left out that Kate hated guns and did not like handling the large pistol. He did not think that Diego needed to know that.

Carson kissed Kate on the cheek and wrapped his arm around her shoulders. "I'll be back before you know it."

She looked up at him. "You'd better."

Diego looked up when Carson joined him. Sweat had begun forming on his brow and his breath was shaky. Carson knew how he felt. The idea of going back outside and possibly running into more monsters unnerved him as well.

"You ready to go?" Diego asked, not looking at Carson.

"As ready as I'll ever be," Carson answered. "Let's get this over with."

Diego checked his weapon and made sure the spare magazines were in their pouches on his vest. Carson did the same, working the charging handle halfway so that the ejection port opened. A round sat in the chamber. Carson ejected the magazine and, upon noting that it was half-spent, decided to swap it out and stick in a full one. He nodded to Diego when he was ready.

Diego took a deep breath and slowly opened the heavy metal door. He peered outside as the door opened. Carson tried to look over Diego's shoulder, but since Carson was several inches shorter than the man, he could not see much of anything except the orange-tinted sky.

The sun was setting.

He had not expected to see a sunset and realized that he had lost track of time. How long had they been at the school? He had been at the school for hours. The realization formed a pit in his stomach. It will be dark soon.

Once Diego stepped outside Carson could see clearly. Nothing moved nearby. He could see the parking lot, the curb where parents would park to pick up their kids, and the road beyond. Across the street was the after-school club building on one side and an open field on the other. He fixed his gaze on the tall grass in the field, watching for movement. He stared for a moment and then realized that Diego had already walked around the corner of the building. With great difficulty, Carson turned his attention away and walked quickly to catch up.

"Don't fall behind," Diego said quietly.

"I didn't," Carson said. "I was watching the field across the street. We don't want one of those freaky bastards sneaking up on us."

"True, but we need to stay together. You see something you let me know. You watch my back, and I watch yours."

"Copy," Carson said in agreement. He quickly glanced back over his shoulder, his attention on the field once again. "No movement behind us."

Diego began moving again, his rifle pointed ahead. Carson kept his rifle in the low-ready position. If anything came at them from the front Diego would have a clear shot. Carson made himself responsible for the rear while also checking the rooftops.

Their progress was slow and methodical. Diego and Carson had started with the outer building at the rear of the school. They knocked on the doors of the classrooms and glanced into the windows. Each room was empty. Satisfied that the building had been cleared they began moving inwards. Diego continued to take the lead and Carson, lacking the level of body armor that Diego was still wearing, was content to follow.

The next set of classrooms, which was to the right as they approached from the rear of the school, were all empty except one. Diego motioned for Carson to knock on the door as he kept watch. Carson let the rifle hang by the sling as he knocked on the door. He glanced through the window and saw the faces of terrified children. His heart started to beat rapidly as an older man answered the door.

"Sir, Officer Swanson and I have been instructed by the Security Forces Squadron to escort you and your students to the cafeteria," Carson said quickly. The older man squinted at him, clearly apprehensive, and then looked over at Diego in full uniform. The sight of the other man served to placate the elderly schoolteacher.

"Can you tell me what is going on?" the man asked.

"I don't have a lot of information," Carson answered. "The base is on lock-down. We're not sure when the lock-down will be lifted."

Carson decided to leave out the fact that the base was being invaded by nightmare creatures that had already killed one officer. It seemed more sensible to omit the information to avoid starting a panic.

"Then why do we need to go to the cafeteria?" the man asked. "Wouldn't it be safer to keep the kids in the classroom until the lock-down is over?"

"There are… things around the school that are trying to attack and I'm following orders," Carson replied, growing impatient. "Those orders are to secure everyone inside the cafeteria. Please, sir, gather the kids and follow my partner."

The teacher glanced wide-eyed over at Diego, who gave a reassuring nod, and then sighed. "Okay."

Carson stood aside as the elder man lead his students out of the classroom single-file and then brought up the rear. Diego still had his rifle pointed directly ahead as he marched slowly toward the center of the school. Carson held his rifle and kept an eye behind him. The kids began chattering excitedly and Diego shushed them. Carson knew it was a futile attempt. Kids tended to talk more when they were nervous or excited. Diego shushed the kids a second time, his expression tense.

They reached the doors of the cafeteria. Diego knocked and Carson smiled when Kate answered the door, the pistol at her side. She recognized Diego and opened the door, allowing the children and their teacher to go inside. Carson looked back toward the field that had held his attention earlier.

He did not expect to see anyone and was surprised when a scraggly-looking man staggered toward the school. From a distance Carson couldn't make out a lot of detail except the man's unkept hair and jerky gait. Something about the man's appearance filled Carson with dread.

"Hurry up," Carson called over his shoulder, his eyes not leaving the stranger. "Get inside, now."

"What is it, Carson?" Diego asked once everyone was inside. Carson pointed toward the stranger with the barrel of his rifle.

"I don't know," Carson answered, pointing his chin at the new arrival. Something about the man felt incredibly familiar and Carson was overcome by a strong feeling of Deja-vu. His heart began hammering in his chest and his instincts were telling him to shoot.

"Something is very fucking wrong about this guy," Carson hissed.

Diego walked past Carson and held his rifle in one hand as he raised his other hand for the man to halt. "Stop where you are!" Diego called out. The man did not seem to hear him. "I said halt!"

"We need to get inside," Carson pleaded. "I've got a really bad feeling about this guy."

Diego ignored him as he gripped his rifle in both hands. "Stop now!" He yelled. Once again, the strange man seemed to ignore him. The man lurched across the street and continued toward the school. Carson could see the stranger more clearly. The man's eyes seemed to bulge in their sockets, his expression slack. The odd man's mouth hung open slightly and a trail of drool ran down his chin.

"He's not stopping," Carson warned. "Something freaky is about to happen, I can feel it."

"I really don't want to pop this guy," Diego answered, a measure of fear creeping into his voice. "I really, *really* fucking don't."

Before either of them could act the strange man seemed to stumble forward and then stood rigidly. Carson saw the man's head begin to swell. His stomach seemed to tumble over itself at the sight. Carson wasn't even aware that he had begun to back up. The odd man began moving again, his head swelling further.

"What the fuck?" Diego asked just before the man's head split vertically down the middle and opened outward. "Oh shit!"

Carson nearly fell over when the stranger's head opened. Teeth lined both sides of the man's split face. Where there had once been a mouth Carson could see a bloodshot eye peering at them. The man fell forward, and the rest of his body continued to split. An assortment of insectile limbs erupted from the opening, followed by what appeared to be tentacles.

The horror advanced.

Diego and Carson backed up and opened fire.

Chapter 11

Hot lead puckered the monstrosity's hideous flesh, yet it did not seem to notice. Carson felt a familiar wave of panic rising from his gut. He hazarded a quick glance over at Diego and could tell by the young man's face that the feeling was mutual.

"Uh, it's still getting closer," Diego yelled over the noise of gunfire, his voice wavering. "Nothing is working on this bastard!"

Carson wanted to reply but his attention was fixed on the creature, its spider-like limbs scrabbling for purchase as it slithered forward. The freakish beast was tapping into the hardwired phobias that humans all shared. It didn't help that it was also triggering Carson's arachnophobia to boot.

He looked for any sign of weakness in the creature.

Eyes appeared sporadically across the thing's amorphous form and quickly disappeared, leaving small holes in their wake. Carson was thankful that he wasn't afflicted with *that* phobia. Then something caught his attention. The eyes may have been appearing and disappearing, but one always remained: the eye where the mouth of a man had once been.

"The eye! Shoot it in the eye!"

"Which eye? It has hundreds!"

Carson steadied his breathing, knelt down on one knee, and took aim at his target. The first shot missed by an inch as the creature shifted forward, but the next shots hit dead-on. The beast let loose an ear-piercing shriek as it recoiled in on itself.

"That one!" Carson yelled. He didn't wait for Diego to respond. The creature's eye had exploded, leaving a gooey hole but it was quickly reforming. Once again Carson aimed and fired three shots, each striking their target. The creature shrieked again and backed up, its fleshy mass quivering. It withdrew a tentacled appendage and pulled something from within its flesh. A moment later, a gob of chunky flesh flew directly at Diego, hitting him square in the face.

Diego fell back and momentarily dropped his rifle as he desperately wiped the gore from his face.

"What the fuck?" Diego swore.

"They fucking throw shit now," Carson answered back in disbelief. "We need to get behind cover!"

Diego climbed to his feet, retrieved his rifle and immediately ran to the nearest car in the parking lot. Carson followed close behind.

"Keep aiming for the eyes," Carson instructed. Diego nodded. Like one, Carson and Diego stood up and began firing over the hood of the car.

Each successful shot made the beast retreat several inches. By the time Carson and Diego had emptied the magazines of their rifles the creature was back across the street. Carson was not content to just keep it at bay, however. It had thrown several more fleshy projectiles at them and had been lucky to have the car between them.

He ejected the spent magazine and fished a fresh one from his jacket pocket. He slapped the magazine into the empty port, racked the charging handle, and resumed firing. He was being as accurate as possible, making sure each shot hit roughly near where the eye kept forming. In seconds the fleshy socket had become so terribly deformed that the eye could not regenerate. Diego followed suit and riddled the monster with bullets.

The pair exhausted their second magazine when they noticed that the thing had ceased moving entirely. Carson's arm twitched from the repeated recoil and his hands shook. He let the rifle hang by its strap at his side.

"I think it's dead," he said shakily. "Fuck, I hope it's dead."

"I think so, too," Diego replied, his voice mirroring Carson's. "Holy shit. I'm going to have nightmares about that thing for the rest of my life."

Carson nodded. He knew that though the monstrosity may be dead it would live on in his nightmares. He doubted that he would ever get a restful night's sleep again. It would have to share space with the grasshopper-things. Carson's pulse pounded in his ears and exhaustion immediately began setting in. It had been a long day, and Carson had a horrible feeling that it wasn't over yet.

"We need to get back inside and check on everyone," Carson said slowly, his breathing shallow and rapid. "They'll have heard the gunshots. I'm sure they're all freaked out."

Diego stood quietly for a moment as he stared at the corpse across the street. Carson was not sure the man had even heard him until he spoke. "Y-yeah, you're right. I'm sure they're terrified. It'll be safer inside, anyway."

He turned on his heel and immediately walked toward the cafeteria. Carson did not hesitate to follow. He wanted to put as much distance between himself and the nightmare as possible. A pair of heavy metal doors would help, too.

Carson had been right, everyone in the cafeteria looked terrified. The children were borderline hysterical. He didn't blame them. He was terrified too.

Once the doors closed behind them, Carson and Diego ensured they were locked. Carson wished that they could barricade the doors, but there wasn't much in the cafeteria for them to use. He would have to be content that the locks would hold.

Carson slowly made his way through the cafeteria and tried not to look at the terrified faces all around him. He was worried that they would see how scared he was, and they would break. For now, everyone was quiet, save for the sniffles coming from many of the children. He tried to block those sounds out, too. It broke his heart knowing that the kids were scared and that he could do little to help them. Instead, Carson kept his eyes trained directly ahead of him. He caught sight of Irene and Chris in Kate's arms. The pistol he had given her was sitting unattended on the ground by her side.

When Kate's eyes locked on him, Carson could tell that she was both terrified and furious. Why she was angry, Carson couldn't begin to guess. He'd tried for years to understand and predict Kate's mood or reactions but had never managed to anticipate correctly. His heart rate, which had already been elevated, started to speed up once again. His stomach seemed to flip, and he could feel his anxiety spiking.

"Well?" Kate nearly spat.

"What?" Carson asked. His mind began to spin as he tried to figure out why she was angry. He'd done exactly as he said he would. He'd gotten everyone in the school into the cafeteria and had made it back without injury.

"Are we stuck here?"

"I-I don't know," Carson answered. "This is probably the safest place for now."

"What about the dogs? The cats? What are they supposed to do?" Kate snapped. "We're just going to leave them home by themselves?"

"They'll be fine for now," Carson replied. The line of questioning confused him. "They're all inside the house."

"We need to get home dammit," Kate said, shaking her head. "We need to get our shit and get away from here. Those *things* seem to be drawn to the school. I heard the shooting."

Carson agreed up to a point, but he also suspected that the creatures weren't confined to the base. He wasn't even sure if there was anywhere that was safer than where they were. He didn't want to face any more of the creatures, and he certainly did not want to put their kids at risk.

"We will eventually," Carson finally answered. "But we need to wait for directions."

"No, we need to go now," Kate argued.

Carson knew that they had reached an impasse. She was not going to be satisfied until he agreed with her, but she didn't seem to understand the danger of what she was suggesting.

"Is the safety on?" Carson asked, nodding toward the pistol at her side, changing the subject.

"Of course it is."

"Good," Carson replied, nodding. "Why did you leave it on the floor? Anyone could have taken it."

"I was holding Chris and Irene," Kate's tone indicated that she felt insulted that he even had to ask.

Carson grabbed the pistol and, after checking the safety, re-holstered it.

"I left it with you to protect them. What good is it if it's just laying on the floor?" Carson asked. Kate glared at him but refused to answer.

He sighed and sat directly across from Kate and their kids, the rifle he still carried slung over his shoulder. Kate just stared at him expectantly. He knew what she wanted. She wanted him to announce that they were going home. Carson wasn't going to do that, though. Not after what he had just encountered before retreating inside the cafeteria.

He knew Kate was glaring at him, her gaze nearly boring into his skull, but Carson refused to look at her. If he did, she would continue to argue about leaving until he inevitably relented. After nearly five full minutes of uncomfortable silence, he heard Kate sigh angrily. Carson still did not dare look her in the eye, as if it would trigger her to attack. His nerves were already shot, and he did not have the energy to fight with her.

Carson slid across the floor until he was leaning against the wall next to Irene. He felt her lean against him and found it comforting, though it should have been him comforting her. He put his arm around her shoulders and leaned his head back against the wall. The adrenaline was finally leaving his system and before he knew it, his eyes closed.

He hoped the nightmare would end soon.

Chapter 12

The air in front of *Carson shimmered. It looked like he was looking up from the depths of a swimming pool. A moment later the shimmer in the air rippled and then a glowing red seam grew outward from the center, extending vertically. The first thing Carson noticed was a blast of heat. It felt like the hottest day in southern Texas with humidity of one hundred percent. It felt as though a sunburn had instantly formed on his face. The seam stopped growing vertically, the glowing line dancing like a flame.*

Then it started growing again, this time horizontally. It opened like a wound, the red light spilling outward like blood.

Carson shielded his eyes against the glare. It seemed impossibly bright, as if there was a massive red star on the other side of the opening.

He kept his hand above his eyes and tried to look beneath it. His eyes slowly focused and his breath caught in his chest.

Something was moving inside the opening. Something with far too many limbs and, somehow predictably, tentacles.

His gaze was transfixed on the squirming mass, his mind struggling to reconcile the image before him.

Then, somewhere nearby, someone started screaming.

***

Carson smacked the back of his head against the wall as he came to. Pain shot through his head, and, for a moment, he thought he was still stuck in the vision because he *still* heard screaming. It took him a second to realize that the screaming was real.

Carson blinked rapidly and quickly looked around. All around him he saw people screaming, their eyes transfixed on something ahead of them. Carson followed their gaze and once again thought he was still dreaming.

A red seam danced in the air thirty feet away from him, and it was growing.

No, Carson thought. *It's not possible. It* can't *be.*

He wanted to deny what he saw. He wanted desperately to wake up. Yet, despite his efforts, including literally pinching himself in the jaw, the scene before him did not disappear. If anything, it only got worse.

The seam began to open, the light bleeding outward. Screams erupted all around him, but Carson's eyes were transfixed. Unlike in his dream, Carson looked directly into the opening. He already knew what he would see, but he wanted to be wrong.

He wasn't.

Within the blood-red opening he saw writhing limbs and tentacles. A horrifying wailing seemed to emanate from within, and Carson was usure if the sound was generated by the creature at the opening, or something else behind it. Not that it mattered. A foul chemical odor seemed to spill out with the red light.

Over the screaming and crying, Carson heard another voice. It took him a moment to recognize it as Diego, and he was screaming the loudest.

Carson tore his eyes away from the nightmare forming in front of him. Diego was sprinting toward him, but he was looking off to Carson's right. Carson followed his eyes and caught a glimpse of what had drawn Diego's attention. The seam had opened directly above a boy who could have been no more than nine years old.

Nausea hit Carson as he saw one of the thrashing tentacles strike the boy's shoulder and then, as if sensing prey, reached out to wrap around the child's waist. The boy let loose an earsplitting shriek as he was slowly reeled up toward the rift.

Diego roared as he charged directly toward the rift. Carson knew exactly what Diego was going to do. He would have done the same thing had he been able to shake free of his momentary paralysis.

Diego dove headfirst toward the rift and was immediately engulfed by the limbs.

A loud droning sound, not unlike that of a tolling bell, reverberated across the cafeteria. It was so loud that Carson had to cover his ears. He noticed that nearly everyone else did the same.

Then, as suddenly as the sound came, it ceased. And, as if the droning had been a signal, the rift began to shrink.

"My baby!" Carson heard a woman shriek. "Please, give me back my baby! No!"

The woman's screams were enough to jar Carson free from his paralysis. He jumped to his feet and began racing toward the rift. He faintly heard Kate and his children screaming out behind him.

Carson was less than five feet away when the rift closed completely. He stumbled as he reached the spot that it had appeared, the air thick as if made of water. Carson was unable to slow his momentum, and he flew several feet when he exited the mire. He rolled over and sat up, staring at where the glowing red rift had been seconds earlier.

"Fuck!" he screamed in frustration.

He looked across the cafeteria and saw his children staring wide-eyed. Their eyes were glistening, and he saw that their cheeks were wet. They were terrified, as they had every right to be. Kate stared at him; her expression was a mix of fear and fury. They locked eyes for a moment, and then Kate wrapped her arms around Chris and Irene protectively, her expression souring further.

Carson knew he had done nothing wrong. Not really. But this did little to assuage his guilt and shame. His children were nearly fatherless. But that didn't seem as important as what the poor woman who was reduced to a wailing mess on the cafeteria floor was going through. She'd lost her little boy, and Carson had watched it happen. The feelings of guilt and shame struck him again. He should have reacted faster. He should have done *anything* other than stare at the horror that had materialized in their midst.

Kate had accused Carson of wanting to be a hero. In that moment, he felt like anything but.

Then another disturbing thought crossed his mind. The rift appeared immediately after he awoke from his nightmare. Had he had a premonition, or had he summoned it himself?

Carson sat with the thought for a moment and then shook his head, as if doing so would make it disappear. He knew what he was doing. It was the same thing he always did. He was blaming himself.

He didn't summon the rift. How could he have?

No, he didn't summon it. But he didn't do anything about it either. He had just stared stupidly at it as something from within snatched up a young boy.

Carson may not have summoned the rift, but he still felt like the boy's abduction had been his fault. And Diego had gone inside the rift after him, while Carson just gawked. Diego had done what Carson *should* have done, as he was easily ten feet closer.

Carson let his gaze drift first toward the woman wailing on the floor, then to his kids' faces and the abject terror their expressions held, and finally to his wife's disapproving glare. Everything that had occurred that day, the horror that he'd experienced, had threatened to break him, but it was that accusatory glare that finally did him in.

Carson stared at Kate and then he fell onto his side, rolling into the fetal position.

And then Carson fell apart.

For the first time since he accepted the reality of his father's suicide, Carson wept.

Chapter 13

Small hands touched his shoulder, rousing Carson from his despair. He didn't know how long he lay on his side, bawling his eyes out. Something inside him had just broken and he could no longer hold it in. It was no secret that he had struggled with his mental health, particularly after the passing of his father, but never before had he broken down so completely. At least not in the presence of others.

"Daddy?" Carson heard Irene ask. A wave of shame swept through him. His little girl had witnessed his mental breakdown. What would she think? What did Chris think?

Determined to redeem himself in his children's eyes, Carson forced himself upright and wiped the moisture from his face. "I-I'm okay sweetie. I was just sad that I couldn't help that poor little boy."

Irene stared into his eyes and Carson had a sneaking suspicion that she didn't quite believe him. He often forgot how perceptive and empathetic his little girl was, unlike her mother in that way. "Chrissy keeps crying. He's scared that the things will get him, too."

Chrissy was Irene's nickname for her brother. Carson had tried telling her that Chrissy was a girl's nickname, but she called him that anyway.

"He's scared, kiddo. We all are. He'll be okay. The thing left." When he said this, Carson looked over at his son, firmly wrapped in Kate's embrace.

"Come here, sweetie," Carson said gently as he pulled Irene in for a hug. "I'll keep you guys safe. I promise."

Irene glanced at the rifle hanging loosely by Carson's side. "Are we going to be okay? What if more of the monsters come?"

"Yes, we're safe, kiddo," Carson whispered. This seemed to offer Irene a measure of comfort. "And I'll kill them all before they could ever hurt you."

Carson released Irene from his embrace and forced himself to stand. His head swam momentarily, likely from the crash following his adrenaline surges. He crushed his eyes shut for a moment, willing away the white spots that danced in his vision. Satisfied that he had regained his composure, Carson opened his eyes.

Reluctantly, Carson led Irene toward her mother and brother. He knew that Kate could see the expression on his face, his displeasure plain. However, Carson doubted Kate noticed nor cared.

"Why?" was all Kate asked, but Carson understood what she was asking. *Why did you leave us behind to save someone you don't know? Why didn't you try to protect us? Protect* me?

Carson stared at her for a moment, biting back a scathing retort. It would do no good, he knew. She wouldn't listen and he knew he couldn't make her understand. "Because I was closest to him. Diego was too far away and nobody else was doing anything."

"You were too far away, too," Kate replied. "What if another one appeared, huh? What if it tried to get us while you were trying to save them?"

"You were there," Carson replied.

"Right, because I *totally* could have stopped it," Kate snapped. This caught Carson off-guard. Very rarely did Kate ever admit to being incapable of *anything*. "You have the guns, remember? You took the gun from me."

Carson subconsciously placed his hand on the butt of the pistol holstered at his waist, the pistol she had left lying on the ground. "You left it on the floor."

He wanted to argue further, to point out that she had been dangerously careless. He also wanted to snap and tell her that she wouldn't have used it anyway, but once again he knew this would be pointless. Kate was, once again, playing the victim.

"Sorry," Carson muttered before taking a seat against the wall, intentionally placing himself more than a foot away from her. He wanted to hold Irene and Chris, but Kate still had her arms tightly wrapped around Chris's small frame. Instead, Carson motioned for Irene to sit beside him, situating herself between him and Kate.

"We're leaving," Kate said after several minutes. "It's not safe here."

"It's not safe out there, either," Carson argued.

"Then you can stay here," Kate snapped. "But give me the gun so I can take the kids home."

Carson just stared, open-mouthed, at Kate. What was she thinking?

"I won't let you guys go by yourselves," Carson replied.

He knew she was going to do exactly what she said whether he gave her the gun or not. The best chance for Chris and Irene's safety was if he went with them. He didn't trust Kate to be able to protect them on her own, especially after leaving the pistol on the ground.

"But we need to get everyone else out of here, too. They're defenseless."

"And how are you going to do that?" Kate snarled.

Carson sat quietly, pondering the question. How *would* he do that? Would these people even follow him? What about the grieving mother whose son had just been abducted? With Diego gone, Carson would have to protect everyone by himself.

It hit him again that Diego was gone. He hadn't formed a deep bond with the young man, but Diego had slowly started to grow on him. And now he was gone, likely forever.

After what had just happened, Carson doubted he'd be able to protect everyone. He wasn't confident that he could even protect his own children. More importantly, would they follow him? Since he had the only weapons, they might.

Instead of answering Kate, Carson took a deep breath, stood, and walked toward the middle of the cafeteria.

"Listen up," Carson called out, trying his best to project a confidence he did not feel. It must have been evident in his voice because very few people looked his way. Typically, Carson had no issue with public speaking. However, that was usually in a teaching capacity. He wouldn't consider himself to be a natural leader.

Unfortunately, nobody else was stepping up.

"Excuse me," Carson called, louder this time. It appeared to be sufficient as everyone began turning toward him. "We're not safe here, obviously. We need to get out of here and get somewhere safe. I don't know where that is, but we know it isn't here."

Murmurs began to sweep through the cafeteria. Carson hoped that someone would offer up a solution, or at the very least provide suggestions. When he realized that none were forthcoming, Carson spoke up again with the only solution he could think of.

"How many of you drove here?" he asked. He glanced around and saw that several people seemed to realize where his question led.

Fortunately, it seemed that most people had. More than half of the adults in the cafeteria spoke up, stating that they had indeed driven to the school. Carson recalled the destruction inflicted upon the squad car but opted not to disclose this.

"Perfect," Carson said after the replies ceased. "Those of you who drove, I suggest you quickly get your families to your vehicles and make your way home, or to somewhere you think would be safe. We'll make sure you get to your vehicles safely. As for the rest, I am going to assume that you live nearby, yes?"

He could tell that people were less than enthusiastic about what he proposed, but without any other suggestions it seemed that nobody was willing to argue. Nobody wanted to stay at the school, of that Carson was certain. He looked around and saw that people were nodding in response to his question.

"Okay then," Carson continued, after a deep inhalation. "Those of us who walked here are going to, unfortunately, have to walk back home."

He raised his hands before anyone could object. "I know that this is not ideal. Trust me, I don't want to go back out there any more than you do, but we obviously can't stay here. Now, you can follow me across the field until we reach the main residential neighborhood, at least, and go from there in large groups. I know I can't promise to get everyone home personally, but I can try to get all of you safely across the field at the very least, if not further."

He didn't like his plan, and evidently neither did anyone else. But, once again, without another option nobody objected.

Satisfied with a bare framework of a plan, as weak as may have been, Carson could see people start moving. Everyone had been nearly frozen in fear and uncertainty when they had initially filled the cafeteria, but now that a plan was in place it appeared that some life had returned. They had a direction, at least.

Most of them did, that is. The woman who watched her son disappear continued to lay on the ground, weeping uncontrollably. Carson wanted to help her, he really did, but he knew there was little, if anything, he could do. He watched her silently for a moment, his heart breaking for her.

Carson hung his head and then turned back toward his family.

Kate looked pissed, but Carson found that he didn't care. It wasn't as though she had come up with a plan and he doubted she ever would have. So be it. She could stay pissed for all he cared. His kids were more important.

Chris and Irene still looked scared, but his plan seemed to have a minor calming effect on them.

It had an effect on him too.

Something nearing elation, though not quite, crept through him and he felt emboldened by it.

He placed a hand on Chris and Irene's shoulders and looked them in the eyes. "Okay you guys, let's go home."

Not once did he look at Kate.

He didn't need to.

For all her bluster, Carson knew Kate would follow anyway. She would be pissed, sure, but she would choose the option that offered her the best chance of survival.

Out of the group, Carson didn't expect the grieving woman to do anything other than wail. He wanted to help, but there was nothing he could do. His condolences and placations would serve only to add to her pain, not alleviate it.

No, Carson couldn't help her, and that helplessness tore at him.

He certainly did not expect the woman to stop crying as if a flip had switched. He didn't expect her to stand up, wipe her eyes, and walk directly toward him. And he did not expect her to pounce on him, her hand going for the gun tucked in the holster at his waist.

Before he could react, the woman had pulled the pistol free and placed the barrel against her temple. He knew what she intended to do as soon as she went for the gun. He also knew that nothing was going to stop her.

"He's gone!" the woman screamed; her eyes crushed shut. "My baby!"

Carson tried to lunge toward her and opened his mouth to yell for her to stop.

The words never left his mouth.

The report of the gun was deafening. The screaming that followed was louder.

Chapter 14

Carson stood in awe, his eyes refusing to accept what they were seeing. It seemed unreal. The woman had been right there, inches away from him, alive. But now? For a moment Carson had the irrational thought that she had just vanished, teleported away perhaps.

On the ground she lay, blood pooling around her head in a macabre halo. The 9mm round had done a fair amount of damage, but not as much as he had expected. The exit wound was barely larger than the entry wound, but it had been enough to get the job done.

A bout of nausea struck Carson at the same time as reality returned. He doubled over, his vision swimming. It took every ounce of willpower to keep from vomiting, which he was thankful for. He would not have been able to handle *that* on top of the guilt he felt.

She was dead, and she had used *his* gun to do it. He could tell himself that it wasn't his fault—it wasn't—but the guilt came just the same. He'd had the gun. She had gone for it, and he didn't react in time. And now she was dead. Worse, nearly every child in the cafeteria had witnessed it.

Carson recovered from the wave of nausea and knelt to recover his pistol, but he hesitated, his hand inches from the grip. Apprehension stayed his hand as if the woman's suicide was an infectious disease and merely touching the weapon would infect him. Another irrational thought, he knew, but he couldn't shake the feeling. Worse still, he worried that recovering the weapon would somehow incriminate him.

Eventually Carson was able to move, and he quickly grabbed the pistol. He checked the safety—hadn't it been on? —

and holstered it before anyone else could follow the woman's lead. He told himself that he had to secure it so that it couldn't harm any of the children, as if the pistol would act of its own accord.

All around him, Carson heard the cries and screams of the horrified children, and the desperate pleas from their parents to calm down. Above the noise he heard Irene and Chris's voices. Kate's voice, however, was oddly absent. When he turned, he immediately knew why.

Kate held both children in her arms, but she wasn't looking at them. No, she was staring at Carson with what could only be described as utter loathing. He knew she blamed him.

"We're fucking leaving," she hissed, her eyes boring into him. "You can keep your fucking guns, but I'm taking the kids."

"W-what?" Carson stammered. "Why?"

Kate released Irene and pointed at the corpse near Carson's feet. "*That* is why. You and your fucking guns caused *that*! If you didn't have that thing on you, she would still be alive. And I will *not* let you put my children in danger."

Carson stood shell-shocked. She *did* blame him. He should have expected as much. Hell, he blamed himself, but it hurt. For the first time in years, Carson acted without thinking.

He strode right up to Kate and, his voice shaking, got in her face. "The gun is what kept us alive! That gun is the reason I was able to get here in the first place! Without it I would be lying dead out in that field! What the fuck do you think you're going to do against those… those *things*?! You going to stare them to death? Make them feel weak and insignificant, too? Well?!"

Carson knew he was shouting. He knew his kids were watching. But, at that moment, he absolutely did not care. This was too much.

If his outburst frightened Kate, she didn't show it. Instead, she matched his intensity. "You're such a fucking asshole! Stay the fuck away from us!"

He expected someone, anyone, to intervene. When nobody did, his anger grew. He ground his teeth; his pulse pounded in his head. Carson had already begun to feel horrible about losing his temper, but she *had* pushed him. He could choose to continue his tirade and scare his kids more, or he could regain his composure. As usual, Carson chose the latter.

"They're not going anywhere without me," Carson nearly whispered after taking a deep breath. "Not with the monsters out there."

"Then get rid of the fucking guns," Kate snapped.

"No," Carson replied, shaking his head. "But they will stay holstered unless we're attacked. We need the protection."

Kate stared at him, and he knew she was attempting to stare him down. It had worked in the past, but he would not allow it to work now. He simply matched her stare, fully prepared to stay that way for as long as it took.

Eventually, Kate looked away. Carson knew he would pay for it later. She would make sure of that. He used to care about the consequences in the past and the inevitable fallout, but he realized that that was no longer the case. He could honestly care less about her displeasure. It was not important. Not while Irene and Chris's safety was at stake.

"Whatever," Kate eventually said, barely loud enough for him to hear. Then she turned her gaze back toward him, her expression hardening once again. "Do whatever you want. You always do. But if you want to come with us, then you will have to give the gun to someone else. I won't have it around my kids."

There it was again. She referred to Chris and Irene as *hers*, not theirs.

He noticed but chose not to say anything. Not now, anyway.

He also wanted to argue that, no, he never did what he wanted. He always did what *she* wanted, what *she* told him to do. But he knew that was an argument that he would lose, merely because she refused to admit to being in the wrong. Nothing was *ever* her fault, and she wouldn't see this as being any different.

"I'll turn over the rifle," Carson answered. It wasn't complete acquiescence, but it would hopefully be enough to suffice. For now, at least.

Kate didn't answer at first. She just kept glaring at him. After what felt like ten minutes, he saw her shake her head. "Fine."

He didn't realize that he'd been practically holding his breath until he exhaled. The tension in his shoulders and the pounding in his head seemed to immediately disappear with the exhalation.

Carson turned and asked if anyone was trained on the rifle. People said they had, and Carson chose to hand the weapon over to a man closest to him. The man, who identified himself as Tim Roe, a K-9-unit instructor, certainly looked like he could have been security forces. Carson felt he was the best person to handle the M-4. Carson felt that *anyone* else would be better at handling the M-4 than him.

After relinquishing the rifle to Tim, Carson turned and walked over to Irene to grab her hand.

Without another word, they headed for the exit.

Chapter 15

The sky had grown dark during their time in the confines of the concrete building; a reminder that time still moved. Carson was dazed and wondered how that could be. How could the world keep turning when all hell was breaking loose? *His* world seemed to stand still. Everything had changed. And nothing would be okay.

Or perhaps that was just his depression talking.

Carson let Tim Roe take the lead. As people began to filter out into the night, Carson noticed that nobody would meet his gaze. Either they were afraid of him or reviled him. He wasn't sure which could have been worse. Nor could he blame them. He *had* brought a gun into the cafeteria, and now a woman was dead. Suicide using *his* gun. Didn't that make him responsible? Culpable?

Kate pulled Irene and Chris along with her, brushing past Carson without so much as a passing glance. Oh yes, she was pissed. He doubted she would get over it this time. Then again, did she ever really get over anything? She claimed to never hold grudges, but her actions told a different story.

"What now? You seriously holding a grudge now?" Carson asked. "If anyone has a right to hold any kind of grudge, it's me. Do I need to remind you of when you cheated, huh?"

"Oh fuck you," Kate snapped back.

Carson sighed and stared upward. "Wow."

It happened a year ago. Kate had gone to help a man who had claimed to be Carson's friend pack up his house, the same man who had hung out with them on many weekends. Carson had suspected, but not really known, that the guy had feelings for Kate. His suspicions were confirmed when the next day Kate had made a show of "confessing" that she had let him "snuggle" with her at some point in the evening, confessing his feelings for her. She swore nothing happened, but the man's behavior told the truth. He'd been inexplicably terrified of Carson finding out.

But why? If it was just snuggling as Kate had claimed, then Carson couldn't be furious, could he? Hurt, sure. Betrayed? Certainly. But enraged? It didn't add up. Unless something more than "snuggling" had occurred.

Then, as if to add insult to injury, Kate had suggested that they try being polyamorous. Worse still, she tried to pass it off as if she was doing Carson a favor. She had tried to convince him that it was what *he* wanted and would make *him* happier. He very nearly agreed, too. But the more he thought about it, the more he rejected the idea. He told Kate this and she seemed okay with it, but he caught the flicker of emotion on her face.

Disappointment.

He knew she had stepped out. He even suspected that it wasn't the first time. Yet, he still stuck around.

Why?

Most likely for their kids. The same kids that she was now claiming were *hers* and not theirs. As if he had lost all claim to them.

No, it wasn't fair. Not at all.

After all, Carson wasn't the one who had put the gun to the woman's head. It hadn't been Carson who had pulled the trigger. He just happened to have a gun and the woman, so completely destroyed by the abduction of her son, seized an opportunity to end her grief.

Carson ground his teeth and fought back the rage that was building inside him. No, he would deal with those feelings later, once they were safely home. Then again, would they be safe there? Would they be safe anywhere? Would they ever be safe again?

Without a word Carson stepped out into the night and pulled the door to the cafeteria shut behind him to become a tomb for the grief-stricken woman.

The moment Carson stepped outside he remembered the creepy man across the street who had transformed into a horrific mass. The memory made him freeze up in fear. The temperature hadn't dropped drastically since the sun had set, yet Carson felt an intense chill shoot through him. He wouldn't have been surprised if icicles formed on his limbs. He would have stayed that way, stock still, had Irene and Chris not gotten his attention.

Irene and Chris grabbed his hands and tugged. The contact was enough to break Carson free from his temporary paralysis. Carson blinked rapidly as though he had just woken up. Everything around him seemed to come back into focus. The first thing he noticed was the sound of sirens. It was enough to make his heart sink.

Everything that had happened in the last few hours hadn't been a twisted dream. It had been a nightmare, but Carson had been awake.

It had all been real.

"Daddy, come on," Chris begged. "Please. I wanna go home."

The fear in his little boy's voice broke his heart. He knew they were as frightened as he was, if not more so. He had to get control of himself. He *had* to be brave for them.

"Okay, buddy," Carson said gently. "Okay. We're going home. I'm going to make sure we get home safe."

Irene squeezed his hand. At that moment, Carson didn't think they believed him. Or maybe they didn't trust him.

He gave their small hands a gentle squeeze. He would prove that they could trust him. He *had* to.

Carson glanced around and took in his surroundings. The streetlights had come on, casting everything in an amber glow. Instinctively, Carson looked across the street where the man had been.

The body wasn't there. In its place was a dark stain that looked like spilled motor oil. The absence of a corpse did nothing to comfort him. It could still be out there, alive. Carson's stomach tightened in a knot.

Everyone had gathered in front of the school. Nobody spoke. The only sounds that could be heard were their breathing and the occasional sniffle. Even the kids were silent. Carson was thankful because that meant he would have an easier time hearing the horrible grasshopper-things if they tried to sneak up on them.

He didn't hear anything. Nothing at all, other than the distant sirens.

Tim Roe stood with the M4 at the other side of the crowd. He was looking both everywhere and nowhere at all.

Carson probably should have given the weapon to someone else. The man looked completely out of his element for someone tied to Security Forces. Even from a distance Carson could tell that the man had not disengaged the safety on the rifle. He began to doubt that the man had held a weapon in quite some time. Or maybe it was the panic clouding his mind. Either way, it wouldn't do anyone any good if the man didn't come to his senses and soon.

Nobody else seemed to notice, though. People crowded near the man as they tried to move slowly toward their vehicles.

Carson hoped that nothing would jump out at them because they would be fucked.

"Let's go," Kate hissed. "What the hell are we waiting for?"

Carson wanted to snap at her, to say something scathing, but he did what he always did. He put his head down and bit his tongue.

Carson gave the crowd a parting glance and then turned toward the rear of the school. What was perhaps only two hundred yards seemed to Carson to span a million miles. Everything inside him begged him to go back inside the cafeteria. Being out in the open made him feel incredibly vulnerable. But he knew that there was nothing back there for them.

Nothing but misery and death.

He swallowed the lump forming in his throat and began walking, keeping the gun holstered just as he had promised.

Hopefully he won't need to use it again. He didn't think he would be able to.

Chapter 16

None of the grasshopper-things, which Carson decided to call death hoppers, jumped out at them as they made their way across campus. He wasn't sure if he should have been relieved or more unsettled. He and Diego hadn't killed *all* of them. He knew that.

So where were they?

He wanted badly to hold the pistol in his hand, just in case something attacked them, but he had assured Kate that he would keep it holstered unless they needed it. He *could* have just said fuck it and drawn his weapon anyway, but that would invite an argument that he was not prepared to deal with. Not now.

Several people had begun to follow them, and Carson suspected they lived in the same neighborhood. These were the people who had not driven to the school, then. It was then that he realized that they were looking at him to protect them.

Just go on ahead, Carson begged silently. *Please. Please just go.*

He half expected Kate to walk out in front, as far away from him as possible, but instead she stayed close behind him.

Don't hate guns that *much, do you?* Carson thought bitterly. *Or are you just hoping that something gets me first?*

Unfortunately, he couldn't rule out that possibility. Not after their exchange at the school.

Carson found himself starting to crouch as they approached the overgrown field. After all, he *had* been attacked there. Once again, he wanted to draw his weapon and nearly did, his hand grasping the grip of the pistol. Against his better judgment, Carson moved his hand away from the weapon. He would unholster it if he heard movement, he told himself.

Anything that sounded like something stalking them, hunting them from within the thigh-high grass.

He moved slowly, hunched over, straining his ears as he stepped onto the field. So far, all he heard was the collective breathing behind him. He glanced over his shoulder and noted that nearly everyone had adopted his stance, half-crouched and moving slowly. He was thankful that he didn't have to issue directions. Probably a herd mentality, he guessed.

They walked fifty yards across the field before he heard anything. At first Carson wasn't sure he had heard anything at all.

He paused and held his breath. Suspecting that it had been his imagination, he exhaled and began moving again.

This time he was *sure* he heard something. It sounded like a plastic grocery bag blowing in the wind, but there wasn't so much as a gentle breeze.

No, something was *definitely* moving out there.

Carson stood still and slowly looked around. He heard it again, but he couldn't seem to pinpoint its origin. It seemed to be coming from nearby, but every time he turned his head it seemed to move. Where was it?

More importantly, *what* was it?

A blood-curdling scream ripped through the air behind him, and he spun to face it. What he saw confused him.

Among the group a woman was thrashing, something wrapped around her head. Carson thought it might have been a plastic bag. It would fit with what he heard. But, to his horror, the thing clinging to the woman was writhing. As he watched he could see the faint impression of limbs within the near-transparent membrane. The thing shifted, moving around the woman to situate itself behind her, draping over her head and her shoulders.

With her mouth covered the woman was no longer able to scream. She clawed desperately at the cloudy thing clinging to her, but it didn't seem to notice or care.

In moments her movements became jerky and uncoordinated. She lashed out with her left hand, shooting the limb out straight, and her fist collided with the young girl beside her. The movement seemed to throw the woman off-balance, and she fell to her side, directly on top of the girl who was now clutching her face and crying.

Carson drew his pistol, letting it hang at his side, and began making his way toward the fallen woman and the girl beneath her. He didn't know what he hoped to do with the firearm. Whatever had clung to the woman had fully encased her head. If he tried to shoot, he would undoubtedly kill her.

With his luck he would probably end up shooting the girl beneath her.

He got within two feet from the woman when she seemed to go stiff. The sudden change made Carson hesitate.

In the half-second that Carson faltered, the woman sat upright and then slowly rose to her feet as if lifted by an invisible wire. He held the gun out to his side, his left hand raised in front of him, and his fingers spread. The woman seemed to sense him and cocked her shrouded head to one side. Carson's heart pounded and all he could hear was blood rushing in his ears.

Whatever had given the woman pause seemed to disappear, as a moment later she lunged forward, legs and arms moving awkwardly. The explosion of motion made Carson jump backward and begin backpedaling. The woman's movements were unnatural, like a stop-motion monster in an old film.

Carson fell backward as his heel struck something—probably a rock—and landed hard on his ass. He looked up and saw that the woman was nearly within arm's reach.

Up close, Carson finally got a good look at what had draped itself over her. It was a milky-white, translucent thing with too many eyes dotting the surface. It may have had limbs beneath the surface though most of the thing's size was made up of wings, but it didn't look like any winged creature he had ever seen.

Rather than fight the fall, Carson allowed himself to fall backward and let the woman advance. Just as his shoulder blades hit the dehydrated, unyielding earth, he planted his feet against the woman's stomach and launched her over him. He heard her body hit the dirt.

In seconds Carson was back on his feet, the pistol thrust out in front of him in a two-handed grip as he watched the woman's prone form struggle to rise. He was tempted to shoot, but doing so would kill the woman and likely piss off the creature attacking her. Instead, he stuffed the pistol back into the holster and yelled "RUN!"

Nobody needed to be told twice.

Carson grabbed Irene and Chris's hands, pulling them toward the edge of the field and into the neighborhood beyond. They struggled desperately to keep up and he had to adjust his pace before he dragged them off their feet. He heard Kate somewhere behind him, her breathing coming out in frightened gasps.

Carson felt a pang of guilt when he remembered the little girl who'd been punched by, he assumed, her mother. But he hadn't been able to think clearly. Panic had overwhelmed him and all he could think of doing was to flee. He turned to go back, but a wave of terrified people barred his way. Dejectedly, Carson had to give up and move with the crowd, rather than against it.

As they approached the first row of houses Carson heard a sound that sent a chill coursing through his veins. The sound that he had first mistaken as a plastic bag. More of those things were coming, and Carson suspected that they were catching up.

A scream ripped through the night, followed by another.

He didn't dare look back.

He kept his eyes firmly directed ahead, mentally trying to gauge the distance.

Twenty yards.

Fifteen.

Ten.

They were less than five yards away when he heard the sound again and it sounded like it was right above him.

Chris happened to look up at that moment and his scream likely saved Carson's life. Without hesitation, Carson dropped to the ground and pulled his kids down with him. Irene cried out as she roughly bounced off the hard-packed dirt. Chris sounded like the air had been forced from his lungs.

Carson felt, rather than saw, the creature crash to the ground off to his left. It had dive-bombed him and, thanks to his quick reaction, had missed by inches.

He pushed himself up into a crouch aimed upward, tracking the flying thing. He hesitated until it seemed to stop in the air for a moment, and then he fired.

The creature flopped about wildly only ten feet away, its limbs appearing broken and useless as it tried to right itself.

This time Carson didn't hesitate.

He lined up the sights on his gun and fired.

The bullet hit and the creature unleashed an unholy screech. Carson expected bright red blood to erupt from the wound but instead saw a spattering of milky grey fluid pump from the opening.

He stared, a million questions running through his mind. He would have stayed transfixed had the creature fallen still, but it continued to thrash. Carson's breath caught in his chest when the creature seemed close to righting itself.

Carson fired more shots in rapid succession. One round skipped across what he presumed was the creature's back as it thrashed, but the other shots hit their mark. The second shot struck near the thing's eyes, and it immediately fell still.

Unwilling to wait to verify that the thing was dead, Carson scrambled to his feet and, after holstering the pistol again, grabbed his kids' hands. Irene seemed rooted to the spot, staring at mound of ruined flesh, while Chris seemed to melt in Carson's grasp.

"We need to go," Carson implored as he tugged on Irene's hand. He pulled Chris to his feet as he spoke. "Before more come after us!"

This seemed sufficient to get Irene's attention, and she immediately started moving. Carson noticed that she refused to look back at the monstrosity. Chris hadn't seemed to hear Carson's pleading, so he lifted the small boy onto his hip and pulled Irene along.

To her credit, Irene did her best to keep pace with his strides, only lagging a step behind.

Above and behind them, Carson could hear more of the bizarre fluttering sounds. He knew more were chasing them. He was tempted to carry Irene as well, but it wasn't necessary. She heard the sounds, too.

They ran and Carson didn't bother to check that Kate was following. He knew she would be, but the kids were his priority. And, as guilty as the thought made him feel, he realized he didn't care if she followed or not. Even worse, he considered that it might be better if she didn't.

But she did. Fortunately, she didn't say anything. All that could be heard were the whimpers, the heavy breathing of the remaining people as they ran, and the fluttering in the sky above.

Chapter 17

The houses rose up from the gloom and Carson nearly wept.
They were close and, for now, they were alive. A pang of guilt
accompanied this thought.

The woman that had been attacked in the field was lost,
of that he was certain. He did not think it likely that the woman
would be the same, or even alive, if the thing that smothered her
came off.

Then there was the kid.

Cason assumed that the child had belonged to the
doomed woman. The way she had reacted to the attack and her
proximity during their march across the field seemed to indicate
as much. If not her mother, then an aunt or older sister.

And they had left her behind.

Carson wanted to go back, to save the poor girl, but he
knew doing so would be tantamount to suicide. He was
depressed, sure, but he wasn't quite *that* depressed.

At least, not yet.

He also doubted that the girl survived. He did not see her
among the crowd. He scanned those terrified faces and, though
he had only seen the child briefly, he did not see her among
them.

No, the girl was lost, too. Perhaps that was a small
mercy. She would be with her mother, or aunt or whatever,
right? He tried to reconcile the thoughts, but that did little to
lessen his guilt.

Bile rose in Carson's throat as he thought about the
child's possible fate, and that seemed to shake him out of his
head. No, he could not dwell on that now. There would be time

later for that. There was always time later to chastise himself for his failings.

But not now.

The crowd slowed as they approached the first row of houses, which allowed Carson to catch up. The plastic fluttering died down as they reached the side wall of a beige, two-story duplex. He doubted that the meager cover was enough to dissuade their attackers. Which meant something else was nearby. His face began to tingle at the thought, and he realized he had begun to hyperventilate.

Fucking anxiety, Carson thought angrily. There was a time and a place for that, and this was not it. With considerable effort, he forced his breathing to slow. In turn, his heart rate began to follow.

Pressed against the wall, Carson glanced behind him. Some of the followers looked around confused. But it was the others, the ones whose faces clearly showed panic, that told him that they had come to the same conclusion: something else was out there.

Carson looked at Irene and Chris, his index finger pressed against his lips. "Don't make a sound," he whispered. "I'm going to make sure the coast is clear, 'kay?"

Irene nodded and Chris followed suit. Kate scoffed but did not offer her input.

He shook his head, making sure it was barely perceptible. Kate didn't seem to notice.

Eyes shut, Carson leaned his head back against the rough texture of the wall and took several deep breaths. No matter what, he knew he would not be prepared for what he saw. He had not been so far.

As calm as he was going to manage, Carson quietly drew his pistol and glanced around the corner of the house. His eyes darted around, searching frantically. And he saw...

Nothing.

He had been prepared to face another nightmare. But a quiet street? It did not make sense. Why had the flying monstrosities backed off? He realized that he was trying to rationalize the behaviors of creatures beyond understanding. Did they behave like terrestrial predators? Or were their motives beyond human comprehension?

He continued to scan the street and the houses, desperate to catch movement somewhere. The absence of life only added to his unease, rather than dispel it. People feared what they did not understand and the unknown. In that moment, Carson experienced both.

After a full minute, he leaned back behind the wall.

"I don't see anything," he whispered.

"Then what are we waiting for?" someone asked.

"Let's fucking go, then," another added.

Carson shook his head. "Something doesn't feel right."

"None of this is right," the first voice snapped. "Nothing that has happened in the past few hours has been fucking *right.*"

The speaker was a man only a few years older than Carson. He could see panic on the man's blocky face. The other was a younger Hispanic man. He reminded Carson a bit of Airman Hernandez, but older.

"Are you *sure* you didn't see anything?" a woman in the crowd asked, bringing Carson back to the present. His mind seemed to be drifting quite a bit lately.

"I looked," he replied. "I didn't see anything, but it's dark. It's hard to see much."

"Then fucking look again," the first man hissed.

Carson bit off a retort. He wanted to tell the man that *he* could check if he was so dead set on it.

"Fuck, fine," he replied instead.

He glanced back around the house, searching the street and windows yet again. He was about to pull back to tell the others that it was empty when he caught movement near a house several houses down.

Squinting, Carson focused on the spot. Had he imagined it?

Unfortunately, he had not.

There, crouched in the shadows near a house at the bend in the street, was a shape that was vaguely human. After his encounter with the ragged man outside the school, Carson was on full alert. He ducked back quickly.

"I see someone, I think," Carson whispered. "Down the street. I think it's a person, but it's too dark."

Gasps and whimpers rippled through the small crowd. He caught several hopeful stares. They didn't know. They had not seen the man that seemed to split apart across from the school. If they had, they would not be hopeful at all. No, they would be terrified just as he was.

"Maybe they need help?" the young Hispanic man offered.

Carson shook his head. "I'm not sure, but I don't think we should get close to them. They may not even be…human."

Now more people began to speak up.

"What the hell does *that* mean?"

"Not human? Then what, an alien?"

"Oh god, it's another monster!"

Panic was starting to infect the crowd and Carson winced as voices rose above a whisper. He tried to shush them, but nobody seemed to hear.

"Oh shit, oh shit!" another voice nearly shrieked. Carson thought for a moment that someone had spotted something that he had missed. Some hideous monster slinking toward them from behind. He was relieved when this wasn't the case, which quickly turned to anger.

"Shut up," he nearly snapped. "All I meant was I can't tell what I saw. Just movement, that's it. It could be a person, but it could be something else, too. Either way, we need to all shut the fuck up and get ahold of ourselves."

"Excuse me?" a woman scoffed.

"Shit, I'm sorry," Carson apologized quickly. "What I meant was we need to be smart about this. And that means staying quiet. At least until we get somewhere safe, or until we can see better."

Several people grumbled but, thankfully, nobody else protested. Better still, nobody was panicking. If they were, they were at least staying quiet about it.

"I wish I had a scope, or binoculars, or *something,*" Carson said to himself. "Shit, night vision goggles would be perfect."

But he had none of those things, and his vision—though corrected with eye surgery—was not strong enough to make out the details of the figure in the shadows.

"Does anyone live on this street?" Carson asked, hoping desperately that nobody in the group did. Again, he found himself disappointed.

"I do," the previously offended woman said. "And I've seen him in the driveway a few houses down."

The woman pointed at the young Hispanic man.

Shit, Carson silently cursed. He could let them break off and make a run for their homes, but they would be defenseless if they got caught out in the open. He wished he had kept the rifle. At least he would have been able to cover them. His pistol was not ideal for the task.

"How far down?" he asked.

"What?" the woman responded.

"How far away is your house?" Carson clarified.

The woman blinked as though she had just woken up. "Oh, sorry. I dunno, about three houses down and on the left side of the street."

Carson ground his teeth. The figure was only a house or two away from where the woman described. "And you?" he asked the young man.

"Across the street, and a couple of houses away from us," he offered.

That was better, but not by much. It still put them closer to the figure than Carson would like.

"Then we will make our way to your house first," Carson decided. "We can follow the fences for the backyards."

"Why are we going to his house first?" the woman asked stupidly.

"Because it's closer you idiot," the man snapped.

"Excuse me?" she snapped back.

Carson could see this getting out of hand quickly. For a moment he wanted to slap the woman.

Only briefly.

"Stop it," Carson interrupted as he massaged his temples, a headache beginning to form. "We go to his place first and then we'll go to yours, okay?"

The woman huffed but didn't argue.

Carson sighed. These people were going to start tearing each other apart. All he wanted was to get home, rather than babysit a bunch of grown adults.

But he had the only gun, and he was now responsible for the group.

Maybe Kate was right. Maybe he *was* trying to play the hero.

Or maybe he just didn't want to see anyone else die.

Yeah, that made more sense. A spiteful part of him wanted to believe it, if only for Kate to be wrong.

Either way, they were going to have to risk it. Or split up. Kate would probably jump at that. And that put Irene and Chris at risk. What was he supposed to do?

Carson could feel himself beginning to freeze with indecision. Risk the kids by trying to escort people home, or let everyone fend for themselves to keep the kids safe? His paternal instinct leaned toward the latter. His altruistic side argued against it.

Fuck. Why was it so difficult?

Carson ran a hand over his closely shaved scalp. His paternal side eventually won out.

"You two, stay close to each other and head to your house," Carson said, his tone leaving little room for argument. "We'll stay close by until you get inside. Once the sun comes up, we all need to get somewhere safer. Maybe near the middle of the base." *If the base is still standing*, Carson didn't add.

The woman opened her mouth to protest.

"It will be too loud if we all go," he quickly added. "If anything starts moving toward you, or you see something that doesn't look right, then you can both hole up in his house."

"But…" the woman began before Carson waved his hand to cut her off.

"I'm sorry, but that is the best way," he interjected. The woman looked as though she were about to argue further, but the young man grabbed her arm and started pulling her along with him. Three children, two of whom looked like they were Kindergarten age, followed them. A pit formed in Carson's stomach as he watched them go.

<h1 style="text-align:center">Chapter 18</h1>

He should never have let them go alone. Carson had been watching the shape fidget in the dark as he slowly crossed the street. The thing did not seem to notice, even when he reached the other side of the street and ducked behind the wall of the pinkish house. Perhaps he *had* imagined it, or maybe it was a pet that had gotten out.

But it wasn't. Not even close.

Carson caught the change in its posture as the woman, along with the young man and the three children, drew near. When they were within a hundred yards of the man's home the thing rose to its full height.

It was not human, and it most certainly was not someone's loose pet.

The thing was vaguely human shaped, if only giving the faint impression of such. It was like a bizarre interpretation of a human being, reminiscent of something a young child would draw, and claim was a person.

For one thing, it stood nearly eleven feet tall. Second, the limbs were disproportionate and oddly numbered. Carson counted three arms and maybe four legs, attached to a lumpy torso and topped with a horribly misshapen head.

Then it moved into the light cast by a streetlight and Carson's mind, for maybe the dozenth time that day, nearly broke.

Carson wished he had never had corrective surgery for his vision, because then he would not have been able to clearly see the thing shuffling across the street.

Another nightmare given life, impossibly formed and almost as impossibly mobile. Its gait was a mix between lumbering, shuffling and skipping. And it made Carson sick to his stomach.

Mottled flesh was stretched across the thing's structure, seemingly bruised in odd places and stretched to near translucency in others, all the while tinted vaguely green. It was also hairless, at least from what Carson could tell from his distance. The bulbous head had a smattering of glistening black jewels embedded across it.

No, not jewels.

Eyes.

Dozens of eyes spread across the surface of its grossly misshapen head.

He was not surprised that the thing had spotted the smaller group. Carson suspected that the thing could see quite well in the dark, or perhaps its vision was in another spectrum entirely. He had no way of knowing.

As the grotesque creature loped across the street Carson noted that it did not seem to have ears.

Or so he thought.

The woman finally noticed the creature as she moved between the houses and let out a gasp. The beast stood ramrod straight and, unfurling from just above its shoulders, Carson spotted what appeared to be large disc-shaped mushrooms. The growths quivered and swiveled in the woman's direction.

Soundlessly, the creature reoriented itself toward the group and began its bizarre loping gait anew. Its arms reached out and Carson saw that the limbs were multi-jointed, unfolding once and then unfolding again. At the ends of the limbs were waving feelers—at least that's what Carson's strained mind could equate to—and pointed digits groping as it neared the group.

The man noticed the creature and moved to position himself between it and the group behind him. Carson heard the man yell, instructing the woman to find a rock to shatter the sliding glass door at the rear of his home. Carson also heard the woman's shrieks and the children's screams. His heart broke at the sound.

Pissed that, once again, he'd been frozen with fear, Carson growled and pulled his pistol free. Had he emptied the magazine? He was afraid to check, fearful that the creature would move at impossible speed, the moment he took his eyes off it.

Instead, he held the pistol straight in front of him, ejected the magazine and tilted it toward him. He caught the glint of brass and knew he had at least two rounds left, one still in the chamber.

Carson slid the magazine in place without taking his eyes off the creature. The monster moved at such a bizarre pace that he had a hard time keeping the pistol sights lined up on it. He was about to pull the trigger when the thing seemed to fall forward. Carson released the pressure on the trigger as he attempted to aim again, but his adjustment was too slow.

The beast's momentum brought it within reach of the man and, to Carson's terror, its head seemed to peel apart like a burst orange, tendrils and teeth emerging from within. The poor man did not have enough time to scream before it was upon him.

Multi-jointed limbs jabbed into his torso and swung him upward, the feelers burying into his flesh. The tendrils sprouting from the thing's head stretched and wrapped around the man's head and shoulders.

With a swift, powerful jerk, the thing tore the man's upper torso free from his body. The creature's tendrils reeled in the man's head and shoulders into its gaping maw, crunching wetly as it bit down. Blood spurted through its teeth and spilled across its flesh.

One of the children let out a bloodcurdling scream. The creature, previously focused on scooping up the viscera that spilled from the man's remains, jerked upright and began its loping movements toward the child.

Carson felt the air escape his lungs and immediately fired. He continued to squeeze the trigger, though the slide had locked back. He fired three rounds and then the magazine was spent.

Somehow, the bullets all hit.

The creature had been in the middle of chewing—if you could call it that—and the impact of the bullet seemed to cause its head to lose its structural integrity. The head seemed to deflate. The second and third rounds hit a mushroom-like growth and the joint where one of its arms attached to its torso.

He watched as the thing stumbled as the folds of flesh that drooped over its shoulders seemed to obscure its vision. It toppled to the ground and started dragging its bulk toward where the child had once been.

Carson's intervention had served its purpose. The woman and children had disappeared behind the house and, a moment later, he heard breaking glass. They had made it inside.

The thing continued dragging itself across the ground before shuddering and falling still. Carson wasn't sure if it was dead, and he chose not to find out. The gunshots would draw unwanted attention. The bulbous thing may be dead, but Carson suspected that other nightmares lurked in the dark.

He wanted to get home before they showed themselves.

Despite Carson's concerns, they managed to make it down several more streets without incident. Nobody spoke or made a sound, barely even breathing as though their exhalations would be enough to draw monsters to them. Carson found that he held his breath at every errant sound. Even the children in the group remained silent. He saw tears moistening cheeks, but he did not hear so much as a sniffle. And he couldn't blame them.

He made sure each family made it into their homes, staying close by to avoid making the same mistake as before. Carson and his family were the only ones outside.

The nightmare seemed endless, and he suspected that maybe it was. He no longer heard sirens in the distance. This fact nagged at him, and he couldn't figure out why.

As did the nearly suffocating silence.

Something felt…wrong. More so than what they had already experienced, that is.

He let out a sigh of relief when he saw the street sign at the corner. Then he caught sight of something that had once felt so mundane but was now the most beautiful thing in the world. He saw the aged wooden boards and the pale-yellow walls of his house.

He used to think that the house was bland and a bit ugly.

It wasn't anymore.

He may as well have been gazing upon a magnificent gothic cathedral or some form of renaissance-era architecture.

Better still, the house seemed undisturbed. With everything he experienced, Carson started to believe that maybe there *was* some unseen force. He just wasn't sure if it was malevolent or not. Whatever the case, Carson felt immense gratitude and relief. He wanted to sprint toward the structure, desperate to be within the safety of its walls. It seemed odd to think it had only been a few hours since he'd left home. It felt like a lifetime had passed.

Then it struck him, the reason something had seemed wrong—again, aside from the obvious. The sirens, or rather, the lack thereof. He had been, in essence, an active shooter. Why hadn't the base been locked down and emergency vehicles swarming the streets? He had run into only two security forces officers. Where were the others?

Another disturbing question came to him.

How far did this nightmare spread?

Chapter 19

The house was silent and dark. This would have once been of little significance, but now it felt oppressive. Anything could be hiding within, waiting to pounce and tear limb from limb. Far too many eyes could be peering out from the depths, watching and drooling in anticipation.

The kids seemed to sense this, too.

Carson felt his chest tighten as he slowly opened the door, his spent pistol in hand. He wished he had brought a spare magazine, but he hadn't expected to use the thing.

Irene and Chris huddled close behind him, adding to the growing claustrophobia that had begun to encroach upon him. He should have felt comforted by their proximity, and a part of him was, but he felt trapped as well. If something rushed out from within the house, he would have nowhere to go.

Taking a deep breath, Carson stepped across the threshold, shoulders tensed in anticipation.

Nothing happened.

No hideous creature pounced. Nothing but silence greeted him.

Fearful of becoming complacent, Carson remained tense and cautious. He may not have gotten jumped, but that did not mean the coast was clear. Something could still be lurking inside.

Carson looked over his shoulder at the huddled forms behind him and brought a finger to his lips. Irene and Chris both gave a feeble nod. Kate stood back, a scowl on her face. He half expected her to grab their kids and pull them away. She didn't, but he did see a flash of something cross her eyes. She may have considered doing exactly that.

He scanned the living room and the stairway, the light cast by the streetlight barely illuminating the room. Carson stepped fully inside and paused to listen. After several moments of silence, he started to relax. He felt the tension in his muscles begin to subside. His eyes adjusted to the gloom, and he could see that the living room, stairwell, and dining room were empty.

He also spied the empty crates, and his heart skipped.

The dogs.

Bella and Doll had been in the backyard when he had left several hours earlier. He should have heard them barking when he opened the front door. Instead, he had heard nothing.

Fearing the worst, Carson turned to Kate and their kids, his hand raised to stop them.

"Wait here," Carson whispered.

Kate opened her mouth to reply, but Carson cut her off with a glare. Normally this would have done nothing. However, Kate seemed to have picked up on the fact that something wasn't right. She didn't figure it out right away and he was thankful for that. If she had, she would have started panicking.

Without hesitation, Carson headed for the sliding glass door at the end of the dining room, careful to check the kitchen as he went. It was difficult to see in the yard, the illumination of the streetlight blocked by the house. The other side of the glass was pitch black, but the lack of movement told him that either something horrible lay beyond or the dogs had escaped the yard. He prayed to any entity that may listen that it was the latter.

His hand slowly made its way to the light switch on the wall that would turn on the lights in the backyard. A chill crept over him as his fingertips brushed the switch, and he hesitated. At that moment, Carson felt the urge to turn away. After the nightmare he'd endured, he wasn't sure if he could handle anything else.

But the kids would start asking about the dogs and panicking. Then Kate would get pissed and check herself. If something happened to the dogs and Carson hadn't checked, she would inevitably blame him and get the irrational notion that their fate could have been prevented if only he had not been such a coward. She would not have been completely wrong.

Fuck, Carson thought as he pressed his forehead to the cold glass and squeezed his eyes shut. *Please be okay. Please be okay.*

He flicked the switch and sucked in a breath simultaneously, bracing himself for the worst.

The light flooded the overgrown backyard and the deteriorating fence. Carson pressed his face against the glass as he tried to investigate the rest of the yard. He saw nothing. No gore. No monsters. And no dogs.

Across from where he stood, Carson made out the disturbed earth at the bottom of the fence. He felt a mixture of fear and relief when he realized the dogs had escaped. He exhaled and leaned back from the glass door.

"Well?" Kate asked from behind him, so close that it startled him and made him spin around.

"Jesus Kate!" he exclaimed and then winced at the volume of his voice. "Don't do that."

"Are they okay?" she asked, ignoring his reaction.

"They got out. Doll was digging again."

"We need to find them! They could be hurt!"

Carson shook his head. "Absolutely not. We barely made it inside. There's no fucking way I'm going back out there, especially in the dark. I'm sure they're fine."

Kate looked as though she'd been slapped. "But…"

"Then *you* go look for them," Carson snapped, his patience at its end. "I'm staying here with Chris and Irene. The dogs can handle themselves. *Our* kids can't."

"Fuck you," Kate spate and then stomped away. He heard her call him an asshole under her breath.

Well, that settles that. He hated the thought of leaving the dogs to fend for themselves, but there was no other choice. Searching for them in the dark would be suicide, especially since neither dog was particularly well-trained. He had chased Bella up and down the streets far too many times and she had not once come when called. Doll was young and hyper. He hadn't had time to train either of them and Kate hadn't even bothered.

He just hoped they were smart enough to stay out of danger. They could probably outrun anything that came after them, he told himself

Carson peered out into the yard for several minutes before letting out another sigh and shutting off the light. Kate had gone back to the living room and sat on the couch with Chris and Irene. He heard her trying to reassure them that everything was going to be okay, yet her expression said differently. She glared at him over their heads.

Too exhausted to care, Carson walked past the couch and slowly began to ascend the stairs.

He was thankful that the house had been built recently, as the stairs didn't creak when he stepped on them. He had holstered his pistol when he began his ascent and wanted to head directly to the master bedroom, but he would have to pass both of the smaller bedrooms and the bathroom.

He balled his hands into fists and tried to mentally prepare himself as best he could as he opened the door to the first room. He started to hate that he insisted the doors be closed whenever the rooms weren't occupied.

He was relieved to see that the room was empty. The same was true for the next bedroom and the bathroom. Tension began to leak from his muscles with every step toward the closed door of the master bedroom, fatigue slowly taking over.

His hand on the doorknob, Carson pressed his ear to the door. He was about to pull away when he thought he heard movement. Had it been his imagination? With his nerves as frayed as they were, it wasn't outside the realm of possibility.

Then he heard it again. Something was *definitely* moving inside. The hair on the back of his neck stood on end. He was unarmed, exhausted, and terrified. It would be exceedingly easy to overpower him.

Carson thought that his body would be incapable of producing more adrenaline, but it seemed that it had kept some in reserve. His heart rate once again jumped up and his face started to tingle as he hyperventilated. Darkness began to creep in from the edges of his vision and he had to force himself to slow his breathing. He stood there, hand on the doorknob, for several heartbeats before he finally began to slowly turn the knob.

The door squeaked faintly as it opened, and Carson's heart seemed to leap into his throat. He paused with the door opened nearly halfway and waited. Carson tried to listen over the pounding of his heart. His pulse was deafening in his ears. He let his eyes dart across the room, scanning for movement.

He saw the hem of the comforter hanging over the bed shift and he once again froze.

Maybe whatever it was hadn't heard him.

Or maybe it was because Kate had left the fucking bedroom window open.

Carson almost laughed. A faint breeze drifted from the window and passed over him, the hem of the comforter shifting gently. Why was the window open? He was thankful that nothing lurked under the bed.

At least he hoped nothing did.

He slowly made his way toward the bedroom closet, careful to keep his eyes on the bed in the center of the room. Carson reached behind him and opened the closet awkwardly. As soon as the door swung inward, he backed in and closed the door.

His hands shook as he tried, and failed, to punch in the combination to the small gun safe on the shelf at the back of the closet. He took a deep breath and tried again. His finger hit two buttons at once and he knew that he messed up the combination again. The safe beeped after he tried a third time, and the lock disengaged. Carson reached in and grabbed the magazine that he had kept loaded.

Carson didn't bother to catch the empty magazine when he pressed the eject button on the pistol. It hit the carpet and bounced, hitting his shin, but he barely noticed. He slammed to fresh magazine in place and racked a round into the chamber.

The added weight of the full magazine was welcome and had an immediate calming effect. Now armed, Carson emerged from the closet and slowly advanced toward the bed. He kept his breath shallow as he tried to approach silently. He stepped within a foot of the bed and got down on one knee, pistol held at his side with the barrel pointed straight ahead. With his free hand, Carson grasped the comforter.

He let his finger migrate toward the trigger as he lifted the comforter.

A dark shape leapt out from under the bed and Carson let out a yell as he fell backward. He was so surprised that his finger had hit the trigger well rather than the trigger itself.

He was immediately thankful for that. He caught sight of a bushy tail as the thing dashed out of the room.

He'd forgotten about the damned cat, their black and white shorthair named Gabby.

Carson couldn't help it. He lay on his back and started laughing. The stress of the day, the constant surges of adrenaline, and the horrifying creatures finally got the best of him. All of it spilled forth and the laughs slowly transitioned into sobs. He curled onto his side and set his emotions free. He stayed like that for several moments, alternating between laughter and sobs.

He had gone crazy. He *had* to have. No other explanation seemed possible. And yet, Carson knew that he hadn't. It was all real.

All the strength fled from his limbs and unconsciousness began to overwhelm him.

Once again, the nightmares returned.

Chapter 20

The structure felt *familiar, but he couldn't quite figure out where he was. It was some kind of residence. He knew that he'd been here before. It had once felt homey and comfortable. Now it felt...off. An eerie silence enveloped the space, punctuated only by heavy breathing.*

It was him. He was breathing heavily. His exhalations were joined by those of Chris, Kate, and Irene behind him, as well as several people he didn't recognize. He felt that he knew them somehow.

He stepped into the house and immediately felt the hair on the back of his neck stand on end. When he first arrived at the house he had felt relief, but that quickly fled as dread replaced it. He wanted to go back out and run as far from the house as he could. Something on an instinctual level, rooted in a primal survival instinct, was begging to be heeded. Yet he could not.

Because someone else should *be here. No, not just one person. Several.*

But from what he could tell, the house was vacant.

He was wrong.

The walls began to form lumps, like pustules or pimples. Something about this struck him as both familiar and terrifying. Part of him seemed to know to stay clear of the growths as contact would spell disaster. He once again wanted terribly to leave this place. He would find nothing but pain and death here.

But he had to be sure. He had to know.

Several steps carried him past the stairway that led to the second floor, containing only one room. He stood in the open expanse of the living room and peered across into the cluttered dining room. He knew on the other side lay the kitchen and the laundry room beyond that. Underneath the stairwell was a hallway that led to three bedrooms.

He wasn't sure which direction to go. Would he find what he was looking for in the kitchen? Maybe, and so he decided to check there first.

He didn't even get to the dining room before he caught movement off to his right. Something had emerged from the bedroom at the end of the hall and off to the right. That alone made him sick with dread, but what he saw coming toward him nearly made his heart seize.

Drifting like a helium balloon, suspended nearly a foot off the floor, was a large white mass. It reminded him of the artist's illustrations of white blood cells. It undulated and tendrils seemed to reach out to touch the walls, propelling it forward. The glob radiated intelligence, and with it, malevolence. He had his answer, and it broke his heart. He felt a terrible loss and now only wanted to shield his children from it.

***

Carson jolted awake and felt something touch his shoulder. He immediately tried to roll away.

"Are you fucking kidding me?" Kate chastised. "You fell *asleep*?!"

"What?" Carson asked stupidly, the nightmare was already fading. He looked over his shoulder and saw her staring down at him, her face red with anger.

"We've been waiting this whole time for you to make sure the house is safe, and you're fucking *sleeping*?!"

He turned away and ran a hand over his head. How long was he out for? With his other hand he grabbed his pistol and awkwardly tried to slide into the holster but sitting up made that incredibly difficult. He stretched his legs out in front of him and leaned back, finally getting the gun into the holster.

"I passed out," he answered, hoping she would back off. She didn't.

"Yeah, and we've been huddled in the living room scared to hell," Kate snapped. "Feel better now? Refreshed? You get your beauty sleep?"

"I didn't mean to, dammit," Carson snapped back. "Gabby jumped out from under the bed, and I passed the fuck out."

Kate scoffed. "Yeah, okay."

He didn't dignify this with a response. Instead, Carson crouched at the edge of the bed and, after checking that the damn cat was hiding under it again, pulled out the long, hard case beneath. He fished in his pocket and pulled out the key ring. He quickly found the correct key and jammed it into the padlock on the front of the case.

"Now what are you doing?"

"Uh, getting the gun out of the case," Carson answered with an exasperated sigh. "What's it look like?"

"Wow," Kate scoffed. Carson felt his blood beginning to boil.

He just shook his head and didn't look back. The lock popped open, and he roughly pulled it free. He waited until he heard her leave the room and then opened the case. Carson pulled the AR-15 out of the padded case and grabbed one of several full magazines, sliding it into the magazine well.

He made sure the safety was on before he pulled the charging handle to load a round in the chamber. He grabbed the other magazines, putting some in the pockets of the vest he was still wearing and slipping another into his pocket where he had had his keys.

Carson was prepared for more vitriol as he left the room and made his way down the stairs. It shouldn't have been able to upset him anymore, but Kate always seemed to know exactly what to say to get under his skin. She was an exceedingly small person, only about four foot seven inches tall—if that—and her words were her only real weapon. But she wielded it like a trained expert.

He had the rifle slung across his back as he stepped heavily down the stairs, thankful that someone had the presence of mind to turn on the lights in the living room. But it would also allow him to see Kate's expression. Couldn't she leave him be, just this once? Hadn't they been through enough already?

As expected, Kate had a scathing remark the moment he came into view.

"There he is, our hero," her words dripping venom. Carson chose to bite his tongue. He didn't have the energy to engage.

"Upstairs is clear," he said. "I'm going to check the garage and then lock everything up."

"Please don't leave us again," Irene begged.

"Yeah daddy," Chris added. "Stay with us, please. Please daddy."

Carson could see tears welling in their eyes. Once again, he could feel his heart breaking. He wanted nothing more than to shield them from the nightmare, to hold them and never let go. He told himself that it was the only way to keep them safe, but he knew better. He *had* to check the garage, if only to dismiss his fears.

"I'm just going to open the door, turn on the light, take a quick look, and then close it," he offered as a compromise. "Just a few seconds, that's it."

"No, don't," Chris began.

"I promise, buddy," Carson quickly interjected. He knew his son's emotions would quickly turn into a runaway train if he didn't get in front of it early. "I'll be super-fast."

Chris didn't argue, but the quiver of his lower lip told Carson that he only had seconds before Chris fell apart. Without hesitation, Carson turned and nearly ran into the kitchen.

He stood before the door to the garage and immediately opened it, momentarily forgetting about being careful. He instantly began to panic and slapped the wall just inside the doorway, looking for the light switch. He found it and flipped it on. Inside the garage was empty, other than several boxes that they still had not unpacked despite being the house for nearly a year.

With a deep sigh, Carson turned off the light and shut the door, locking it. He walked into the dining room and slipped the latch on the sliding glass door to lock that as well.

"See?" Carson asked when he walked back into the living room. "Lightning fast."

Chris and Irene nodded. It looked like they were finally starting to calm down. He didn't bother to look at Kate—he could see her expression in his peripheral vision—and headed toward the front door to lock that as well.

With the front door locked and the deadbolt engaged, Carson finally felt his tension subside.

Chapter 21

"Daddy, we're hungry," Chris whimpered from under his mother's grasp. Irene nodded enthusiastically, as if to reinforce the point. Carson had been so engrossed in his efforts to keep them safe that he realized he didn't know what time it was. No wonder they were hungry. And the presence of the living room lights was enough to confirm that electricity was still flowing, for now.

"Okay, you guys," Carson said with a small smile. "I'll make us something to eat."

The effort to cook a sizeable meal, one Carson hoped wouldn't be their last, had served to push the nightmares to the furthest reaches of his mind. It was a welcome distraction. He used to love cooking, but over time it had become a chore as he was the only person in the house who prepared the meals. Yet, after the insanity of the day, he felt immense relief in the task.

It wasn't anything special. A simple meal of baked chicken, white rice, and steamed vegetables, but both children shoveled it into their mouths as though they hadn't eaten in days. Carson sat at the dinner table and pushed the food around his plate with his fork. He knew he should eat, but the persistent anxiety—which returned in full force the moment he finished cooking—twisted his stomach into knots.

Kate picked at her food in silence. Carson didn't believe in the reading of auras and a lot of that new-age stuff, but he felt at that moment that he could *see* her anger radiating from her. The silence was almost worse than her consistent needling. He found himself imagining the litany of insults and accusations running through her mind. He wasn't psychic, but she was predictable.

The meal continued in this fashion until Chris and Irene, after having a second helping for the first time in a long time, scooted their chairs away from the table and announced that they were stuffed.

Kate was sure to order them to rinse off their plates and put the dishes in the dishwasher. Carson found the silence at the table following their departure too much to endure and quickly excused himself.

Despite his exhaustion, Carson couldn't keep himself from pacing around the living room and checking out the windows at regular intervals. His brief nap may not have fully recharged his batteries, but his anxiety seemed up to the task of keeping him awake.

Kate plopped down on the couch, Irene and Chris flanking her, and opted to turn on the television. The noise made Carson jump. If he could hear it, something else could, too.

"What are you doing?" Carson asked in a loud whisper.

"The kids were bored," Kate replied. "What do you want them to do?"

He shook his head and, after a long sigh, leaned against the wall near the front door. "I'm sorry, but we can't have the TV on. It's just too noisy."

"After everything we've been through, we deserve to relax," Kate snapped.

"I understand that," Carson said calmly. "I do, but we can't take the risk. It's too dangerous."

She glared at him and stayed silent for a moment. Another tactic she often employed, knowing that the prolonged silence and unbreaking stare would make him incredibly uncomfortable. Normally he would concede, but not this time.

"We can't," he said after several moments.

"Turn off the TV, kids," Kate said, her glare still firmly directed toward Carson. "*Daddy* says you can't watch it."

For fuck's sake, Carson thought angrily. *What the hell do you want from me?*

He held her glare for several minutes and realized that his hands had curled into fists. As if sensing this, Kate's eyes flicked to his hands, and her expression hardened further.

For seemingly the first time, Carson saw Kate; *really* saw her. The mask had slipped completely and what stared back sent a chill up his spine. This wasn't the woman he had fallen in love with. In her place was vicious, manipulative and horribly insecure woman who seemed to thrive off the discomfort of others.

Carson had a sneaking suspicion that the woman who glared at him from the comfort of their living room couch was the *real* Kate and had been since the beginning. In that moment, Carson chastised himself for not recognizing the signs. The red flags, the flashes of her fiery temper, and her toxic attitude toward anyone who challenged her suddenly flooded his mind. The signs had been there, but he'd been too blind to notice.

"But I'm scared mommy," Chris begged beside her. "Can we *please* watch something funny or something?"

"Yeah," Irene chimed in. "Like funny cat videos?"

A smirk tugged at the corner of Kate's mouth, yet her eyes remained cold and hard as she stared at Carson. "Ask your dad."

That wasn't fair. She was making him the bad guy and all he was trying to do was keep them safe. What else was he supposed to do? He couldn't sit by and let the noise bring all manner of nightmares down on them. In that moment following his painful epiphany, he found he had started to hate her.

"Maybe your mom can put a video on for you on her phone," Carson offered after a moment, returning Kate's glare.

That was it. No further discussion. It was a small victory, sure, but a victory, nonetheless. Kate glared a moment longer and then, with a huff, pulled out her cell phone.

Carson hid the smile that was creeping on his lips by turning to peer out the window. The streetlight cast its yellow glow over the front yard, the shadows cast by the vehicles in the driveway a nearly impenetrable gloom. For a moment, everything felt peaceful.

Until it didn't.

Something shifted within the darkness near his truck. For a moment, Carson thought that maybe Gabby had gotten out and was hiding under the truck, but this assumption was quickly dashed when the cat rubbed against his calf. The touch alone would have been comforting on any other occasion. This time, however, it filled him with dread.

Without a word, Carson reached out and flipped the light switch, plunging the living room into darkness. Chris and Irene squealed simultaneously and Kate, having apparently already forgotten about the events that had transpired, took the opportunity to question Carson's actions far louder than was necessary.

"What the hell are you doing?" Kate yelled.

Carson quickly turned and put a finger to his lips, making a shushing sound.

"Don't you *shush* me," Kate hissed.

"Dammit, shut up," Carson whispered firmly. Fearing another retort due to the harshness of his words he added, "Please."

Fortunately, Kate seemed to detect the tremor in his voice because no further response came. She went so far as to whisper quietly to their children to calm them.

Carson turned back to the window and, with the glare from the living room eliminated, he could see further into the shadows.

He quickly wished he couldn't.

At the edge of the shadow cast by the truck, Carson saw a spider-like limb reach out. Then another, followed by a pale green, round body, and two more limbs. At the rear was a long, whip-like tail. The thing scuttled completely out of the cover of darkness and Carson knew his face had gone white as a sheet.

"Oh, fuck you," Carson moaned. "That's not fucking fair!"

"What? What is it?" Kate, having picked up on Carson's fear, began to panic.

Carson had suffered from arachnophobia all his life. He had thought, wrongly, that his exposure to the freakish creatures would eliminate his fear of spiders. If anything, it had made it worse. The recent appearance hammered it home.

The spider-like thing seemed to have heard him, or Kate's near screams, and turned toward the house. It moved just like a spider and shared a few similarities, but it had only four legs rather than eight. Additionally, its body did not appear segmented into two parts. It was just a round, lumpy greenish mass. He couldn't see any eyes on its surface. Yet, how come this didn't make him feel any better?

The creature quickly scurried right up to the house and Carson instinctively jumped backward, eliciting a shriek from everyone in the room. He unslung the rifle from his back and raised the barrel of the weapon toward the window, his hands shaking uncontrollably.

He heard the clicking of the creature's appendages against the outside of the house and knew it was trying to climb up toward the window.

Once again, the forelimbs crept up into his line of sight and a wave of nausea slammed through him. The small, twitching motions identical to those of a spider. This was it. This was the moment that would break him, if nothing else would.

Bile rose in his mouth, and, with a supreme level of effort, Carson kept it from spewing forth. That is, until the thing's underbelly came into view.

The creature quickly scuttled up the glass and there, situated on its belly, was a distinctly humanoid face. The "mouth" was open in a silent scream and there were dark pits giving the impression of empty eye sockets. It quivered and uttered a piercing cry, the sound nearly identical to the cry of an infant.

Carson's vision swam and he pitched forward at the waist, vomit erupting from his mouth and nose. He retched several more times and then looked back up. It was still there, staring at him and wailing.

That was it.

His mind shut down and he fell on his face.

For the first time since the waking nightmare began, Carson didn't dream. He was completely unaware of anything at all. He experienced only blissful nothingness.

But this didn't last.

He first registered someone shaking him. Then voices muted as though underwater. His mind begged to stay oblivious, pushing back against the attempts to rouse him. But the attempts won out.

"Wake up!" a voice cried out. It was distinctly female and sounded very young. "Please daddy, wake up!"

Carson slowly opened his eyes, his vision still swimming. His face felt wet and sticky, an agonizing pain radiating out from the middle where his nose was. It was broken, of that he was certain.

"Daddy!" Irene shrieked when he turned to face her.

He tried to reach out to put a calming hand on her shoulder, but his vision refused to clear. He fumbled clumsily and finally felt the bony slope of her shoulder. "I-I'm okay, I think," he said, but it came out distorted.

"Daddy, you're bleeding!"

"It's my nose," Carson replied as he gingerly touched his face. Yes, his nose was definitely broken. He'd fallen face-first on the floor.

"I'll get the first-aid kit," Irene said and immediately ran off. He and Kate had complained about Irene sneaking the first-aid items to school in her backpack, but now he was thankful. It would, at least, give her something to do other than panic.

He sat up and wiped the back of his hand across his eyes. After a moment, his vision finally began to clear. Conscious of his appearance—he must have looked like a mess with blood all over his face—he brought his hand over his nose and mouth before turning to look at Kate and Chris.

"What was that?" Kate asked, her previous anger no longer present. In its place was fear. "Carson, what the fuck was that thing?!"

Carson knew that he couldn't accurately answer, just as he knew she didn't expect him to. The question was rhetorical, her mind coming undone just like his was. She was clawing at anything to rationalize what they had just seen. Unfortunately, there was no way to rationalize or understand *any* of the things they'd seen.

"Where'd it go?" Carson asked, ignoring her questions and refusing to look toward the window. "Is it gone?"

"I don't know," she replied weakly. "It kept climbing up. I-I think it climbed on the roof."

He was thankful for that, too. At least the wailing had stopped, and he wouldn't have to look at the thing again. He hoped he wouldn't, anyway. He didn't think his already fragile psyche could handle it.

Irene ran back into the living room with the small first-aid kit in her hands. She dropped to her knees and immediately began to sift through the contents. Carson doubted there was much of anything in the kit that would work for a broken nose, but he chose to let her look anyway.

"Will this work?" she asked, holding up a wrapped square with a label indicating that it was a non-adhesive gauze pad. Carson nodded. It would be better than nothing.

Chris continued to stare; his face as white as Carson's had been before he had blacked out. He could see Chris's lips moving, but no sound came out. At that moment Carson feared that Chris had shut down, his mind rejecting the terrors he'd been subjected to.

After rolling up the gauze and stuffing it in a nostril, followed by another, Carson stood up and made his way to the bathroom on the main floor, just off the kitchen. He turned on the light and looked at his reflection.

What peered back was barely recognizable.

Blood was caked across his face, nearly covering everything below his nose. His eyes were bloodshot, and his face was still pale. A bruise was already beginning to form across the bridge of his nose and under his eyes. He turned on the tap and let the cool water run over his hands, the rifle slung across his back.

He felt the rifle hit his back as he leaned forward, but the sensation barely registered. Carson was effectively numb. Perhaps that was a good thing. At least for the time being.

He splashed water on his face, the cold causing the pain to flare up where it hit his nose and cheeks. As gently as possible, Carson began scrubbing the blood from his face.

Several minutes later, the basin of the sink effectively dyed pink, Carson stepped out of the bathroom and grabbed a hand towel off the handle of the oven. He winced when the cloth touched his face.

Almost dreamily, he walked back into the living room. His eyes remained unfocused as he sat on the couch. He only vaguely registered the weight pressed against him.

For a long while he just sat there, his mind nearly blank.

None of this could be real, could it? The monsters, the weird portal, or the deaths. No, surely not. After all, nothing like this happened. Nor had it ever.

Try as he might, Carson could not convince himself that the last few hours had been nothing more than hallucination. His mind wanted to reject it, but he'd always be keenly aware of everything that happened around him. He had a powerful imagination, sure, but he could always distinguish imagination from reality.

Carson's mind finally climbed back to the present. No, it hadn't climbed. His mind had been dragged back against its will, kicking and screaming.

Chris was pressed up against him.

"What are we going to do?" Kate asked quietly, more to herself than to him.

He shook his head. He seemed to be doing that a lot today.

"I don't know," Carson finally answered. "I have no clue. What *can* we do?"

Carson looked over and saw a tear roll down her cheek. It was a rare moment of genuine emotion. He felt the compulsion to comfort her, but he couldn't simply forget the nasty behavior from earlier. Maybe, once upon a time, he could have, but not now.

Instead, he reached over and pulled Chris in tight, the boy's small body shaking. For perhaps the hundredth time that day, he felt his heart break for his kids. They didn't deserve this. Hell, Carson wasn't sure *he* deserved it. Nobody did.

His eyes burned as tears welled up and spilled down his face, tracing hot tracks down his bruised cheeks. He leaned back on the couch, ignoring the rifle against his spine.

Chapter 22

For a long while, Carson sat on the couch and stared at the ceiling. The comforting weight and heat from both Irene and Chris pressed against him from either side. For a moment, he could almost forget about the monsters.

Almost.

Far above, somewhere on the roof, he could hear scratching and thumping. The thing with the face and baby-like screams was still searching for a way inside. He was thankful that he couldn't hear the screaming anymore. He never wanted to hear that again.

At every thump, Carson felt Irene and Chris jump. Their nerves had to have been as frayed as his own. He felt the desire to turn on the television just to provide a distraction. The cat videos that Kate had played on her phone could no longer distract them from the horror above.

"Will it get in the house?" Irene asked, barely above a whisper.

"I don't think so," Carson answered, though he wasn't confident in his answer. "I think it would have by now, if it could. But we'll stay down here, just in case."

"What if it does?" Chris asked in a small voice.

"Then I'll kill it."

"What if there's more?" Irene asked.

"I'll kill those, too."

His answers, and the absolute certainty in his voice, seemed to calm them. Carson had been telling the truth. He *would* kill anything that tried to get inside or die trying. He felt a measure of comfort in the certainty of this thought. It gave him purpose.

The thumps persisted but seemed to slow. The thing was possibly tiring itself out. Carson hoped so. Maybe it would get bored and move on. *Maybe moving off to hunt easier prey,* Carson thought morbidly. He immediately chastised himself for the thought.

He considered sneaking outside and trying to shoot the fucking thing, but the thought terrified him. The thing may not be alone, and Carson did not want to face more of them. He couldn't handle one and doubted his psyche could handle others. However, he knew he couldn't just sit by and hope the thing disappeared on its own.

Coming home began to feel like a mistake. Sure, Carson had been able to arm himself and restock his ammunition, but had it been worth it? They were effectively trapped.

At least until morning.

"We need to leave," he said, the beginnings of a plan starting to form. "In the morning, we'll pack what we can and get out of here."

Kate gave him an incredulous look. "And go where?"

Carson thought for a moment. There was no way of knowing how far the nightmare spread. It was possible, though remote, that the attacks were confined to the base. "We'll head to your parents' place, or my mom's," he offered. "It would be better than staying here."

Kate was quiet for a while and Carson started to think that she hadn't heard him. "We'd have to go back out *there.*"

"That spider-thing almost got in *here,*" Carson countered. "As far as we know the whole base is now crawling with those things. You think it's a good idea to stay put? What if they find a way in?"

"Fine," she said after a moment, her face going white. "I'll call them now and tell my parents that we're coming."

Before Carson could respond, Kate had her phone up to her ear. He could make out the dial tone from the speaker as the call went through. His heart started to sink when it kept ringing. It rang several times and then he heard the answering machine pick up.

"Try again," he offered, and Kate complied. Once again, it rang until the answering machine picked up.

"Maybe they're at the store?" Kate suggested.

"At eight at night?" he asked in return. "Yeah, I don't know about that. Maybe try their cell phones?"

Several moments, and a half dozen attempts later, Kate dropped her phone on her lap. Her face had started to go pale, and Carson could see the panic in her eyes.

"What if something happened to them?" she asked, her voice trembling.

"Then we *really* need to go," he answered. "I'd say we go now, but I'd probably pass out behind the wheel at this point. And the kids need sleep, too."

Kate nodded but remained quiet. Her body began to shake as she started to succumb to the grips of terror. He knew she feared for their safety. Her family were the only people Kate seemed to genuinely care about. She might care mostly about herself, but she certainly held real affection for her parents. Her sisters, too, for that matter. To a certain extent, that is.

A question began to form on Kate's lips. Carson suspected that he knew what she would ask and wasn't certain how he would respond. What if the monsters got them, she would ask. And what would he say? He couldn't tell her that it wouldn't be possible. She'd argue if he did, and he didn't believe it in any case.

Instead, Kate remained quiet, the question not forthcoming. Carson felt relieved. He suspected that she knew there would be no satisfactory answer to her inquiry and chose to forgo giving voice to her fears.

Nearly half an hour passed in virtual silence, with only the occasional thump coming from the roof. Nobody spoke. After a while, the thumps no longer elicited a reaction. Even the kids seemed to have tuned it out.

Sleep initially seemed an impossibility, but as time wore on their eyelids grew heavy. Even Kate, who had been silently spiraling into panic and despair, had begun to sink lower into the couch and her chin seemed to creep closer to her chest.

Before long, Carson heard Irene and Chris's breathing slow down. Their heads rested against his shoulders and their bodies relaxed. He knew without looking that they had both fallen asleep and for that he was glad. He just hoped that they weren't plagued by nightmares.

Carson, on the other hand, couldn't seem to sleep at all. He was terrified of falling asleep and facing the nightmares that seemed to routinely prevent him from resting. He knew that fatigue would quickly overrule his fear if he continued to sit idle on the couch.

Carefully, Carson eased Irene and Chris off his shoulders and rose from the couch. His movements, subtle as they were, got Kate's attention.

"Where are you going?" Kate whispered, intent on letting their children sleep. From the heaviness of her eyelids and the grogginess in her voice, Carson suspected that she'd been asleep as well.

"I'm going to start gathering some things for when we leave."

"Oh," was all Kate offered in response. His answer appeared sufficient, as her eyes closed, and she leaned back against the couch.

The first task would be to grab the emergency to-go bag he had purchased shortly after moving into the house from the closet near the main entryway. It was heavy and contained the basics necessary to survive for roughly three days. Carson had also bought a box of meals-ready-to-eat, or MREs, and stored it in the garage. He decided to unsling his rifle from his back and, instead of switching on the light in the garage, turned on the attached flashlight.

The beam illuminated the boxes stacked inside the small garage. He'd been told that it would fit more than one vehicle. Carson suspected that it had applied to small vehicles, like motorcycles, and not a regular sized car as they had struggled to fit their Toyota Camry inside without scraping the side mirrors. The garage instead became a storage room.

He was thankful that he'd had the presence of mind to keep the box of MREs near the door to the garage. He located it and, after quickly sweeping the beam of the flashlight around the garage, chose to return the rifle to its place on his back. With one foot holding the door to the house open, he grabbed the heavy box by the thick plastic bands and dragged it inside.

Carson carried the box into the living room and set it down on the floor beside the to-go bag.

The next task on his mental checklist would be harder to accomplish, though not physically. He did not want to head back upstairs and, in turn, closer to the thing crawling on the roof, but he needed to make sure he had all the ammunition for his pistol and the rifle gathered. He would also need to pack a bag with several changes of clothes, toiletries, and any other necessities.

He also had bought tactical gear but never expected to use it. He had a cheap imitation of the plate carrier vests that he'd seen security forces wear, minus the capability to carry an armored plate. Essentially, it was just a vest with ammo pouches and MOLLE compatibility. He'd thought the vest, tactical gloves, belt and drop holster were cool when he bought them. Now he just felt like an imposter. He wasn't Special Forces. Hell, he wasn't even *Security* Forces.

The gear was functional, and would probably come in handy, but wearing it would feel wrong, like an ill-fitting suit. Carson caught himself spiraling down the well of depression and yanked himself back. It didn't matter if people thought he was legitimate or not. What mattered was the safety of his family.

Before he left the bedroom, Carson grabbed up a pair of long-range walkie talkies—the range likely exaggerated as a marketing ploy—and the charging dock. He'd make sure to charge them before they left the house.

He had a suspicion that they would not be coming back.

Reluctantly, he headed upstairs and set about gathering everything he could as quickly, and quietly, as possible. Even at an accelerated pace, it took him over an hour to get everything he thought they would need. Kate would have to pack a bag of her own, since Carson wasn't sure what she would choose to bring along. He would help the kids pack their bags when they woke up.

Carson hefted the bag onto his shoulder and carried it down the stairs to place it with the rest of the supplies. It hadn't taken up as much time as he had hoped and, without anything else to do for the time being, he chose to retake his place on the couch. This time, he made sure to unsling the rifle and set it with the supplies.

He sat on the couch and asked Kate for her phone. She protested at first but eventually relented when Carson assured her that he only needed it to make a call.

Carson stared at the screen and tried to remember Booker's phone number. It took an embarrassingly long time. He typed it in and held the phone to his ear. Hopefully, after telling Booker what had happened, the man would stay away from base.

"Hello?" Booker asked groggily. *"Who's this?"*

"It's Tanner," Carson answered. "I'm using Kate's phone."

"Tanner? What's going on?"

Carson proceeded to tell Booker about everything he had been through since their last conversation. To his credit, Booker stayed quiet and listened to all of it. When Carson finished Booker was silent for a long time before he spoke again.

"It's all real," Booker croaked out. *"Damn, man. I'm just glad you guys made it out of there."*

"Barely," Carson said, nodding. "But I couldn't save all of them, man. I fucked up."

"Tanner, buddy, you did what you could. You were in a seriously fucked up situation and people died. I get it. But you could only do so much, and it sounds like you tried."

"Yeah, but still," Carson's voice shook. "People are dead because of me. That…woman is dead because of *my* gun. I was too slow to rescue her boy, and she fucking killed herself."

"Don't do that man," Booker said quietly. *"It wasn't your fault. Beating yourself up about it won't change anything. Right now you need to focus on keeping your family safe."*

"Did you get anything from Command? They must know by now that shit hit the fan," Carson said, trying to change the subject.

"*Hang on a sec,*" Booker answered. After a moment his voice returned. "*Yeah, an emergency notification went out. Not a lot of detail, though. Just an order to evacuate as quickly as possible. Fuck man, it looks like you were right: I'm not going to work tomorrow.*"

"Son of a bitch," Carson exhaled. He'd hoped that the situation had gotten under control. "Okay, we're getting out of here at first light."

"*You can't leave now?*"

"Not safely. We're exhausted and I will probably pass out behind the wheel. I'm going to keep watch and have Kate drive after she sleeps."

Kate looked over at the mention of her name and arched an eyebrow. Carson stared at her expectantly. After a moment she sat back and mumbled, "fine."

"*Okay Tanner. Okay,*" Booker said, though Carson could hear that he was not comforted by the decision. "*Just get out of there.*"

"What are you guys going to do?" Carson asked.

"*For now we're going to stay put. The creatures attacked the base and were about forty-five minutes away from there. But, if I see even one of the fuckers, we're going to high-tail it out of here.*"

"Oh, okay," Carson said after a moment. It would be hypocritical to tell Booker to leave now, after he already told the guy that they were waiting until morning. "Let me know if you guys have to bail. Just call this number. My phone is busted so I can't answer mine."

"Sure thing, buddy. Stay safe."

"You too."

Carson hung up and passed the phone back to Kate. She had already started falling asleep and was not happy about being woken up. She grumbled, put the phone in her purse, and then went back to sleep. Carson sat on the couch, going over his conversation with Booker. The base was pretty much lost. The sense of security that had influenced his decision to live in the housing development within the gates had evaporated. Rather than feel safe, he felt trapped.

Carson put his head back and stared up at the ceiling, listening for any noises that would indicate one of the spider-creatures was still there, but all he heard was silence.

He had intended to stay awake and watch over his family until the morning, but fifteen minutes later his eyes closed of their own accord and, before he knew it, he fell asleep.

Chapter 23

He had closed his eyes and the next moment he was being shaken awake. It was almost as if he'd been put under anesthesia. To him, no time had passed. But when he opened his eyes and looked around, he noticed the sun shining through the living room window.

Carson didn't jolt upright. His anxiety didn't immediately spike. He awoke slowly and calmly, which was also a first in a while.

The house was quiet and, for a moment, peaceful. It took him several minutes to remember the terrors of the previous day. In fact, Carson wasn't sure if the whole thing had been a very long, very vivid nightmare. He would have chalked it up as such, but then he saw the gear piled in the center of the living room and knew that it had all been real.

He wanted to cry.

Why couldn't it have been a nightmare? Hadn't he suffered enough? If Carson believed in karma, he would have tried to understand where the negative karma came from, and what he had done to earn it. But life didn't work that way. He hadn't seen karma work the way people always said it did. The nasty, vile people always seemed to get away with everything.

He noticed his spiral into despair and mentally applied the brakes. He had to pull himself together. If that meant suppressing his emotions in that moment, then so be it. There wasn't time to feel sorry for himself; he could do that later when they were safe.

Irene came down the stairs, the top of her head barely visible over the wall. A *thump thump* followed every step. When she came into view Carson saw that she was dragging a Hello Kitty suitcase. Either Kate had seen the pile of stuff in the middle of the living room and had instructed the kids to pack their things, or Irene had seen it and decided to pack on her own. Sadly, Carson suspected the latter.

Chris called out for help at the top of the stairs. "I need help."

"What do you need help with buddy?" Carson called up.

"I can't carry my suitcase."

"Okay, okay, I'm coming."

Carson felt as though his bones had been filled with lead. It took a concerted effort to rise from the couch. He may have slept so deeply that he hadn't dreamt, but it hadn't been sufficient to refresh his body and mind. His back popped as he finally stood upright, and his neck felt stiff. Pain ran down his left shoulder from his neck as he tried to look to his left. Carson tried to roll his shoulders and stretch his neck, but he knew the kink in his neck would persist through the day.

"Daddy," Chris called down impatiently. "I need help."

"I'm coming buddy," Carson called back. "Hold your horses."

He stepped around the pile of gear, which had grown a bit since the night before, and made his way sluggishly toward the stairs.

There, at the top of the stairs, Chris stood next to a suitcase that was nearly as tall as he was.

"What do you have in there?" Carson asked.

"I have my stuffed animals, and my toys," Chris began, as though this was the most normal thing in the world. "And my clothes. And some undies…"

Carson chuckled as Chris listed off all his "necessities" he had chosen to pack. He was glad Chris hadn't loaded the suitcase down with books, but it was surprisingly heavy, nonetheless.

"Bud, we're going to have to go through this and make sure you have everything you need," Carson said as he lifted the suitcase. He could see the zipper straining to remain closed.

"I got everything I need," Chris replied, clearly confused.

"Well, we're going to make sure anyway."

"But…" Chris began.

"Just trust me, okay?"

Chris stuck out his bottom lip and his shoulders drooped. "Fine."

They made their way back to Chris's bedroom and Carson laid down the suitcase. The moment he pulled on the zipper tab, the suitcase nearly burst open.

Chris had been honest. He had packed *every one* of his stuffed animals. And beneath that, a smattering of toys—including a fair amount of Lego pieces—along with a single pair of underwear and several mismatched socks.

"Buddy, this isn't going to be enough," Carson said as he held up the articles of clothing. "You need to pack a lot more clothes."

"But I won't have room for my stuffies," Chris complained, tears welling in his large brown eyes.

Carson felt his heart melt in that moment. He wanted to let Chris bring all his dearest possessions, but that simply was not possible.

"Let's pack your clothes and stuff first, and then we can see how many stuffies we can fit in the suitcase," Carson offered.

"But they won't all fit," Chris argued. "I need them."

"Let's just see, okay buddy?" Carson countered.

"But…" Chris prepared to argue again.

"Just pick out the *most* important ones and we can come back for the rest later," Carson lied. He knew they wouldn't be coming back to the house for a long time, if ever. "Is that okay?"

Chris didn't appear to enjoy this idea, but he eventually nodded. "Okay daddy."

"And we can't bring all your Legos," Carson chuckled. "But we can put some in a Ziploc bag," he added quickly.

"Oh okay," Chris appeared to perk up a little. "I'll go get one."

Carson watched as Chris raced out of the room. Glancing back at the suitcase lying open, Carson felt a pang of sadness. He considered grabbing another suitcase just so Chris could bring his prized possessions, but there wasn't enough room in the vehicles. They had to make sure they had room for everything they needed to survive. Unfortunately, Chris's toys didn't qualify.

Chris ran back into his room, a gallon-size Ziploc bag clutched in his little fist.

"I got a bag," he proclaimed proudly. "*All* my Legos will fit in this!"

"That works," Carson replied, a small, sad smile pulling at the corners of his mouth. "Let's get you packed buddy."

The task of packing Chris's belongings had the pleasant side effect of distracting Carson for a short while. They sorted through Chris's dresser and selected articles of clothing that would be appropriate for different weather conditions. Chris picked out his favorite shirts and started pulling as many pairs of underwear out of his dresser as he could before Carson had to tell him to slow down.

All told, it took about forty-five minutes to get Chris's suitcase repacked. They had had to leave out over half of Chris's stuffed animals, and it had taken some convincing to get Chris to let Carson close the suitcase. Carson suggested that they arrange the leftover toys to defend the bedroom while they were gone. Chris eventually acquiesced, though Carson knew it had been difficult for the boy.

Carson picked up the suitcase, which wasn't any lighter than when they had started, and headed toward the stairs. Chris insisted on helping carry the suitcase, which amounted to him grabbing one of the handles and "carrying" it with Carson. They made it down to the living room and added the luggage to the growing pile.

Kate was nowhere to be found on the main floor. Carson suspected that she was in their bedroom, packing her own belongings. He had the momentary urge to go up and help her repack her suitcase just like he did with Chris. Though the thought made him chuckle, he knew it would go over about as well as lead balloon. He hoped that she had the forethought to grab what was absolutely essential. Sadly, Carson doubted it.

She had always overpacked whenever they were going to be away from home for more than a day, and yet she was always missing something crucial. Carson couldn't understand how she could pack so much and *still* not have what she needed. But he also knew she'd get pissed if he tried to help her, stating that she was perfectly capable of doing things herself. Instead, Carson decided to leave her to it. If she left something behind, oh well.

While they waited for Kate to finish up, Carson fixed a quick breakfast of scrambled eggs and bacon. It wasn't a large meal and would be considered meager in most circumstances, but he suspected it would be the last decent meal for a while. Besides, the eggs and bacon would end up going to waste otherwise.

Sitting at the dinner table, Carson and his kids ate their breakfast in silence while Kate busied herself upstairs. It was peaceful, but he knew it wouldn't last.

They'd have to face the nightmare again before too long.

<h1 style="text-align:center">Chapter 24</h1>

Carson set about gathering the assortment of bags and gear from the living room. Kate came down as they were finishing breakfast and, surprisingly, didn't complain that they hadn't waited for her. Carson found this odd but decided that he appreciated the change.

As predicted, Kate brought down two large suitcases. Carson was tempted to sort through them and remove whatever would be unnecessary but thought better of it. It wasn't worth the fight. Instead, he resolved to load them into the truck last. If they didn't have room, then Kate would have to downsize. It would be a necessity rather than Carson's idea. She'd protest, sure, but she wouldn't be able to accuse him of singling her out or belittling her decision-making.

"Did you hear from your parents?" he asked when she made it to the bottom of the stairs.

"Oh, yeah," Kate said. Carson wondered if she got much sleep. Dark circles rimmed her eyes. "Yeah, they called me back, but I didn't hear it last night. They were out because mom worked late, and dad had to pick her up. They got home late."

Carson sighed a breath of relief. "Oh good. They know we're coming, then?"

"I told them that we were coming to visit. They asked why, since it's the middle of the week," she answered. Carson sat silently, waiting for her to continue. When she didn't, he began to grow restless.

"And?"

"I told them that you got some time off," she answered, as though everything was completely normal. This struck Carson as odd.

"That's it?"

"Yeah, why?"

"Don't you think they'll ask questions when we roll up with a bunch of shit in the bed of the truck?" Carson asked, bewildered. "Or, you know, the guns?"

Her eyes narrowed and she scowled before answering. "Just keep the guns in the truck. And I don't know, I'll tell them something."

It became clear that she had no interest in continuing the conversation. He wasn't sure how to feel at that moment. He supposed it was a bridge they would cross later. The main priority was getting away from the base.

He pulled his phone out of his pocket and looked at it for the first time since the fiasco at the school. As he feared, the screen was a spiderweb of cracks. Since it was purely a touch screen, it was completely useless. He couldn't reach out to his guys to check on them.

An idea came to him. Not a great idea, mind you, but better than nothing. He knew where Paul Booker, his only real friend and his coworker, lived. And, since it would be along the same path that they would be taking, he decided to drop in on his friend. That is, if Booker didn't go to work. Carson very much doubted that.

"We're making a stop on the way," he called out.

Kate whipped around and glared at him. "The fuck for?"

Carson held up the ruined cell phone in his hand. "I can't contact any of my people. I need to make sure they're safe, too. And Paul will probably be home."

"Probably?" she scoffed. "And if he's not?"

Carson chewed the inside of his cheek for a moment. If that were the case, then there really wasn't much else he could do. It wasn't like he could call any of them from *her* phone. Mostly because, as with most people, he didn't have their numbers memorized. "Then we keep going," he said finally.

Kate continued to stare daggers at him, until she finally shook her head and turned away. "Whatever," she said over her shoulder.

With the conversation concluded, Carson began gathering up their things to load into the truck.

He started by dragging the MRE box and his suitcase to the door but could not bring himself to open it. The creature that had crawled on the house had most likely moved on, but he was terrified that it was lurking nearby.

Sweat broke out on his forehead and he felt a bead run down his spine.

Please be gone, he silently begged. *Please, please be gone. I can't handle seeing* that *again.*

His heart pounded in his chest and his hands started to tingle.

This is ridiculous, he chided. *Stop being a bitch and just open the fucking door. Act like a fucking man.*

Carson ground his teeth and slowly stretched his hand toward the doorknob. The knob felt unnaturally cold in his hand. He realized that his hands had begun going numb and determined that the chill was in his head. With a deep breath, he turned the knob and threw open the door.

Nothing was waiting on the other side.

A whoosh of air fled past his lips, and he felt his heart begin to settle. He silently thanked whatever deity might exist that the creepy spider-thing was gone.

But what if it was on the roof?

Carson propped the door open with his foot and grabbed his suitcase, the MRE box balanced on top. He almost dropped everything when he rolled the suitcase down the first step but managed to keep it under control. Once on the main path he had significantly less trouble with the load.

Hefting the suitcase and box into the bed of the truck was only marginally more difficult. He arranged them in the truck bed to allow space for the rest of the luggage so that he could cover all of it with a tarp and tie it down.

After several more trips, Carson loaded everything—including both of Kate's suitcases—in the truck and grabbed a tarp from the garage. Two ratchet straps crisscrossed across the load secured it.

Satisfied that they had everything they needed, Carson walked back inside the house.

Kate sat on the couch, their house cat Gabby in her arms. Shit, he hadn't thought about the cat. Carson turned back toward the truck and began mentally unpacking the bed. He hated the idea and began trying to come up with an alternative plan.

Well, there was room inside the truck for the cat's food bowl, the clear container of food, tub of cat litter, and litter box. He would have to empty the litter box completely, though, and he'd have to scrub it clean, so the truck didn't end up overwhelmed by the ammonia smell of cat piss. He couldn't leave the cat behind, though, so he would just have to suck it up and do what needed to be done.

Carson suspected that would become his mantra from that point on: just suck it up and deal with it.

Without a word, he went about gathering up the cat's belongings and washed out the litter box.

The process of getting ready to leave took longer than Carson had wanted. He had grown irritable by the time everything was done, and he couldn't wait to hit the road.

Kate had insisted on trying to call out for the dogs. Carson protested, but she did anyway. After several moments, Kate finally gave up.

He herded the kids into the truck and, after unloading the AR-15 at Kate's insistence before loading it in the vehicle, crawled into the driver's seat. He gave the house a final look and then quickly backed out of the driveway.

They made it a block down the road before he slammed on the brakes.

"Forgot the fucking walkie talkies," Carson offered in explanation as he turned the truck around toward the house.

"Do we really need them?" Kate asked.

He could tell that she wanted to get away from the house as much as he did. She would refuse to admit it, but she was terrified. Not that anyone could blame her. Nothing about what had happened was normal. *Any* rational person would be terrified, yet she *had* to put up a front. She wouldn't dare show any weakness, not to Carson and not to the kids. But Carson could tell. She thought she hid it well, but it was written all over her face. She was petrified.

And so was Carson.

He irrationally believed that getting away from the house would make everything better, as though the *house* was to blame for their enduring nightmare. It wasn't, of course, but the thought still stuck around anyway.

Carson jumped out of the vehicle as soon as he put it in park and dashed toward the house. Then, feeling like an absolute idiot, he had to go back to the truck to retrieve the house key.

They were all jumpy. Irene and Chris hadn't spoken since entering the truck, but he could see it on their faces just as plainly as Kate's.

He grumbled to himself as he made his way back to the house and jammed the key into the lock. He had to exert control over himself as he turned the key so that it didn't break off in the lock. Carson would have probably just thrown his hands in the air and left the walkie talkies behind. Fortunately, the key didn't break, and he opened the door.

Dread washed over him as he stepped inside. He couldn't explain why, but it felt as though a malevolent presence was in the house with him.

Carson chalked it up to the trauma from yesterday.

There, on the dinner table where he left them, were the walkie talkies on the charging dock. He shook his head as he walked over and unplugged the dock. Not wanting to linger any longer, he snatched up the dock and walkie talkies and turned back toward the door.

Something moved in his peripheral vision.

Carson jumped and dropped the equipment in his hands, then cringed when the radios hit the floor. He looked around frantically, expecting to see something lurking.

He didn't see anything.

I'm losing it, he thought.

Carson shook his head, stooped down, and grabbed up the radios and the charging dock. Satisfied that nothing was broken, he stood up and then froze.

There it was again. Lurking at the edge of his vision. An indistinguishable shape seemed to huddle near the back door, but when he turned to look it was gone.

No, not gone. It had moved, staying at the edge of sight.

Once again, Carson wondered if he was losing his grip on sanity.

But there was *definitely* something there.

It didn't move toward him, but it didn't move away either. It just lurked there, seemingly watching him and waiting.

Whatever it was, it was large. The thing seemed to stoop beneath the ceiling, implying that it was easily over nine feet tall. The house had nine-foot ceilings, and the thing had to bend down to fit.

The thing also seemed to shift and churn in place. Carson tried to take in as much detail as was possible without looking directly at it, but he couldn't make sense of its general form other than its size.

From upstairs he heard glass shatter, followed by a skittering noise. One of the spider creatures made it inside.

"Yeah, fuck this," Carson said after a moment and then raced toward the front door.

The thing kept pace the entire way, staying out of reach but always there.

He had to keep from screaming as he dashed out of the house and yanked the door shut behind him.

Carson blinked as the light flooded his eyes.

It was gone.

He couldn't stop the laugh that burst out of him. It suddenly felt absurd. It was just his mind playing tricks on him, it had to be. There was no shadow figure. No spider-creature breaking in. It *had* to have all been in his head.

He walked back to the truck and tossed the bundle of radios and the charging dock into the back seat between Chris and Irene.

"What was that about?" Kate asked. Carson knew what she was referring to. She'd seen him run out of the house as though the devil himself were on his heels.

"Nothing," Carson said after a moment. "The house just gave me the creeps for a minute."

He didn't have to look over at her to know she was staring at him. Yeah, he didn't believe his answer either. Rather than offer another explanation, Carson instead put the truck in reverse and backed out of the driveway.

"Let's try this again," he said more to himself than anyone else.

As he drove down the road, Carson swore he saw something hovering near the living room window.

Something very large and dark.

Something he couldn't quite see.

Chapter 25

They didn't get very far. As soon as Carson pulled the truck around the bend in the road leading to the elementary school, and the south gate of the base further down, he found himself stuck behind a parade of cars. The moment he saw the gridlock his heart sank.

For a moment he considered trying another exit from the base but knew immediately that the other two gates would be just as backed up. They were stuck and vulnerable.

"Fuck!" Carson yelled as he slammed his palms on the steering wheel. "We should have just left last night."

Irene and Chris whimpered in the backseat. Carson knew his outburst scared them, especially since until recently he'd always been relatively mellow. He hated raising his voice and losing his temper. The loss of control both angered and frightened him, so he often clamped down his emotions. He knew it wasn't healthy, but constantly scaring his children wouldn't be either.

"Now what?" Kate asked as she stared out the windshield, the cat clutched in her arms.

Rather than respond immediately, Carson leaned his head back and closed his eyes, breathing heavily through his nose. As irritating as the question was, he couldn't deny that it was valid. She was right. Now what? Every egress point from the base was gridlocked.

Carson considered taking an…unconventional route. Since most of the base consisted of open space often occupied by cows it wouldn't be too difficult to take the truck off-road. However, when they first moved in, the privatized housing representative had told them that the base had once been a tank garrison and still had land mines buried around the fields. Hell, a cow found one by accident and had turned into ground beef instantly. Despite the base's best efforts, there was bound to be more that had been missed.

He did not want to be the next unfortunate victim. Turning into a pink mist was undesirable, especially after surviving the horrors of the day prior.

No, off-roading was not a viable solution. So, what did that leave?

Would they have to return to the house? Carson immediately dismissed that option. As far as he was concerned, going back home would be akin to digging your own grave.

The car in front of them moved up several feet. That was a good sign, at least. Carson took a small measure of comfort in the fact that traffic was moving, albeit at a dying snail's pace. If they waited, they could be at the in-laws' house this time next week.

Somewhere up ahead a car honked. Carson scoffed. Why did people think that honking their horn would make a traffic jam move faster? It never worked. All it ever did was serve to incite road rage.

Worse still, the horn would draw unwanted attention. This thought immediately made him sick to his stomach. They had pretty much set up an all-you-can-eat buffet for any number of nightmares that were no doubt still lurking about. Carson wanted to get off the menu as quickly as possible.

Traffic began moving faster and Carson couldn't suppress his chuckle of disbelief. Honking the horn had worked? Had someone up ahead fallen asleep at the wheel or something?

He was surprised when they were able to accelerate to 15 MPH. As they moved beyond the school Carson involuntarily gasped. The remaining cars in the parking lot had been demolished. As had the cafeteria and several other buildings.

Something *very* large had come through some time in the night. He was immensely thankful that he hadn't been around to see whatever *that* had been.

Further down the road they could see the firehouse and beyond that the gas station. Carson didn't realize he'd been bunching his shoulders and breathing shallowly until he relaxed. As they approached the gate, he figured out why traffic had started moving faster.

Someone had decided to drive through the fence to the right of the outbound lane and now everyone was taking full advantage of the opening. Carson saw the bodies of two young men in uniform who had tried, and failed, to control the situation. He felt bad for them. Security Forces always seemed to draw the short straw, and these two poor bastards were proof.

And for what? There was no protocol for an invasion of monsters. No standard operating procedure or technical manual telling you how to subdue a Cronenberg monstrosity. No amount of training prepared any of them for what they had faced in the last eighteen or so hours. Shit, they were more likely to be prepared for a zombie apocalypse than what they now faced.

The trip to the in-laws would take about two hours on a normal day, and the detour would make the trip even longer. But today was anything but normal. Drivers seemed to completely forget about traffic laws and drove erratically. Most of them probably had no idea where to go. They just fled without a plan. Carson was glad he wasn't one of them. As tenuous as their plan was, it at least gave them direction.

The drive would take them south through Wheatland, and then west through Marysville, where Booker lived, and Yuba City before hitting a long stretch of empty road. Carson figured traffic would be hell until then.

And he was right.

Traffic on the road to Wheatland was a nightmare. Vehicles seemed to travel without rhyme or reason. Cars drove down the wrong sides of the road, or along the shoulder. Some even decided to forgo the road entirely. Carson used his truck's horn more in twenty minutes than he ever had before. He was thankful that Wheatland, the small town that it was, wasn't gridlocked. He turned right onto Highway 65, which turned into Highway 70 as they passed through West Linda and began the drive northwest toward Marysville.

As they rounded a bend and approached the city limits of Marysville, traffic had become even more chaotic. People ran across the streets, nearly getting hit by cars driving on the wrong side of the road. Panic had fully set in.

The chaos confirmed his worst fears. The nightmare was not isolated to the base. It had spread much further. The question was, how much further? He had a sense of foreboding as he thought about arriving at his in-law's house. If the horrors were widespread, then the house would not be a refuge. Especially since Kate's parents abhorred guns. The house would be essentially defenseless. And they were heading right toward it.

Carson thought about voicing his concerns. He knew they were valid, but he also knew Kate had already made up her mind. Nothing he said was going to change that. Instead, he continued driving in silence, desperately hoping he was wrong.

The traffic in the town made it extremely difficult for Carson to think about anything other than avoiding an accident, which nearly occurred a half dozen times in the span of several minutes. At this rate, it would be a miracle if they made it out to booker's place unscathed.

Moments later, a speeding car clipped the side of the truck, and he had to tightly grip the steering wheel to make sure they didn't go off the road. The drive side mirror was ripped free, and he knew that a sizeable dent would be on the side of the truck.

The speeding car didn't even slow. The panicked driver continued on and tried to take a turn, but they were going too fast. The car jumped the curb and flipped over as it struck a glass storefront. Shattered glass and dust rained like diamonds on the pavement as smoke began to pour out of the engine bay. Screams erupted from inside the store and, Carson imagined, from inside the overturned vehicle.

His instinct was to stop and help. And he truly wanted to. However, with the ensuing chaos he knew that doing so would only get them injured or killed.

Sure enough, another vehicle, an old red pickup truck, careened off a parked car and slammed into the overturned vehicle. The force shoved the vehicle inside the building, eliciting more screams. What had been screams of terror had turned into screams of pain.

Carson slowed just enough to go around the traffic accident and the people started to flood the street. He once again felt guilty about leaving the scene as he watched the mess shrink in the rearview mirror.

Fortunately, the route to Booker's apartment was along the backroads of Marysville. It was a rough neighborhood, but he doubted anyone else would be heading *toward* it. Everyone was trying to get out of town.

After turning off the main road, traffic practically disappeared. Carson let out a sigh of relief. At the very least, if Booker wasn't home, he would have a chance to breathe and collect himself. He continued driving slowly down the road, still cautiously observing the side streets for any other crazed drivers. He was relieved further when he turned down another street and saw the apartment building up ahead.

He pulled the truck into the parking lot and saw it was emptier than he had ever seen before. It made sense, of course, as everyone had likely fled. He continued to scan the parking lot, ignoring the myriad of parking spaces available. He was looking for one vehicle in particular: Booker's red Ford pickup.

A moment later, he saw the truck. He had never been happier to see the beat-up old thing. Carson parked right next to the truck and switched off the engine. He looked over at Kate and noted that she was looking away from him, out her window. Wonderful.

"Are you coming in?" he asked, even though he knew the answer.

"Nope," she replied without looking at him.

Carson heaved an exasperated sigh. He'd have to make the visit quick. "Fine. I'll run up and check in with Booker. The kids can stay here."

"No," Kate began, finally looking over at him. "Take them with you. They probably need to pee anyway."

Carson had anticipated this, too. Fortunately, Booker quite liked children and had one of his own. Carson figured he would be happy to see them.

"'Kay," he said and then looked up at the rearview mirror, catching Chris's gaze. "Let's go guys."

Extricating the kids from his truck, Carson decided to ask Kate if she was sure she didn't want to come in. She was sure. Kate offered a half-assed excuse along the lines of keeping Gabby company. Carson reminded her that Booker wasn't allergic to cats, but Kate refused to budge.

It was going to be a very quick visit.

Carson left the rifle in the truck cab but made sure to take his pistol with him. After the trauma he had endured in the last eight hours, he refused to be unarmed. He took Chris and Irene's small hands in his and led them to Booker's apartment.

As they traversed the parking lot, Carson heard the sound of helicopter rotors overhead. He looked up and spotted two solid black military helicopters flying back toward the base. Were they finally getting it under control? He hoped so, but there was no way he was going back until they were given the all clear.

They walked up to the door and Carson hesitated before knocking. What if nobody answered? Or worse, what if they were inside, but *couldn't* answer? He ground his teeth and steeled his nerves. He knew he was being ridiculous, his anxiety dictating his every thought. Booker had promised to call if something happened and they needed to leave, and he hadn't called. Carson knocked rapidly on the door and waited.

He heard movement inside. Carson's hand unconsciously moved closer to his holstered pistol. When the door opened, Carson's hand dropped to his side. Booker looked out of the narrow crack between the door and the frame.

"Tanner?" Booker's eyebrows knit together. "What're you doing here?"

Carson realized he hadn't expected the question and began stumbling over his words as he tried to answer. "I uh…well, we were in the neighborhood."

Booker opened the doorway wider and held up a hand to silence Carson's rambling. "You saw more."

It wasn't a question. And when he saw the look in Carson's eyes, he just nodded. "Yeah, you did. You guys okay?"

"Yeah, I-I guess so," Carson answered shakily. "Booker, the things I saw…there were things that the news reports didn't even show."

Booker nodded again. "Yeah, I saw 'em too. Freaky little fucks." He looked over at the kids. "Oops, sorry."

Carson didn't respond. He was looking over Booker's shoulder—as much as he was able considering the height disparity—to peer inside the apartment. Booker followed his gaze. "We're alright," he said. "We just holed up in here and stayed away from the doors and windows. Nothing saw or heard us."

"You guys were lucky," Carson said, his shoulders relaxing. "I saw what those things can do to people, and it's fucking awful."

"Yeah, I bet," Booker replied. "You guys wanna come in?"

Carson shook his head, despite wanting to do just that. "Can't. I just needed to check on you. Speaking of, have you heard from the others?"

Booker stepped outside and shut the door behind him. "Yeah, Benson and his wife are okay. For once, moving to of base was a good idea. Trejo and Velasquez were on base and holed up in Trejo's dorm. I guess the SecFo guys told them to stay put until they could evacuate. Hernandez is the only one I haven't heard from."

"Oh," Carson said slowly. When he left it looked like the base was ruined. Maybe the other side where the dorms were located was still intact. "Hernandez never answers right away, but he lives down in Roseville, too. How long ago did you try to contact him?"

"It was only about twenty minutes ago," Booker said. "So yeah, he'll probably respond soon."

Carson nodded but didn't reply. It was reassuring to know that at least some of them were okay. Hernandez was the only one truly unaccounted for. Carson considered waiting until

Booker got a reply, but he knew Kate would be irate if they took too long. He hated that his phone was useless.

But Kate's wasn't.

"Hey, look," he said after a moment. "We gotta go, but I want you to let me know when you here from Hernandez. And please check in with me. I wanna know if anything changes. I'll fucking drive my ass all the way back if you guys need to pop smoke and get out of Dodge."

"I appreciate it, Tanner," Booker said as he pulled Carson in for a hug. It took him by surprise. "I'll stay in touch. You guys be safe too."

"We will," Carson answered. "I hope this shit ends soon."

"Me too."

"You sure you want to stay here?" Carson asked again.

Booker shook his head. "Doesn't look like there's enough room in your truck and my vehicle is out of commission." He nodded out the window toward his truck. Carson saw that a large puddle formed under it, a rainbow glittering on its surface.

"You can't stay here, though," Carson argued. "You guys need to get out. I don't think help is coming."

"Not much we can do, buddy," Booker said sadly. "Only thing we can do is hunker down and try to stay quiet so none of those things come after us. You go get your family somewhere safe. I'd send my kids with you, but you don't have any room at all."

"I… We could…" Carson stumbled. He tried to think of something, but his mind was coming up with nothing.

"Go, dude," Booker said. "Get out of here."

Without another word, Carson turned and led his kids back to the truck. Kate rolled her eyes when he slid into the driver's seat. "All good?"

"Yeah, all good," Carson lied. He knew things weren't good at all, but telling Kate would do nothing. She might even blame him.

Surprisingly, Kate nodded. "That's good. Can we go now?"

Carson stared out the windshield at the apartment building and then slowly nodded.

He turned the truck on and backed out of the parking spot. With a final glance at Booker's apartment, he put the truck in drive and pulled out of the parking lot back onto the side roads before getting to the main streets of Marysville.

Several nerve-wracking moments later, they exited Marysville on Highway 20 and headed through Yuba City. It was almost exactly the same story. Chaos and terror in the streets. Vehicles shooting through intersections and bouncing off other vehicles. Someone drove up behind Carson's truck and hit the tailgate. He heard a crunch and figured that one, or both, taillights had been shattered. Everyone in the vehicle lurched forward from the impact and Carson strained to keep control of the truck. He wrenched the steering wheel to the left just as a woman darted out into the street.

The woman shot them a glare as they passed by. Carson didn't blame her, but it irritated him just the same. He barely missed her, and he would have hit her had he acted a second later. Instead of a bloody smear on the pavement, the woman stood angrily in the street. Carson just shook his head and continued on.

The rest of the drive through the small city was similarly stressful, but they managed to avoid further incidents. Carson breathed a sigh of relief as they passed the Lowe's Hardware store that marked the end of town. Up ahead he saw the road was mostly empty. It was as if everyone was confined to the towns.

Confused and unsettled, Carson stared ahead and pressed down harder on the accelerator, intent on getting as far away as fast as possible. He was relieved that he didn't have to merge on any more highways for a long time. Highway 20 would eventually join with Highway 29, but that was at the last stretch. He hoped that the drive would be easier from that point on.

Yet, deep in Carson's heart, he knew it wouldn't be.

Paul Booker looked out of the living room window as he watched his friend depart. He had a feeling that they would not see each other again. Not for a long time, at least. Ally, Booker's wife, slowly walked out of their bedroom. The walls in the apartment were incredibly thin. Ally had heard the entire conversation as easily as if she had been standing right beside her husband.

"Do you think it was a good idea to let them go?" she asked. "What about strength in numbers?"

"Honey," Booker said softly. "We don't have room. Not with our kids. It would be more dangerous if something tried to get in. Someone might get shot by accident."

Ally nodded. They had a shotgun and that was it. And shotguns aren't known for their precision. She pressed her head against Booker's chest, and she hugged him.

Booker knew how Ally felt. If it hadn't been dangerous, he would have urged Carson to stay. And forget about leaving. Booker and Ally had an irrational need to stay in their own home, around their own things. The familiar surroundings offered them comfort.

Movement caught Booker's attention. He looked out of the window again and scanned the parking lot. A moment later, he saw the last thing he ever wanted to see: the weird creatures—what did Carson call them? Killbugs or Doomhoppers? Something like that—and there was easily a dozen. Crawling around the grasshopper monsters were much smaller, spider-shaped creatures. The small ones began climbing over vehicles and up along the walls of the apartment complex. The larger monsters followed close behind.

"Shit, we should have left sooner," Booker hissed. "Ally, grab the kids and hide in the master bathroom."

"Why? What's going on?"

Booker turned to face her, his eyes wide with fear and his face drained of color. "Baby, now. Just do it."

Without a word, Ally immediately darted toward the back of the apartment. Booker heard his sons whine in protest. He stood still, watching the monstrous creatures outside until he heard the door to the master bedroom, and then the bathroom, shut.

Tearing his gaze from the nightmare heading toward the apartment, Booker went to the coat closet and pulled out his pump-action shotgun. Anything that came through the door would catch a face full of buckshot.

Unfortunately, the creatures had other ideas. The thin walls, which Booker had complained about for over a year, provided little resistance when the creatures started their attack. The large monsters broke through the sheetrock and drywall with ease, releasing a flood of the skittering spider-like things into the apartment. The grasshopper monsters crawled through the opening and slowly approached Booker.

"Fuck you!" Booker bellowed as he aimed the shotgun at the nearest monstrosity and fired.

From outside, you could hear the blasts of a shotgun.

Then a second.

Followed by several high pitched, bloodcurdling screams.

Then silence.

Chapter 26

The drive remained clear for all of fifteen minutes before they encountered another blockade. This time several vehicles had collided and blocked both lanes of the highway. Carson found it bizarre that people were at a complete stop as though waiting for emergency services to arrive, contrary to the erratic driving he'd encountered so far. Why now?

Rather than wait, Carson pulled the truck off the road and drove along the shoulder. He caught confused glances as he passed the stopped line of vehicles. He almost laughed at the ridiculousness of it all. Evidently, his detour inspired others to follow suit.

Dust filled the air as vehicles drove through the dirt. Carson had to slow the truck significantly as visibility was reduced to several feet. He knew that at any moment he'd pass through it, but the risk of hitting something debilitating was far too high to drive at the pace he had been. Sure enough, a large boulder reared out of the gloom and had he been driving faster they would have hit it. He was able to swing the truck to the right to avoid the obstacle, the tires of the truck slipped momentarily in the grass.

An instant later the dust cloud cleared. What Carson saw made his heart stop. Several feet above the ground were several glowing red rifts. He counted easily a half dozen spread out across the horizon. The nearest rift was roughly one hundred yards ahead and it began to grow.

Carson was immediately transported back to the school cafeteria when the small boy and Diego were engulfed by an identical tear. Panic swept over Carson, his breath coming in short gasps. His face and hands started to grow numb as they slowly approached the blood-red opening.

His instincts warred against each other. He struggled to decide whether to turn around, or to plow straight ahead. Turning back would be a death sentence, but nearing the rifts would likely be suicide too. Carson didn't realize that he had taken his foot off the accelerator as the truck began to coast to a stop. A car horn behind him pulled him out of his head and back to the present.

No, going back was certain death. At least going forward had a chance of survival. So, forward they went.

Carson pulled the truck onto the asphalt and sped toward the widening rift ahead, intent on swerving around it before they got too close. The previous rift hadn't grown very wide, and he suspected that would be true again.

He was wrong.

As the truck neared the rift, it seemed to sense the approach and started opening wider. The hellish glow spread from the edges and spilled out. Indiscernible shapes moved within, bulging like a tumor. The appearance of the rift called to mind the trauma videos Carson had seen during his first aid training. The red glow spilled out as though it were a viscous substance, like a hemorrhaging wound. And that's what it looked like; a hemorrhage in the fabric of reality, spilling forth something that should have stayed on the other side.

As he looked, more of the rifts began to open and spill their contents. Tentacled things and insect-like limbs began to crawl out of the gaping wounds. Carson tried to look, but it was as though his eyes would not focus. It was his mind trying and failing to comprehend what he saw.

The rift ahead of them pulled ever wider, nearly twice the width of the truck. Carson pulled to the right, intent on skirting around it. The edge of the rift stretched outward and continued to bar the way forward.

"That's not fucking fair!" Carson yelled. His outburst seemed to shock Kate and the kids out of their terrified trances. Chris and Irene burst into tears and Kate shrieked. Even Gabby panicked and tried to claw her way out of Kate's arms.

"Turn around!" Kate screamed.

"I can't!" Carson yelled back. "There's nothing fucking back there!"

Kate continued to scream, adding to the cacophony inside the cab of the truck. Carson felt his ears start ringing. At the same time, his vision was starting to narrow as he hyperventilated. His abdomen felt tight, and the sensation moved up to his chest. If he hadn't known better, he would have thought he was having a heart attack.

The opening of the rift gave Carson his first clear view of what lay on the other side, but his mind struggled to process it. Odd land formations that defied physics, at least the laws of physics as they applied to our reality, and the sky swirled as though made of liquid. Things seemed to fly and other things that should have been land-locked seemed to move in defiance of the landscape, floating along. A viscous fog spilled out, which explained why the red glow had looked like a liquid.

Carson felt a pounding in his head that seemed to intensify the longer he looked. His eyes watered and his face, which had been numb, suddenly felt hot. He pulled his gaze from the eldritch nightmare before him, fearful that his flesh would literally melt. The pounding in his skull immediately began to subside.

"What the fuck is that?!" Kate shrieked. Carson looked back at the gaping chasm and saw an enormous shape approach. At this, Carson's heart stopped in the space of two beats before hammering again in his chest. His head swam as the thing came into view.

He had no frame of reference for what he saw. It was as though the light from our sun could not penetrate through the tear, leaving the colossal figure cloaked in shadow. It appeared larger than a mountain, and that was just what was visible. If that was just the head, then the rest of it was truly titanic. Around the silhouette of the thing, before the blood-red sky was blocked from view, the figure seemed to undulate and writhe.

"Oh, sweet Jesus!" Carson blurted as the thing started crossing the threshold. Its very existence seemed to destabilize reality as it tried to push through. Carson had no doubt that the things were from a separate dimension entirely. The air began to shimmer and distort the more the thing tried to force its way through. At that moment, Carson genuinely believed that everything was about to end.

The titanic mass shuddered and a low, rumbling moan filled the air that made Carson's bones vibrate. His vision blinked out and he immediately slammed on the brake pedal. He heard the tires squeal and could feel their momentum shift as the truck came to a halt, but he could not see anything.

What Carson hadn't expected was the smell. Or at least the vaguest concept of a smell. It was more akin to having lightning shooting up his nostrils and stabbing through his brain. It triggered an instinctual revulsion. With it came an excruciating tightening of his abdomen as though he'd been vomiting for hours.

A louder roar shook the ground. He pressed his hands against his ears, but the roar was so loud that this did nothing to dampen the sound. A sharp pain bloomed in both ears, and he felt something wet and warm roll down the sides of his face.

An instant later the noise stopped, and the smell faded. With it came Carson's vision and his stomach seemed to unknot. He pulled his hands away from his head and saw them wet with blood. He blinked rapidly, trying to force his vision to steady and clear. His hearing slowly started to return, the sounds around him muffled and distorted as if he were underwater.

He glanced around the cab of the truck. Kate looked pale and seemed to stare blankly ahead. Small trails of blood ran down from her ears and eyes. Her exposed skin was covered in bloody scratches from Gabby's frantic attempts to escape. He immediately looked behind him and saw that Chris and Irene still had their eyes squeezed shut. Thankfully, he could not see blood anywhere on them. The cat had buried herself under Chris's feet and the supplies on the floor of the cab.

He turned back toward the windshield, and he saw the rift, which had been so massive that it could have easily swallowed four lanes of traffic, rapidly shrink. As the rift closed, reality seemed to crash back into place like a wave. Carson's hearing and vision immediately returned and set his head to pounding once again, though this time from the influx of information.

With hands gripping the steering wheel in a white-knuckle grip, Carson laid his head forward and shut his eyes. He tried to will away the debilitating headache. The sounds of car horns, crumpling metal, and shattered glass pierced his brain. For a moment he almost wished that the loud roar would return, if only to deafen him.

His mind seemed to stabilize as it began to sort out the sensations flooding in. With a deep, painful breath, Carson slowly lifted his head and opened his eyes.

The rift had closed. The others seemed to shrink as well. What caused them to open and close? It seemed so incredibly random. Carson couldn't seem to pinpoint anything that could be recognized as a catalyst, though he suspected he wouldn't recognize it anyway. Such things were very likely beyond his understanding.

As he glanced around, Carson noted that several vehicles had collided. Somehow, they had managed to get through the chaos unscathed. He looked out at the horizon as he tried to determine if the colossus made it through, but there was no evidence that it had. He wondered if maybe the thing hadn't been able to alter reality enough to come through.

Up above, several jet-black helicopters had appeared and began to circle the area. Carson only glanced at them for a second before returning his attention to the road.

In the interest of avoiding an accident, Carson pulled off the highway entirely. The tires crunched in the dirt as the truck bounced over uneven ground. Once they stopped, he shut off the engine. The truck went silent, the only sounds the ticking of the engine as it started to cool.

He pried his fingers painfully from the steering wheel. Faint indentations marred the surface from the force of his grip. He always knew he had a great deal of grip strength, aided by his disproportionately large hands, but he had never caused a steering wheel to compress permanently.

Several deep, painful breaths later, Carson finally felt his heart rate begin to slow. Just as he managed to calm down, Irene and Chris began screaming from the back seat. The sudden noise made Carson jump in his seat, the seatbelt keeping him from hitting his head on the ceiling of the cab.

"Are we dead?" Irene cried out, her eyes wide with fear.

Chris began wailing.

"No, no kiddo," Carson answered as calmly as possible. "We're okay."

"But th-that thing!"

"It's gone sweetheart," Carson said gently. "It couldn't get through."

"But what if it tries again?" Irene shrieked.

Carson cringed from the pitch of her voice. The headache hadn't fully subsided. "It can't kiddo. It was too big."

He didn't quite believe his answer, but he wasn't about to show his kids that.

"But what if it does?" Chris whimpered.

"I don't think it can," Carson tried to reassure them. "I think our reality won't let it through. We'll be okay. Trust me."

Irene and Chris shook as tears continued to well in their eyes. He could tell they didn't believe him, but they seemed to settle for that answer after a moment. No doubt it was easier than considering the alternative. Carson hoped that he was right.

As he turned back toward the front he glanced at Kate. She was still staring straight ahead. The bleeding from her ears and eyes appeared to have stopped.

For a fleeting moment two feelings arose simultaneously. He was concerned about her well-being, yet also hopeful that her influence was at an end. That second thought made him feel terrible. What kind of awful person would wish harm to another? Yet again, she was an admittedly terrible person.

The realization sickened him.

Maybe fate had spared them.

Then again, maybe not. Kate began to stir and let out a groan.

Shaken from his ruminations, Carson switched back into his role as the caring husband. Yet, this time, it felt fake. He'd been angry with Kate many times in the past and had had less than positive thoughts, but he'd always pulled out of it and resumed his blind affection. Not this time, though.

Perhaps it was the events of the past twenty-four hours, and Kate's behavior during this time, which had brought about the change. Or, most likely, it had been slowly growing, and their shared trauma had been a catalyst.

Either way, Carson found that the love he'd had for Kate had disappeared. He also knew that tolerating her behavior would be exponentially more difficult. But he would do so for the sake of their kids for as long as he could. At least until they were safe.

Now there was a conversation that he did not relish the idea of having. How would he tell Kate that he was done and didn't want to continue their marriage without her losing her temper?

Carson silently chastised himself for the thought. She didn't care how she made him feel. Why should he give her that courtesy?

Because he realized he was not capable of apathy. He felt things too much and too strongly to disregard even *her* feelings.

Kate mumbled something incomprehensible, and Carson had to ask her to repeat herself. Once again, she tried to speak, but he could not decipher what she said. She sounded drugged. Carson looked at her and saw that her eyes continued to wander, unable to focus on any one point.

From what he could tell, Kate was suffering from a concussion. They hadn't collided with anything, and he didn't think she had hit her head, but perhaps the roar of the enormous…thing rattled her brain. If so, how come Chris and Irene weren't acting the same way, or worse?

"Kate, can you understand what I'm saying?" Carson asked. He noticed that it was difficult to say her name, which hadn't been an issue in the past. Oh yes, something had changed indeed. He couldn't deny it.

Kate mumbled and her head lolled. The chaos had certainly rattled her cage something fierce.

He reached out to steady her head and his hands hesitated an inch from her face. He ignored it and held her head straight. Kate blinked rapidly for several moments before her eyes finally seemed to fixate on him.

"W-what was that," Kate managed, though it came out as all one word.

"No clue," Carson said, which was true. He had no idea what the thing was or how to describe it. His mind seemed to be trying to eradicate any impression of the thing, rendering any memory a murky haze. Within minutes the memory was as faint as an old dream.

Chapter 27

Carson thought about the portals that had appeared. He had only ever seen one appearance, but something told him that the appearance of multiple portals meant things were getting worse. Moreover, he hadn't been able to see if anything had come through them. His blackout, which he couldn't remember the cause of, lasted until the portals closed.

Over half a dozen portals had opened simultaneously. For how long, he wasn't sure. No doubt long enough for *something* to come through. And with that many portals? The implication made him sick.

One thing was certain: the invasion—which is how Carson decided to view it—was not isolated to the base and the surrounding area. He was afraid to find out just how widespread it was. His pessimistic side said the whole world, but his more practical side argued that it hadn't spread that far…yet.

As if in confirmation of his fears, Carson spotted close to a dozen of the death hoppers moving like a swarm of ants out in the open field to his left. They were rapidly travelling toward town. He knew that just one of the things could cause havoc; more would be catastrophic.

Above the pack Carson saw a flock of the bizarre flying creatures that looked like plastic bags. They, too, were headed to town. Anyone who managed to evade the Death Hoppers would have to contend with those nightmares.

Carson wasn't sure which was worse: getting torn apart or turned into a mindless puppet. Neither was enviable and he hoped he would never have to find out.

Rather than continue to take inventory of the horrors spilling across the landscape, Carson kept his eyes locked straight ahead as he pulled the truck back onto the road. As long as he could avoid an encounter with any of the interdimensional freaks, they would be okay.

At this point Carson suspected that the rifts were exactly that: portals to another dimension hemorrhaging nightmares into ours.

The road seemed to be clear as they travelled further away from Yuba city. Either most people had already gotten out, or the mass exodus would occur following the appearance of the Death Hoppers. Carson hoped for the former.

In the best conditions the drive would take roughly two hours. Carson suspected that it would take far longer than that. Worse still, the fuel gauge was already situated at the halfway mark. They would have to stop for gas at the gas station that was forty minutes away.

He hoped that the nightmare hadn't fully hit there yet. They would need to grab snacks to hold everyone over at a minimum. There was no way they would stop somewhere for lunch. They *could* dig into the MREs, but Carson wanted to avoid that if at all possible. Who knew when they would need them later?

"Daddy," Chris called from the backseat. "I'm hungry."

Carson sighed in frustration and tried to think of something to hold them over until they reached the gas station. Unfortunately, he hadn't packed anything for them to snack on, and he doubted Kate had bothered.

"Can you hold on for a little bit?" he asked.

"I think so," Chris answered. Carson was not confident in the answer. He suspected Chris would ask about eating again in fifteen minutes or less.

"You didn't pack snacks, did you?" Kate asked. He could tell by her accusatory tone that he was about to be berated once again.

"No, I didn't get a chance to."

Kate scoffed. "Why the hell didn't you think to grab something for them to eat before we left? They were going to need to eat at some point again."

"Yeah, I know," Carson answered quietly.

His response did little to stem her tirade.

"What if we can't stop at the gas station, huh? What then? I really fucking hope you packed *something* in all that shit you put in the truck. Or did you just pack *your* shit? I bet you have plenty of bullets, don't you? You made sure to bring *those*."

Carson had enough. All the stress and trauma from the past twenty-four hours came to the surface and boiled over.

"Did *you* pack anything?" he shouted. "No, you didn't! You just sat there and watched everyone else. *You* had plenty of time to give the kids breakfast. *You* had time to pack snacks while I loaded everything in the fucking truck! But no, you were too fucking busy dicking around on your phone to do *anything* to help. I swear Kate, you expect everyone *else* to do everything for you! It's time for you to grow the fuck up and start acting like a fucking adult for once!"

"You're such a fucking asshole! You happy now? Look at what you did!" Kate snapped back. Carson expected her to continue, but to his surprise she went quiet. It was then that he heard both kids crying in the back seat.

Shit.

"Hey, hey," he called over his shoulder. "I'm sorry guys. I'm just really stressed and scared. I didn't mean to scare you."

He heard Kate mutter "Yeah right."

Chris and Irene continued to cry, though their volume lowered a bit. "I know you're scared," he continued. "But I'm going to do everything I can to keep us safe, okay?"

Kate opened her mouth to interject, but Carson shot her a look that told her to keep it to herself. To his surprise, she did exactly that.

He didn't know how long her silence would last. He doubted it would be for very long. She would inevitably start attacking verbally in any way she could to do maximum damage. What she didn't know was that he no longer gave a shit.

"Okay daddy," Irene said softly. Chris nodded in agreement.

Despite their response, Carson saw tears continue to roll down their cheeks. He suddenly felt bad about losing his temper. Not because he'd been nasty to Kate, but because it scared the kids. It was rare for him to yell at all, and rarer still for him to lose control. He could only recall a handful of times when he had gotten really angry.

Kate, on the other hand, seemed to lose her temper almost daily. As such, the kids didn't seem to react much anymore. Sure, it made them flinch and he could see the fear in their eyes, but that was about it. Neither of them would cry as a result. Not like they were now.

Guilt formed a lump in his gut. Carson opted to shut his mouth and just focus on the road. He doubted anything he said would help assuage their fears.

Besides, anything he said would inevitably be used against him when Kate found her voice again.

They made it all the way to the gas station before Kate spoke up. Carson considered it the most peaceful forty minutes he'd had in days.

"You better get them something to eat," Kate hissed. "Or are you planning on letting us starve the whole way?"

Carson glared at her. "Don't worry, *I'll* take care of it. *After* I get gas."

"Fine," Kate snapped back. "Take them with you. I'll stay in the truck."

Carson rolled his eyes as he maneuvered the truck across the two-lane highway and into the gas station parking lot. He immediately noticed that there weren't many vehicles around. The easy explanation was to chalk it up to the early hour, but something told him this wasn't the case. He was relieved to see that none of the vehicles looked damaged. Perhaps his apprehension was misplaced.

He pulled up to an open gas pump and put the truck in park. Normally, Carson would shut off the truck and immediately hop out. However, after the portals had appeared, the idea of leaving the truck made his stomach turn. He felt the familiar sensations of an impending panic attack. His nose and lips began to tingle, as did his fingers.

Carson shut his eyes and forced himself to slow his breathing. He would have to overcome his anxiety if they were to have any hope of surviving. After a moment he felt the tingling sensations fade and he opened his eyes. Without looking at Kate, Carson fished the pistol out of the center console and shut off the truck.

Before Kate could fire off another insult, Carson stepped out of the truck and shut the door. When nothing immediately leapt out, Carson allowed himself to relax a fraction.

Complacency would get them killed, but so would blind panic. Instead, he resolved to use his anxiety to focus his attention.

Stuffing the pistol in the waistband in the front of his jeans, Carson popped open the gas cap and pulled out his wallet.

The next several minutes passed quietly as the pump poured gasoline. He heard the rhythmic clicking of the gas pump as the numbers on the screen climbed. The rumble of the occasional engine echoed from the highway. For a moment, everything seemed normal. Carson knew that wasn't true, but he allowed himself to enjoy it for the time being.

The handle of the gas nozzle clicked off and snapped Carson out of his reverie. He didn't bother looking at the total on the screen. It didn't seem important now.

After replacing the gas cap, Carson climbed back into the truck and started it up. He was thankful that the parking spaces in front of the truck stop were open. That meant they wouldn't have to be out in the open for long. Even though he couldn't see anything around, Carson suspected that monstrous things lurked.

Carson took a moment to carefully examine their surroundings and, satisfied nothing was stalking them, climbed back out of the truck. Kate, true to her word, stayed in the truck. Chris needed help out of his booster seat, so Carson chose to focus on the task rather than give Kate his attention. He knew she wanted him to apologize and beg her to join them. He refused to give her that.

Irene hopped out on the opposite side and Carson immediately felt his stomach clench as she dropped out of sight. Panicked, he roughly unlatched Chris's seatbelt and pulled him out of the truck. He left the door open and Gabby, seemingly sensing a chance of escape, darted out. An instant later, she was gone. Carson chose to let the cat go. Irene and Chris were his priority.

"Ow," Chris whined.

Without looking down, Carson offered an apology as he pulled Chris along. They circled around the bed of the truck, and he felt a surge of relief when he saw Irene standing on the other side.

Feeling stupid, Carson breathed a sigh of relief and took her hand.

Together they made their way into the truck stop.

Chapter 28

The truck stop was as quiet inside as it was outside. Carson had expected to see people milling about as they purchased snacks or beverages, or absolute destruction. Instead, what greeted them was neither. Overhead lights blinked occasionally, illuminating the entire convenience store. Everything appeared perfectly normal, aside from the complete absence of people.

It was as if everyone had just vanished into thin air. The registers were still on, as were the cold storage units and the television behind the counter. Carson knew immediately that something was off. No employee in their right mind would leave the place completely unattended without, at a minimum, locking the doors.

Tentatively, he stepped forward. He kept Irene and Chris behind him just in case something decided to ambush them. Every step seemed way too loud to him. Carson felt like their presence was like ringing a dinner bell for some malevolent being. Their breathing sounded exaggerated, their steps a cacophony. They were most likely being very quiet, but Carson's nerves were already frayed and were unravelling further.

Chris started to speak, but Carson spun immediately and pressed a finger to Chris's lips to silence him. "Shh," Carson whispered. "Something's off."

Chris's eyes bulged. The color began fading from his round, innocent face. A moment later, tears began welling up in his eyes.

Carson felt a pang of remorse. He hadn't meant to scare the boy.

He heard Irene's breathing speed up as she started to panic. Carson met her gaze and put a hand on her shoulder. "Hey, hey. Take it easy. It's probably fine."

From somewhere behind him he heard a skittering noise, like a rodent scampering across the floor. Now it was his turn to start hyperventilating as he whipped around, his eyes darting everywhere as he tried to pinpoint the source of the sound.

There was another monster that he hadn't considered coming through the portal. One that, in his opinion, was far worse than the Death Hoppers of the flying parasites. One that was far too similar in appearance to his biggest phobia: spiders.

It was at that moment that Carson decided to spin the kids toward the door, intent on vacating the seemingly vacant store as quickly as absolutely possible.

However, something was blocking the door.

He wished he had had the presence of mind to grab the walkie talkie. That was the whole damn point of bringing them.

Crawling across the wall near the entrance was exactly as he feared: the nightmarish spider-thing with the humanoid face. Even worse, it wasn't alone. More began to crawl from behind boxes against the walls.

The pressure of small hands in his grasp seemed to flip a switch in his brain. Fury replaced fear. The monsters represented, in that moment, everything that posed a threat to his children in the world.

Carson moved Chris and Irene behind him. As he did this, he quickly looked over his shoulder. None of the aberrations were behind them. He turned his attention back in front of them and moved his hand slowly toward the butt of his pistol.

A magazine of nine-millimeter would, in theory, be enough to eliminate the creatures crawling on the walls barring their way out. He counted eight of the things so far. No doubt more were making their way out. Carson didn't want to think about where they had come from, or what they'd been doing, before he had stepped inside.

Careful to avoid any rapid movement for fear of enticing the things to attack, Carson carefully grasped the grip of the pistol and pulled it free.

The monster directly ahead of him stopped and its legs twitched. Carson sucked in a breath and froze. He held his breath in a standoff that seemed to span minutes. The creature slowly resumed crawling toward the door and Carson, his vision starting to fill with black spots, finally exhaled.

As slowly as humanly possible, he raised the pistol and lined up the sights on the monster. Over his shoulder, without looking away, he whispered, "get down and cover your ears. Now."

Chris and Irene whimpered. Carson allowed them a moment, hoping that they were doing what he asked. If not, they were about to temporarily lose their hearing.

He squeezed the trigger slowly as he controlled his breathing, the barrel of the Beretta barely wavering.

The sound of the gun going off was deafening.

An unholy shrieking came from the creatures across the store. The one he had been targeting erupted in a mess of bile-colored viscera. The other monsters immediately scattered away from their fallen companion, only to alter their course and head straight toward him.

Carson dropped down to one knee and quickly sighted in on another before pulling the trigger. Without concern for his hearing—it was pretty much fucked at this point—he took aim at another and fired.

The next round missed as the creature he'd been aiming at seemed to flatten itself to the floor. The second round did not.

As Carson took down five of the freaks, the others seemed to retreat. He couldn't be certain, but it seemed like the things understood the danger their target presented. They hopped backward when he tried to line up another shot.

It was worse than he had first imagined. Not only were the things terrifying, but they were also intelligent. At least enough to recognize a change in circumstances warranting an adjustment to their tactics. Instead of coming straight toward him, the things fanned out.

Carson immediately recognized what they were trying to do. He quickly glanced over his shoulder and saw that none of the things were behind them…yet.

"Get up!" Carson yelled. "Stay behind me! Back up! Back up!"

Before either of his kids could respond, Carson began to backpedal. Fortunately, Chris and Irene did not hesitate.

He continued to aim at the spider-like monsters, hoping to keep all of them where he could see them. He knew that if any of them managed to flank him it would all be over.

He would die before he let that happen.

As he continued to retreat, Carson fired off more rounds. He wasn't focused on hitting the things. Rather, he was more intent on keeping them at bay. Therefore, he was pleasantly surprised when several shots managed to hit some of the creatures. Only one was a lethal shot, but the other shots managed to injure a few of the monstrosities bearing down on them.

The creatures were advancing too quickly for Carson to maintain a two-handed grip on the pistol. He turned away and, with a free hand, pushed Chris along. Irene had managed to stay ahead by a foot or so, but Chris was smaller and therefore slower. With his other hand, Carson continued to fire off rounds at the skittering little monsters.

It was so much harder than movies made it look.

As they neared the rear of the store, a sound echoed from the other end. Carson looked over and saw Kate standing at the entrance, her eyes bulging as she screamed Chris and Irene's names. The added noise had an effect that she certainly had not intended.

The spiderlings at the rear changed direction and began heading toward Kate.

From his position, Carson was helpless to stop them from charging her. His focus was tethered to the monsters that were continuing to try to flank them. Against his protective instincts, he had to let Kate fend for herself.

Kate decided staying inside the store was a bad idea and ran back outside. As soon as the door shut, the monsters that had been targeting her changed direction once again.

Carson didn't know if should be relieved or pissed. Kate had left them to fend for themselves, but it wasn't as though she would have been able to do anything about it anyway.

More likely than not, Kate would have become another victim. And then Carson would have to deal with the fallout. His feelings toward may have shifted, but the kids' feelings had not.

However, Carson didn't have time to concern himself with what *could* have happened. He was too busy trying to make sure nothing happened to his children. That meant trying to find an exit. As much as he hated it, he had to turn away from the advancing nightmares and search the rear of the store. The creatures decided to seize the opportunity that just presented itself.

"Daddy! Look out!" Irene screamed.

As he turned around, Carson saw Irene grab a broom and slam the wooden end into the closest creature. The broom handle punched through its flesh, and he watched as its legs shot out straight to the sides. He felt a surge of pride, mixed with pity, for Irene. She was so young but had managed to step up and do what was necessary. He knew she would fall apart when the reality of it finally set in. For now, though, she had bought him enough time to turn and fire at the next creature in line.

"I found a door!" Chris yelled.

Carson didn't dare turn away. His ears were still ringing from the gunshots, and he found it amazing that they were able to hear at all. Without taking his eyes back off the monsters he shouted out to his son.

"Open it! Get out! Both of you!"

"But—" he heard Irene begin to protest.

"Now!"

"Daddy, no!" Chris cried out.

"I'm right behind you! Go!"

Without another word, Carson heard the crash bar on the door slam and a breeze rolled over his neck. An instant later the fire alarm went off. The creatures darted around manically, the pitch of the alarm seemingly causing them significant distress. Carson took advantage of the momentary distraction and raced out of the doorway, slamming the door closed behind him.

Immediately, Carson slid to the ground with his back pressed against the door. Irene and Chris leapt on him, burying their faces in his chest and their bodies shuddering with wracking sobs. Without realizing it, Carson had joined them. With the alarm still blaring, though muffled a bit, Carson broke down in tears while he held his kids tightly in his arms.

<h1 style="text-align:center">Chapter 29</h1>

An unknown amount of time passed while they just sat outside of the convenience store, the alarm blaring. It was unlikely that anyone was coming to investigate. Even if the alarm was connected to a system to immediately notify law enforcement, the descent into chaos would hold them up. That, and the fact that the closest town was forty minutes away.

Exhausted and feeling broken, Carson dragged himself to his feet. Irene stood up with him, but Chris had fallen asleep. Rather than disturb his son, Carson carefully picked him up and started plodding along back to the truck.

In truth, he was surprised that Kate hadn't come to find them. Then again, after his startling realization, it shouldn't have. Realistically, she had probably taken refuge in the truck and left them to fend for themselves.

As they came around the side of the building Carson saw the truck come into view. For a moment he thought that the truck was vacant, and he began searching around for Kate. The thought of discovering a corpse made him feel sick. She may be a despicable human being, but he wouldn't wish that tragedy on his kids.

Carson suddenly felt awful for thinking that way. What did that say about him? Hadn't they all experienced enough death already? Worse still, was the horrible image in his mind a result of wishful thinking? He tried to shake the thoughts from his head, but as they continued toward the vehicle, he found that the grisly image seemed to become more vivid.

He saw the top of a blonde head just barely poking over the side of the door in the passenger seat. Both relieved and a bit disappointed, Carson led the kids to the truck and helped Irene inside. Once she was safely inside, he went around to the driver's side and carefully loaded Chris into his booster seat.

Kate remained hunkered down in the passenger seat the entire time.

"Thanks," Carson said sarcastically as he climbed behind the wheel. His remark, surprisingly, was met with silence. He glanced over and saw Kate pull her legs up to her body and lay her head on her knees.

After a long while she finally spoke, her voice muffled. "Happy now?"

"About what?"

Kate raised her head and turned to face him. He expected red-rimmed eyes, but instead he saw a coldness that made his anxiety begin to spike. "You got to be the fucking hero."

Shocked, Carson let out a gasp and floundered for a moment as his mouth opened and closed like a fish out of water. His face grew hot from a mixture of shame and rage.

"A-are you serious?" he finally managed. "Happy?"

"Well?"

Anger began to supplant his shock. "No, I'm not fucking happy. We almost got killed. How the hell could I be *happy* about that?"

Kate stared at him; her grey eyes bored into him. Carson suddenly wanted to take his chances with the spider monsters instead. The absolute hatred behind those eyes both shocked and hurt him. How had he lived with this woman for so long?

"Let's get the fuck outta here," Carson said after a while.

"Gabby got out," Kate hissed.

"Then she's the lucky one."

"What the fuck does that mean?" Kate snapped.

"It means I've had enough, Kate," Carson answered quietly. "I want a divorce."

Kate stared at him, her face red. She was furious, but she also looked like she expected him to say that.

"Whatever," Kate grumbled. "I don't want to deal with you, either."

Without another word they pulled out of the gas station parking lot and back on to the main road. A million conflicting thoughts and emotions whirled through him. He was more confused in that moment than he'd ever been, even after the portals had appeared.

They drove in silence for another thirty minutes. Carson was content for about fifteen of those. After that he began to get antsy. Chris was still sleeping in his booster seat, and Irene had nodded off shortly after they left the gas station. Kate was turned away from him, her attention on everything outside the truck. Or, more likely, nothing at all.

He tried to turn on the radio but was met with nothing but static. The truck didn't come with a CD player and cell reception was non-existent, meaning using the Bluetooth connection was useless. No music, then.

The silence made Carson's mind start to wander. He revisited his interactions with his coworkers from what felt like a lifetime ago but had only been the morning before. He thought about how the news reports had seemed ridiculous, and Booker's insistence that something bad was happening. He would have to check in with them to see if they were okay. With his cellphone out of commission, he would have to use the phone at his in-law's house.

Then he thought about the elementary school. His entire concept of reality had been turned on its head and only got worse after. The portals and the things that dwelled within. Things that he couldn't have conjured up in his worst nightmares.

Without realizing it, Carson began thinking out loud.

"What the fuck is happening?" he said to nobody. Kate didn't seem to notice. "None of this makes sense. I mean, it's obvious that those things are from another dimension. The way they move. The way they look. But how?"

His thoughts began to spiral further. "Maybe a government experiment went bad? The super-collider thing fucked up the fabric of reality? What if it was on purpose? And all those portals opening at once. The fuck was that about?"

"Does it matter?" Kate interjected. "Everything is fucked."

"But why? Why now? What changed?"

When Kate didn't answer Carson went back to his musing. "I mean, it could be a coincidence. But I doubt it. Something about this whole thing is off."

"You think?" Kate snapped.

"Well, obviously everything is off," he sputtered. "We have fucking *monsters* appearing out of nowhere. I mean the timing feels off. Everything has been spiraling out of control. Countries are starting to get worked up and wars are on the verge of erupting, then all of sudden portals pop up and shit monsters all over the place. Someone must have *really* pissed God off, or gods. Or something."

"Yeah, maybe it's the fucking apocalypse," Kate muttered.

"Sure as hell seems that way," Carson said, ignoring the bitterness in her voice. "Regardless, something or someone fucked up in a *big* way. This shit doesn't just *happen*."

Kate ignored him. Carson didn't care much anymore about what she thought of him. Yet, the tension made him resort to rambling.

"Huh," Carson let out a soft chuckle. "Maybe it was the Catholic church. The end times because of all those priests diddling altar boys."

Humor was a defense mechanism that Carson often resorted to. He had hoped that the off-color joke would help break the tension. It didn't work.

"Maybe not," he muttered. "Shit, maybe it's aliens. Maybe it's just all random."

"Maybe the super-collider fucked up and transported us to another dimension," Kate said after a while.

Carson looked over at her, an eyebrow arched questioningly.

"Saw something about that on Facebook," she said as way of an explanation.

"That would be some shit, wouldn't it?" he asked. "For once some idiot on social media actually being right about something? And it just happens to be something as colossally fucked up as this. Yeah, that would be a real kick in the nuts…or ovaries. You know, whichever." She saw him looking over and her expression hardened.

Yeah, she was still pissed—or scared, but at least she wasn't screaming at him. The tension had lessened in any case. The rest of the drive would be a little more tolerable. Besides, there was something about finally saying what had been lurking for so long that seemed to alleviate the tension as well. Maybe they had both wanted a divorce, but they were just waiting for the other person to say it.

It was immensely frustrating that he couldn't come up with a plausible explanation for what was happening. He desperately needed something to help him hold together his fragmenting sanity. Carson wasn't sure how much more he could take.

The road began to slowly incline as they approached the mountain pass that would take them into Lake County. Out of all the times that they had taken the road, this time terrified him. Something about the mountains felt oppressive. He couldn't help feeling that they would be trapped in those mountains by something worse than anything they had encountered so far.

As if to reinforce the point, Carson caught a glimpse of a dark shape out of the corner of his eye. However, just like what happens when you notice something floating in your vision and it keeps moving whenever you try to look at it, it stayed just out of sight.

The same indiscernible, evil-feeling figure had caught up to them.

Or it had been right there with them the entire time. But, for now, it wasn't doing anything. It might have been a hallucination from an exhausted mind.

Carson wasn't sure. He chose to focus on driving.

Chapter 30

As they drove in silence, Carson caught himself thinking about *his* family. He was saddened that he hadn't given any of them much thought since everything fell apart. But that was how it always was, wasn't it? So much effort and attention on Kate's family, but none toward his. And he had let it happen. Not only let it but had started doing the same thing.

It was no real secret that Carson was not as close to his siblings as he had once been. Annaise, who was only a year younger than him, had been pretty much his best friend growing up. He had been mocked frequently about being close with his sister, and had endured a fair share of insinuations that made him sick. He would quickly lose his temper and start screaming at anyone who dared to speak ill of her. Surprisingly, those encounters never came to blows.

For the first few years of his life, it had been just him and Annaise. They would play for hours and make up imaginary worlds. They would doodle and laugh. When he started pre-school, Carson hated it. His friend wasn't there with him and the other kids were mean. It wasn't until he reached the first grade that he didn't hate school, because Annaise went to school with him. Without other friends to play with, he had been miserable.

Carson thought about their early childhood in Alaska. Their dad served in the military which had brought them to the arctic. But they loved it. The snow had seemed magical and pure. Not for the first time, Carson felt the longing to return. Was it the snow that he missed? Or was it the happier times? He supposed it was the latter. He also knew that going back would not bring him the happiness he sought. And now, with the world apparently ending, he probably never would.

How *was* Annaise doing? She must have been panicking. She was married now and had children of her own to protect. How were they doing? Were they safe? Carson didn't want to think about the alternative. Losing his father had been bad enough. Losing his best friend and sister, too? Unthinkable.

There was also his mother to worry about. His parents had divorced years ago and that had caused no small amount of tension amongst the family, but she tried her best. For Carson, that was enough. She wouldn't be alone, but with her health slowly declining, it wouldn't be easy for her to flee. Carson hoped that she and her boyfriend— or common-law husband by now? —were okay. And his baby brother too. Well, he wasn't a baby anymore.

And then there was Brianna, his second youngest sibling. She had been a wild child and, Carson suspected, could handle herself better than any of them. He remembered that she had seemed fearless, and nobody would control her. It had caused its fair share if problems, sure, but Carson suspected that it would be a benefit now.

Then again, their father's suicide had had an effect on all of them. Annaise, who already struggled with depression, took it as hard as Carson had. She, like Carson, had looked up to him. The Three Amigos, they once called themselves. The moniker had seemed great at the time, but as an adult Carson knew that it had upset their mother. He couldn't blame her. But he, Annaise, and their father had been close. They went everywhere together. His death created a void that neither of them would ever be able to close or fill.

Michael reacted with anger and Brianna felt betrayed. As the two youngest, they hadn't seen their father the same way. Once they had grown old enough, they saw the broken shell that he had become. Carson and Annaise had known him when he had seemed full of life. Granted, they had also seen his downward spiral, too, but the old memories stuck around. Maybe that was why Carson and Annaise had both become nearly suicidal after he died, while Brianna and Michael had turned angry.

Again, Carson couldn't blame them. He didn't like it, but he had to respect their grieving process too. It wasn't like their father was perfect. He had quite a few flaws, which had become apparent when Carson reached adulthood. Their father had been depressed, angry, and self-destructive. He had been raised to withhold affection and hide emotions and it had a damaging effect on all of them in different ways.

Carson suspected that a part of his depression stemmed from there. That and the feeling of isolation that came with every move to a new school. He had sought therapy after enlisting, but it hadn't succeeded in eliminating the suicidal ideations. It just made them tolerable.

This brought Carson to another realization: Kate had a big part to play in that. She made him miserable, though discreetly, and always had a way of making him feel as though nothing he did would ever be enough. He was gone too long, or didn't make enough money, or didn't help out enough around the house. Despite his best efforts, Carson could never get anything quite right.

Carson glanced over at Kate as she sat in the passenger seat and felt a new emotion eclipse the affection he once held: hatred. Sitting beside him was a woman who was so insecure about her own shortcomings that she had to tear everyone else down around her. Carson, being married to her, was the most common target. Since Carson already suffered from depression, anxiety, and cripplingly low self-esteem, it had been easy for her. And he hadn't noticed! It had taken the apocalypse to make him see it.

But what could he do? He couldn't very well leave her by the road to fend for herself. He may have felt hatred toward her, but Carson couldn't bring himself to be that cold. She was still a human being, right? And after the nightmare that had become his reality, Carson did not want to experience another death for as long as he lived. Impractical, sure, but that was how he felt. It made him feel powerless.

Had Kate been right? Was he trying to play the hero? Once again, Carson felt his face grow hot, because maybe he was. Maybe Carson had taken the opportunity to step up into a role he had always wanted. Be careful of what you wish for. Never before had that adage felt so true.

There was nothing left to do, though. They were on their own. Either Carson stepped up and accepted his role, or they all died. There could be no in between. Carson felt his resolve strengthen at this. He didn't want the responsibility now that he had been saddled with it, but he would take it on anyway.

Filled with this new resolve, Carson gripped the steering wheel and stared ahead. He would get them safely to Kate's family home, and then he would go look for his family.

He just hoped they were all still okay.

Chapter 31

The mountain pass normally felt too open for Carson's comfort. Off to the right the mountains jutted upward as the road hugged its side. On the left was a drop of about two hundred feet or so. He'd always feared that the road would give way, and they would tumble down the slope to their deaths. Now it felt too enclosed. He surmised that this feeling was because turning around would be incredibly difficult, especially with so many blind turns. Unable to see oncoming traffic, he would have to risk a collision with a vehicle going easily 65 mph.

With a white-knuckle grip on the steering wheel, Carson slowly drove along the narrow road. He never understood how people were comfortable going so fast on this road. The posted speed limit was 55 mph, but he always kept the vehicle moving at least 10 mph slower.

When he checked the speedometer, he noticed he was going even slower. It seemed counterintuitive to move slow when he was in such a hurry to get out of the claustrophobic environment, but it would do them no good if they flew off the road. No, going slower was safer, but it would also significantly prolong his discomfort.

Carson resigned himself to the sacrifice. He'd suffer through his paranoia so that they could make it through the pass alive. His hands would just hurt afterward.

Chris and Irene were still asleep in the backseat. When he glanced over at Kate, he noted that she had drifted off as well.

Lucky them.

Not only was he exhausted, but Carson was terrified of sleeping. The nightmares always seemed to return, except when he'd been so worn out that he didn't dream at all. He preferred the blissful nothingness over the monstrosities that plagued his dreams. It wasn't enough that he had to deal with them while awake.

He decided he would push himself to the point of collapse. It was the only way he would be able to get any real rest. Or so he hoped. Chronically tired, he doubted he would ever feel rested again.

Twenty minutes later, Carson found himself struggling to keep his eyes open. The only thing that kept him awake was the frequent surges of adrenaline when his eyes stayed closed for too long. He would jolt upright and force his eyes wide open.

A moment later he no longer had to worry.

Overhead came a loud roar.

Carson almost slammed on the brakes in terror. Leading up to this point, he'd only been concerned about the flying creatures. He didn't think anything else had taken to the skies. Apparently, he'd been wrong.

Fearing an impending attack, Carson leaned forward and tried to look as far above the truck as possible through the windshield. The roar hadn't ceased. In fact, it was getting louder.

He pulled his gaze reluctantly from above. It turned out to be an immensely good idea. When he looked ahead, Carson saw that they had veered into the left lane and had been heading directly toward the edge of a cliff. Had he looked a moment later, it would have been too late.

He jerked the wheel to the right, careful not to overcorrect and run into the side of the mountain. Carson's heart slammed against his ribcage. He would have no trouble staying awake now.

The roar had reached a deafening crescendo. Overhead a dark shape overtook them.

A flood of relief swept over him.

It had been the sound of a jet engine. Overhead flew the shape of a large military cargo plane. He suspected that it was a C-17 cargo plane. Oddly though, it was heading *away* from the base and toward the coast. And it was painted completely black.

Carson knew that the C-17s weren't painted that way. They weren't designed for stealth and as such, were always a steely gray color. Same with the rest of the cargo planes that the military used.

Flanking the massive airplane was a cadre of Blackhawk helicopters. He counted six flying parallel to the cargo plane like an armed escort.

For some reason, the appearance of the plane and the helicopters filled Carson with dread. It would have made more sense if they were headed toward the military base. But away from it? Things must be much worse than he'd thought.

Careful to keep his attention on the road, Carson used his peripheral vision to track their course. They were heading the same direction he was. There was no doubt about it. But why? There weren't any military bases in that direction as far as he knew.

Had it been just the Blackhawks, he wouldn't have given it much thought.

But a cargo plane? Out this far away from a base?

He suspected that things had gone very, very wrong.

The military aircraft disappeared after a short while, but as he drove Carson could still hear the roar of the engines punctuated by the thumping from the helicopters. Rather than obsess over their potential destination, Carson opted to focus his attention on the road and getting to his in-law's house. He'd have time to worry about everything else later.

It seemed like *everything* was going to wait until later.

Eventually, much to his relief, they made it through the mountain pass and into the open. Aside from the strangeness of the plane, he was surprised that the drive had been uneventful. Carson was thankful for this, too, since the stop at the gas station had been a disaster.

Thinking of the gas station seemed to make his stomach growl, and he remembered that he had not grabbed anything for them to eat. Fortunately, Kate and the kids were still asleep. He hoped they would be for the rest of the drive.

He suspected that they would sleep the whole way, considering that even the roar of a jet engine hadn't been enough to wake them. Hell, Kate hadn't even stirred. Not so much as a twitch.

Carson was okay with that. It would be a peaceful drive, at least.

A while later they started nearing civilization. They were nearing the north end of Clearlake. The name of the city had once been accurate, but years of pollution of the city's namesake made it ironic. You were more likely to sprout an extra limb if you swam in it. And forget eating *anything* that came out of it.

Yet, after the things he'd seen, Carson would rather swim in the biohazard that was Clearlake any day. He could handle three-eyed catfish and cycloptic blue gill. Those seemed perfectly normal in comparison.

As they neared the city Carson noticed that the air seemed hazy and thick. Squinting, he saw that the sky was filling with thick, oily smoke. Something was burning. A moment later he found out what.

The entire city looked like it had been covered in napalm. Buildings were burnt down to their foundations, the remnants of their frames jutting like blackened skeletons.

Everything had been scorched. The ground was black. The buildings were black. Even the asphalt looked darker than normal.

"What the fuck?" Carson asked aloud.

Silence. Kate and the children were still asleep.

Ash fell on the windshield like filthy snowflakes. He flicked on the windshield wipers and slowly drove through the destruction. He'd never been fond of the city, but nobody deserved this.

Had there been a wildfire? It wouldn't be the first time the county suffered from a catastrophic wildfire, but the magnitude of this one far exceeded any other. It was no secret that California was suffering from numerous droughts, and this led to rampant wildfires across the state.

But this? It looked like a military strike. The more he looked, the more Carson grew convinced that the destruction was the result of exactly that. Which begged another question: who the fuck did it?

He didn't think it was their military. The United States military wouldn't wipe an entire city off the map in their own territory, would they? And why Clearlake of all places?

A sense of foreboding once again came over him. What if it *had* been a military strike by their own military? If it was, that meant the monsters had been appearing all over and had overtaken the town. That thought terrified him more than anything that had happened so far.

Thankful that his family continued to sleep, Carson drove out of Clearlake and headed south. He hoped that the next town, Lower Lake, had fared better.

It hadn't.

Carson was struck with a feeling of déjà vu. Lower Lake, too, had been completely levelled. For the first time since starting the drive, Carson worried that his in-laws hadn't been spared from the waking nightmare. If so, then they would have to continue and try to find refuge elsewhere. Kate would lose her mind. The kids would, too. Carson knew he would be gutted as well, since he got along well with Kate's family. Even if Kate herself was insane, her family didn't seem to be.

As he drove through the wreckage, he caught sight of the one thing he had hoped he wouldn't see: a burnt human corpse. The remains were twisted from the heat, but it was unmistakable.

The burnt figure solidified his worst fears. Towns had been reduced to ash with people still there. Either there had been an evacuation, and some people had refused to leave, or there'd been no warning. He couldn't imagine what that would have been like.

The terror those people must have felt knowing that everything they once knew was destroyed and they were caught inside. Carson hoped most had not been aware at all; that people had succumbed to smoke inhalation before the flames went to work. It would have been preferable over burning alive.

Tears rolled down his cheeks as he surveyed the devastation around him. He felt the overwhelming urge to turn around and go back the way they had come. He didn't want to find out if his old hometown had suffered the same fate. Sure, not every memory from before he enlisted had been pleasant ones, but there were some sprinkled in there. The pain of that level of loss would likely be too much.

As they continued down the road, he felt the familiar symptoms of a panic attack starting to creep in. He ground his teeth and forced the panic back. There was no time for it and likely wouldn't be for quite some time. Pessimism replaced his impending panic.

Everything was gone, he told himself. If both Clearlake and Lower Lake were demolished, so would everything else be. It was incredibly unlikely that the private community ahead would have been spared.

As they rounded a bend in the road, Carson breathed a sigh of relief. He'd been wrong. Somehow, impossibly, the community looked untouched. He couldn't help the feeling of elation that flooded him. Maybe their luck had finally changed.

He rolled up to the gate and stopped in front of the intercom. The barrier, though flimsy, looked intact. With his window rolled down, Carson leaned out and pressed the call button on the little metal box. He heard the chime, confirming that the intercom was functional.

However, after more than a minute of silence, there was no reply. Confused, Carson pressed the button again.

More time passed without an answer.

A feeling of unease quickly overtook his previous elation.

Rapidly, Carson pressed the intercom button over and over. Still, no reply came. Unease turned to frustration, anger, and then panic.

Something was wrong.

Carson hated blocking the road and was thankful that nobody was behind them. He shifted the truck into park and leaned out the driver window. He could see the small guard shack further ahead, but the window was dark. Nobody seemed to move inside.

Where did this guy go? Carson thought. *He leave to take a piss? What the fuck?*

Beyond the gate and to the left, just a little further up the road, Carson could see the in-laws' house. They were so close. If only the prick manning the gate would just answer and lift the bar.

Kate began to shift in the passenger seat and slowly blinked her eyes. Carson looked over and watched as she got her bearings.

"What's going on?" she asked.

"No answer," he replied.

She peered through the windshield to look at the little shack. Carson knew she wouldn't see anything either. Unless she suddenly developed x-ray vision. After a moment, Kate slumped back in her seat.

"Push the button again," Kate implored.

Frustrated, Carson reached out and jammed his index finger into the button. As expected, nobody answered. "I've been doing that for the past five minutes. Nobody's answering."

They sat in silence for a moment before Kate spoke up again. "Just go around."

Carson laid his head back against the seat and looked at the ceiling of the cab. He squeezed his eyes shut, let out a long exhale and then looked ahead. His hands gripped the steering wheel tight enough to elicit a small squeak from the material.

"Goddammit," he hissed. Without another word, he put the truck in gear and slowly drove off the road into the gravel. He heard the crunch of the tires as they rolled around the gate. He pulled the truck back onto the road and half-expected flashing red and blue lights to erupt behind them. But nothing happened. No guard running out of the shack to yell at them. No sirens. Absolutely nothing.

He felt a knot forming in the pit of his stomach as they drove up the road and turned into the driveway.

The shadowy figure reappeared at the edge of his vision and Carson jumped. He tried to catch sight of it, but just as before, it eluded him.

The thing was starting to feel like a bad omen. The knot in his stomach turned to a brick of lead.

He hoped he was wrong.

Chapter 32

On previous occasions when they would visit, one or both of Kate's sisters would come outside to greet them. Their small children would often be close on their heels, excited to see their aunt and uncle. But today, nobody came out of the house.

The vehicles, of which there were quite a few, were in the large driveway. If any one of them were missing, Carson would have suspected that nobody was home.

He didn't know why, but something felt wrong. Where was everyone? Kate had spoken to her parents just that morning and had told them that they were coming to visit. Her family should have been expecting them. So, why had nobody come outside?

Carson parked the truck under the large oak tree that sat in the middle of the gravel driveway, next to Kate's brother-in-law's SUV. It was an older Jeep Cherokee, painted a hideous beige-yellow color, and seemed to always have some mechanical problem or another. From what Carson could tell—given that the vehicle was covered in leaves and pollen—the vehicle had been in the same spot for a while. His sister-in-law's small sedan was parked on the other side of the Jeep. It was dirty, but not like the Jeep. It had been driven recently, since it hadn't been coated in a thin layer of pollen like the Jeep. And the windshield was clean.

What Carson found most unsettling was the silence. No cars seemed to be driving along the main road outside the security gate, nor around the neighborhood. It was as though everyone had decided to stay inside or had disappeared. That thought made the pit in his stomach feel heavier.

Kate stepped out of the truck first, eager to run inside. When Carson stepped out after her, she quickly came around the front and stopped in front of him, her eyes boring into him.

"Leave the guns in the truck," she hissed as she quickly looked over her shoulder at the front door. "You know my parents hate guns. You don't give a shit that I don't like guns either but at least respect *them* enough to keep them in the truck. You don't need them."

Carson opened his mouth to reply, but Kate had already walked past him to help Chris out of his booster seat. He knew that, despite his paranoia, leaving the weapons in the truck was the more diplomatic approach. He hated the idea of *ever* being unarmed ever again, but he didn't have the energy to deal with a fight.

After all, they *were* safe, right? He shouldn't need the firearms now that they had made it to the house. But the burned out remains of the previous two towns filled him with a sense of foreboding. The housing community had been untouched, for now. But for how long? How long until bombs were dropped here? That would be it for them. Stuck at the house, they'd be obliterated.

Or, what if something *else* was in the house? Sweat broke out on his forehead and his stomach clenched as a wave of nausea overtook him. Was he being irrational?

It made a certain amount of sense. After the adrenaline wore off it wasn't unusual to feel sick and exhausted. And Carson had been running on adrenaline for hours. Even when he'd fallen asleep the night before, he hadn't had time to fully process the events that had taken place.

Just then, images of the dead started filling his mind's eye. The eviscerated remains of Airman Swanson's partner. The young man that had been attacked in their neighborhood and slaughtered before their eyes.

And the portal that had opened in the cafeteria, swallowing up the young boy and Airman Swanson. He suspected they were dead too.

Bile forced its way up his throat and filled his mouth. Careful to turn away from the kids, he bent over and spat on the rocks. He hadn't eaten much so all that had come up had been stomach acid.

Carson stayed hunched over with his left hand on the side of the truck to steady himself. He closed his eyes and felt his cheeks flush. His face felt damp with sweat and his body trembled.

Kate, either unaware or uncaring, did not come to check on him. She continued up the small ramp that had been put in for her grandmother and walked across the wooden deck toward the front door.

An upper deck wrapped completely around the front of the house, covering the walkway in shadows. Sunlight squeezed between the leaves and the gaps in the wood to cast a dappled lightshow over them. Carson had never really stopped and noticed the effect before. It gave everything an ethereal, dream-like quality.

He wiped his face and dried his hand on the front of his pants before standing upright. With a steadying breath, he pushed down the horrors invading his mind and turned toward the house. He would give himself time to fully process everything, he promised himself. But not yet. Not until they were settled.

A growing sense of unease came over him as he walked across the wooden deck to the front door. Carson remembered helping his in-laws rebuild the deck several years ago. It had been in such poor shape that nobody felt safe walking on it, especially since the house sat easily ten feet above the ground in some places. Going through the deck meant an unpleasant drop that would undoubtedly lead to an emergency room trip.

He had never fully gotten into carpentry, but he'd found the experience surprisingly enjoyable. It was hard work, sure, but it felt so rewarding when they had finished. He liked the fact that he could step back and look at the deck knowing that he had helped build it.

Carson tried to use that memory to keep his anxiety at bay. For some reason, he felt off. Perhaps it was the shadowy figure lurking at the periphery of his vision, keeping pace but staying just out of sight. He didn't know what it was, or why it was following them, but it was almost certainly malevolent. It just hadn't struck yet. He wondered if it was just biding its time.

Kate reached the front door well before Carson and their children did. She knocked and waited, expecting the door to swing open and one of her sisters—probably the eldest, Jessie— to greet her. However, no one answered. Carson saw the frustration on Kate's face as she knocked again, harder this time. Once again, no answer.

The door was very rarely locked. Living in a gated community gave people a sense of security and they would often drop their guard. Carson had an inherent mistrust of people so he would lock the door regardless of the neighborhood. He would do so even on base, which *should* be more secure than anywhere else.

Kate turned the knob just as Carson reached her. He followed close behind as she stepped over the threshold.

The house, for all intents and purposes, seemed empty. One thing he knew about Kate's family was that they would lock the door *only* when they weren't home. Kate had a copy of the key for that very reason.

"Perhaps someone had forgotten to lock up before they left?" Carson suggested.

Kate stood quietly, staring into the house. "Maybe."

Immediately inside the entryway there was a stairwell to the right that led straight up to the only room on the second floor, the master bedroom. To the left was the large living room with fifteen-foot ceilings. Natural light spilled in from the west facing windows high up on the walls.

Along the wall immediately to the left was a large wooden entertainment center. Carson knew that there were few places that they could put a television, but where it was meant that in the early afternoon there would be a terrible glare from the windows. Worse still, there were no shades for those windows.

On the wall to the left of the room, opposite the staircase, was a large sliding glass door that opened out onto the deck. A small couch sat in front of the door, which made it difficult to go out that way. Especially with the lounge chair next to the couch. In the corner, between the couch and the entertainment center, was an old-fashioned wood stove that had been converted into a pellet stove. It was the house's only form of heating.

Across from the entrance and the entertainment was another couch, with space behind it to walk from the dining room to the back hall without going through the kitchen. The rest of the living room was open, with a large rug in the center.

A wall behind the central couch separated the living room from the kitchen. A dining room was to the left and open to the living room, with a dining table that was used more for random clutter than for family meals. The kitchen itself had been renovated and allowed for a thoroughfare to the laundry room, garage door, and bathroom, as well as a passage to the rear hall.

The hall led to three bedrooms on the main floor, situated underneath the master bedroom. One on the left at the far end of the hall, with two on the right. Despite being unobstructed from the living room, the bedrooms always got cold in the winter. He remembered waking up freezing on more than one occasion.

Carson looked up at the door leading into the master bedroom and noted that it was, uncharacteristically, open. His in-laws *never* left the door open to their bedroom. Carson's hair stood on end.

He had been so distracted by the open door that he hadn't initially noticed the texture of the walls. Spaced sporadically along the walls were pulsing masses like pimples. Carson immediately recognized them, and in that moment recalled a nightmare that he had had only a day before.

"Fuck! Fuck! Fuck!" Carson yelled in a panic, grabbing Chris and Irene's hands. "We need to go, now!"

Ignoring him, Kate walked further into the house. "Mom? Dad?"

"Kate, we need to go!"

She continued to ignore him as she cupped her hands around her mouth. "Jessie? Maggie? Where are you guys?"

Carson felt his chest tighten as though clamped in a vice. Every breath seemed to make it squeeze harder. His vision was starting to narrow, and he had to glance down to make sure he still held his children's hands in his own as they had gone numb.

"Kate, dammit!" he yelled out as he continued to pull Chris and Irene out of the house. Kate had made it near the threshold of the dining room and was staring down the hallway to the bedrooms, her eyes wide with fear. "Kate! Move!"

Chris and Irene were out on the deck and behind him when he saw the pustules begin to pulse faster, seemingly sensing Kate's presence. Kate continued to stare, standing stock-still. Carson followed her gaze and knew before what she saw before it came into view. This was almost *exactly* how his nightmare had played out.

Floating into view was a large, white amorphous blob. It hovered roughly two feet above the floor, suspended by long, thin white appendages that retracted quickly into the thing's form when it moved. The appendages would reappear and shoot out at the wall, dragging the thing forward. Its movement and existence seemed to mock physics. There was no way it should be able to hold itself off the ground, nor should it be able to move in any direction. Gravity *should* have pulled it to the floor into a puddle of goo, but the thing seemed to ignore gravity altogether.

Thus far, this thing was the most terrifying thing Carson had encountered. Not because of its appearance, though deeply unsettling, nor because of the way it moved. What terrified him was the overwhelming feeling of murderous glee coming off of it. He didn't know how he detected this, but it was undeniable. It wanted only to kill and absorb any living thing it encountered.

Kate had become its new target.

As it moved closer, Carson detected a change. Its demeanor turned into a malicious amusement as Kate began to back up slowly. The numerous eyes across its surface were all fixed on her. What it knew, but Kate didn't, was that she was moving closer to one of the pulsing pimples jutting from the wall.

The gooey surface of the floating thing seemed to quiver with anticipation as Kate came within several feet of the nearest pustule directly across from it.

"Kate! This way!" Carson screamed as he started toward her, but her attention was solely on the milky blob. "Get away from the wall!"

"Mom!" Irene screamed and tried to race past Carson. He reached out and grabbed her, pushing her behind him once again.

The floating mass seemed to halt its forward movement. Kate continued to back up, inching closer to the wall. The pustule that was growing from the wall began to quiver more intensely as though detecting the presence of something living drawing close, a bit like a predator preparing for an ambush.

Kate was oblivious of the growth, having seemingly forgotten all about them. Carson wondered if she'd even noticed them in the first place. Unfortunately, only he knew the danger they posed. He didn't know what the floating mass would do if it came in contact with Kate, but he *did* know what would happen if she touched the evil pimples.

Another backward step brought Kate within a foot of the growth. The pustule seemed to, oddly, move *away* from her.

All of this occurred within the span of several seconds. Carson pushed Chris and Irene behind him and blocked the doorway. He knew what was coming. He stepped forward to grab her and pull her out of the pustule's reach.

"Kate! Dammit! Get away—" he began but was immediately cut off by the sound of a wet thud. Kate stumbled away from the wall as though pushed, her eyes wide with fear.

"Fuck!" he screamed. It was too late.

Carson started to close the door just enough to block the line of sight. He had a feeling he knew what would come next and did *not* want his children to bear witness.

Kate stared at him, her eyes bulging. Blood began to slowly roll down from her ears, nose and the corners of her eyes. She opened her mouth to speak, only for more blood to spill over her lower lip and chin. She stumbled toward Carson with her hands outstretched, silently begging him to help.

Beads of red sprouted across her skin, welling up from every pore. Kate fell to her knees, her hands still held out. Carson tried to move forward, but an invisible force held him in place. Rooted to the floor, all Carson could do was watch. Every fiber of his being implored him to turn and run, but he could not force his body to move.

The floating mass quivered excitedly. If it had eyes, Carson knew they would be fixed on him. He knew at that moment that the thing was holding him in place, forcing him to watch.

Up until then, every monstrosity that they had encountered had acted on instinct. As horrific as they had been, Carson had never detected malice in the things. They hunted and killed, just as any predator from their world might.

But this thing was different. It seemed to enjoy killing. It relished the pain it inflicted and witnessed. Worse still, it took perverse enjoyment of watching the suffering of others. Carson had considered the monsters to be evil, but they weren't. No, *this* thing was evil.

The only thing that he detected that seemed as truly evil as the white floating blob was the shadowy figure that had followed them. Even now, the thing hovered at the edge of Carson's vision, seemingly enjoying the spectacle.

Kate pitched forward and caught herself on her hands, her head hung low. Her dirty blonde hair fell over her face, obscuring her features. She seemed to be deflating, shrinking down to the floor.

No, that wasn't right. Not shrinking.

She was dissolving.

Blood mixed with other fluids in a puddle underneath her. She fell to her side and Carson caught her eyes fixed on him. In that stare he saw a mixture of agony and fury. Her mouth no longer moved as the muscles had liquified. Her teeth tumbled out her open lips. Hair started to fall from her head as though someone were shaving her scalp. Her body was losing shape as it became more liquid than solid, and still she stared at him.

The hate in that gaze was worse than anything else. It was total and absolute. Carson had failed to prevent her demise, and she was making sure he knew it.

That stare stayed on him until her eyes melted and ran from the sockets like candle wax. A moment later, her skull caved inward.

Carson felt his body released from the glob's invisible grasp, yet he could not move. He wasn't sure if he would ever be able to move again. He certainly wouldn't *sleep* again. He continued to stand in the doorway like a statue, terror and shock rendering him paralyzed.

The floating white glob hovered over to the puddle on the floor and once above it, lowered itself. Its mass obscured the remains of Carson's wife, and a wet sucking sound emanated from it.

Quivering with pleasure, the glob seemed to take its time. The sounds it made finally shocked Carson back to reality. He realized that every other sound had been muted because he immediately heard screams from behind him.

From the sound of it, the screaming had been going on for a bit.

Carson slammed the front door, turned to Chris and Irene, and pulled them back toward the truck. He didn't look down at them. He couldn't. He couldn't bear to see the pain in their eyes.

Chris and Irene may not have witnessed the entire atrocity that had unfolded in the house, but they must have caught a fleeting glimpse. The absolute terror and pain in their cries told Carson as much.

Wordlessly, Carson yanked open the rear driver side door and hurriedly pushed his suffering children inside. He shut the door the instant Chris's small foot cleared the doorway. He turned, pulled open the driver's door and collapsed into the seat behind the steering wheel. It was then that he noticed that he'd been crying.

Wracking sobs shook his body. The horror that he had witnessed had been worse than anything he had ever experienced in his life.

Toward the end, Kate had shown her true colors. As a result, Carson had no longer felt love for her. But watching her die was something he had not been prepared for. He knew that Chris and Irene would likely never recover from the loss. He would have to comfort them as they inevitably fell to pieces, but nobody would be there to comfort him.

He had never felt more alone.

Chris and Irene continued to wail uncontrollably in the backseat as Carson stared out at the house. His vision constantly blurred as tears welled up and fell. He was, at that moment, truly helpless. If Chris and Irene weren't in the vehicle, he would likely turn the pistol on himself. The image of Kate's body liquified on the floor of her childhood home would haunt him forever, and he did not think he had the strength to endure it. A bullet would be easier.

Carson sat in the front seat for many long moments, staring at the house. He expected the blob to force down the front door and pursue them, but the door remained closed. The kids had screamed themselves hoarse and Carson sat near catatonic.

Minutes passed before Carson, without a sound, put the truck in reverse and backed out of the driveway. He had no idea where they were going to go.

It didn't matter.

Chapter 33

With no destination in mind, Carson drove. He stared straight ahead, barely blinking. The shock hadn't left his system yet. He had driven through the gate to leave the community, smashing the arm that was meant to bar the way. It was laughable how secure that flimsy mechanical arm had made people feel.

It hadn't done any fucking good.

If the nightmare of his in-laws was any indication, the community was lost. He doubted *anyone* was alive. In twenty-four hours, the community had gone from over a thousand people to a ghost town.

That realization convinced Carson that the end of the world had come. He had never given any thought to the doomsayers that came out of the woodworks every new year. As far as he was concerned, they were delusional and just seeking attention.

How ironic, then, that the real apocalypse came without warning. No doomsday reports. No tabloid articles. Nothing more than a smattering of odd sightings reported on news outlets.

Carson drove in silence as he headed south. Chris and Irene had cried themselves to sleep. He envied them.

So, without hope or direction, Carson drove. He passed through a split in the hills that served as a barrier between the community and the town ahead. How amusing that the town was named Middletown, for now it was in the middle of hell.

All around Carson could see the blackened remains of the landscape. But improbably, the town and community had been untouched. He drove down the road and approached the first of three stop lights in town. Off to the right was the high school that he had graduated from. He had met Kate there, and at the time had thought he would live happily ever after.

What a fucking joke.

There was no such thing. All that he could hope for was as little suffering as possible. Life had felt so promising. His future had seemed full of promise.

Not now.

The world as he knew it had ended, but he had been cruelly spared.

Why? Was this some form of Karmic justice for some past slight? Had he been an absolute monster in a previous life? Why the fuck did he have to suffer? More importantly, why did his *kids* have to suffer? What had they ever done to deserve such a fate?

He had always been a pessimist. A combination of trauma and a negative environment had molded Carson into a cynic. As such, it was hard to be hopeful of anything.

But now? There was nothing. No hope. No future.

So why keep going? Why not put a bullet in his brain and be done with it?

Carson knew the answer. They were sleeping in the back seat. He couldn't abandon Chris and Irene, and he *certainly* couldn't turn a gun on them.

Despite everything, Carson had to keep going. *He* may not want to live another moment, but the kids did. At least for now. Who knew what the future held?

He had been so consumed in his introspection that he hadn't noticed the stop light turn green. It didn't matter much. Nobody else was on the road. Carson had no real reason to obey the laws of the road, but old habits die hard.

Gradually pressing on the accelerator, Carson steered the truck through the quiet town. Middletown was never bustling with activity. People were rarely seen walking down the sidewalks. But despite this, there was still the feeling of absence all around. Carson knew in some way that there was nobody left. They had either fled or been killed.

Carson suspected the latter.

He pulled over, parked, and sat in the driver's seat, his head pounding. He wanted to rage, to scream his lungs out and bang his fists against the dash. Pressure built behind his eyes, signifying a horrendous headache was coming. Carson tried to sit back, but his muscles had seized in place. His body began to shake.

No. Not his body. The ground under them was shaking.

He finally forced his eyes open and, to his horror, saw nearly a dozen jittering, red-colored vertical slits growing in the air around him. As he watched, they began to slowly open on by one.

He knew what they were.

It was hard for Carson to discount that their appearance had something to do with him. The headache, overwhelming emotions, and temporary paralysis seemed to precede their inexplicable appearance.

"No, please," Carson whined. "Not now."

The nearest rift opened wider and from within he could see the twitching needle-like limbs of what he knew were the spider monsters. They scrabbled forward, their grotesque bodies pulled into view. Behind them Carson saw something launch over the spider monsters. Something with grasshopper legs.

"Fuck!"

Without waiting for anything else to appear, Carson shifted the truck into drive and stomped on the accelerator. The engine revved and rocks flew from under spinning tires. The tires finally found traction and the truck lurched forward.

White knuckling the steering wheel, Carson swerved around the growing swarm spilling from the nearest portal. One of the spider monsters had been unlucky enough to be on his path and the truck bounced over its crushed carapace.

"Fuck you!" Carson bellowed.

As if triggered by the kill, the other portals opened faster and spilled their contents. He caught sight of more of the death hoppers launching themselves over the asphalt while a swarm of the spider monsters crawled across the ground.

One of the death hoppers collided with the side of the truck and its weight made the passenger door buckle inward, spraying Carson with a hail of shattered glass. He swerved as he ducked away from the crystalline shower.

In front of the truck was the bizarre creature he'd seen the night before. The one that had been vaguely human shaped. Carson had time to take in the thing's potato-shaped head before the grill of the truck made contact.

The spud monster bent forward, and its bulbous head collided with the hood, splitting open like a rotten gourd. Yellowish white viscera erupted forth and splashed against the windshield. Carson screamed as he fumbled for the windshield wiper toggle.

He pressed his fingers against the side of the lever to douse the glass with cleaning fluid, his foot never leaving the accelerator. The truck bounced and shook as he drove over the mangled remains. The wiper blades squealed as they fought to scrape away the muck.

Enough of the windshield was clear so that Carson could witness a monstrous hand reach out from within a blood-red portal, grasping for the fleeing truck. With a bloodcurdling scream, Carson wrenched the steering wheel in the opposite direction. The tips of the colossal fingers scraped over the top of the truck, and, for one heart-stopping moment, a finger snagged on the bed of the pickup. The truck jolted to a stop and threw Carson against the steering wheel. His forehead struck the top of the wheel and made his existing headache grow tenfold.

Carson's vision blurred as his head felt like it was about to explode. The front end of the truck began to rise, and he remembered the gargantuan hand. He let out an unintelligible yell and pressed back down on the accelerator pedal.

Chris and Irene, who had been violently awoken during the first impact, screamed at the top of their lungs. The cacophony of their voices made Carson panic as he desperately stomped on the pedal. The tires spun over the asphalt and kicked up white smoke. For one terrible moment, the truck moved backward.

The hand tried to use the tips of its fingers to reel in the fleeing truck. As the fingers bent inward, the thing that was attached to the hand chose to open its fingers to get a better grip.

That momentary release was all the truck needed. As the front end of the pickup fell back down, the tires caught and propelled the vehicle forward. Carson tensed as he fought to maintain control. He swerved over the road and overcorrected, nearly driving into the side of a hill. At the last moment, Carson regained control and pointed the front end of the truck toward town.

Without looking back, Carson sped faster than he'd ever driven, away from the growing horde.

He made it to the center of town before he heard the growing roar.

Looking up at the sky through the windshield, Carson expected some new horror to descend upon them. When he didn't see anything, he became confused. For probably the first time since he had driven away from his in-law's house, he scanned his surroundings. The sound seemed to be coming from all around him.

In the rearview mirror, Carson caught sight of a looming shadow advancing quickly toward them. He nearly panicked when the shadow overtook them. He yanked the steering wheel to the left when he felt the tires hit the curb.

The squeal of tires echoed down the street as Carson struggled to regain control of the vehicle. His heart slammed in his chest as he gripped the steering wheel. After a moment, he was able to get under control.

He was breathing heavily, the panic and exertion that came from losing control taking a toll on him. His nerves were already frayed. The near accident didn't help.

Carson looked up again and caught a familiar sight. Up above was the large black military plane. He heard the thumping of the helicopter blades under the roar of the large airplane.

Oddly, the plane seemed to be getting lower. He had no idea where they planned to land. Mountains and trees were all around them. He couldn't remember there being any open expanses of land within the town limits. The plane, it seemed, didn't really care. It flew overhead and he noticed that it was slowly veering off to the right. He suspected that the pilots had located a strip of land suitable enough to land the massive craft. The helicopters, on the other hand, did not have the same limitations. Carson had left the center of town and was on an open stretch of road leading to the casino that was located on the outskirts of town. One of the Blackhawk helicopters landed in the center of the road ahead of them.

Carson had to slam on the brakes to avoid hitting the black aircraft. The truck hadn't even fully come to a stop when black-clad figures jumped from the inside of the helicopter and began surrounding them.

Shocked and confused, Carson glanced around frantically. Maybe the military came after him for going AWOL.

Several more helicopters had landed nearby and in moments, the truck was surrounded by over a dozen people holding automatic weapons. Every weapon was trained on the blue pickup truck. The shadow figure that had lurked since he had left the house quivered and then, inexplicably, dissipated.

It was gone.

"What the fuck is this?" Carson barked. His outburst shocked Chris and Irene awake. They immediately began to scream and cry.

One figure walked right up to the driver's door, a submachine gun in hand, and tapped the end of the barrel on the glass. Carson heard a muffled voice but couldn't understand what was being said.

But he could guess.

Without fighting, Carson raised his hands off the steering wheel and carefully opened the driver's door.

Hands reached in and roughly pulled him from the vehicle. He bucked and pulled against the grip on his arms. He saw Chris and Irene pulled from the truck, though with a bit more care than he'd been. Still, the sight of hands on his kids incensed him. Carson roared and yanked harder.

A pinch in the side of his neck shocked him into stillness for a moment.

His legs seemed to go out from under him, and he pitched forward. His vision started to cloud over.

Carson figured that this was the end. Running away from the monsters had done nothing. Kate was dead and now he feared the men were going to take his kids from him, to never be seen again. All of it for nothing. Every attempt to keep them safe had failed.

A moment later, a black boot collided with the side of his head.

Carson's world faded to black.

Chase MacLeod

Epililogue

Carson awoke in what could only be described as a high-end prison cell. Bright fluorescent lights made his eyes water and his head pound. The light may as well have been stabbing directly into his brain. It felt as though no time had passed since the encounter on the road and waking up in the room. He suspected that someone had used a powerful anesthetic on him, and it pissed him off.

With a monumental effort, he forced himself up into a seated position. Everything hurt. He felt that every movement was taking place underwater. His limbs were sluggish, and his vision was blurred.

Where was he?

How was he alive?

More importantly, where the hell were Chris and Irene?

Who the fuck were those people on the road? They had military training, that much he could tell. But none of them had had any recognizable insignia on their uniforms. Their attire, down to the black masks they wore over their heads, brought to mind some form of SpecOps team. If that was the case, why were they after *him*?

The haze cleared slowly and Carson was able to better evaluate his surroundings. In the corners of the room were video surveillance cameras. It boggled his mind that there was more than one camera in the room.

A heavy metal door stood across from where Carson sat, adjacent to the transparent walls of his cell. He suspected that the walls were made from some form of plexiglass, or something similarly sturdy. Other than a simple bed, sink, and toilet, the room was otherwise empty.

The more he looked, the more questions he had.

Once again, why were they after him? And why his kids?

Who the fuck were they?

Another horrible thought came to mind: did they have something to do with the portals?

Carson hobbled over to the wall across from him and banged his fists against it when he thought of his children. He had no idea where they were or if they were okay. After what had happened to Kate, it was driving him crazy not knowing if his kids were safe. Images of their bodies melting to the floor filled his mind's eye. The horrifying visual caused Carson to pound harder on the wall.

His banging, though undoubtedly muffled, brought two men dressed head-to-toe in black tactical gear. From behind them came another person, a man in his mid-forties and dressed in a nondescript black suit adorned with a symbol that seemed vaguely familiar.

The man had salt and pepper hair that was closely cropped, reminiscent of a soldier. The man's posture and demeanor further implied a military background. His face started to show signs of age, crow's feet spreading out from the corners of his eyes. He was cleanshaven and well groomed. Carson suspected that the man was probably a high-ranking officer, perhaps even a general.

The man, definitely someone important, spoke to one of the men who promptly walked away. Carson couldn't hear what was said and a pit formed in his stomach. What were they going to do to him? A moment later, the man returned with a simple folding metal chair.

The man in the suit sat down across from Carson and produced a manilla folder from inside his jacket. He held open against the barrier between them. One of the soldiers flanking him pressed a button and Carson could hear the man speak.

"Staff Sergeant Carson Andrew Tanner," the man began, his voice deep and rich. "United States Air Force, enlisted in February 2012. Married, with two children. Irene and Christopher Connelly. Odd, they don't share your last name?"

Carson didn't realize that he had been asked a question. The man stared at him; an eyebrow arched inquisitively.

"I was going to change my name," Carson answered after a moment. "Just never got around to it. Kate—" his mouth went dry when he recalled his deceased wife. "Kate and I decided that they would keep her name until I filed to have all of our names changed."

"I see," the man said after a moment. "Okay, let's see…Right, you were born in Alamogordo, New Mexico on June 12th, 1989, to Derrick and Peggy Tanner. Your father served in the Air Force as well, from 1987 to 1998. And it says here…oh, I'm sorry."

Carson detected sorrow in the man's voice, which admittedly caught him off-guard. He knew what the man had read but was surprised that he seemed to be genuinely saddened by it.

"I'm sorry to hear about your father, son" the man said sadly, his grey eyes fixed on Carson. He looked down at the folder and, after a moment, continued. "Father committed suicide twelve months ago, which is a contributing factor to your impending medical evaluation board."

"Wait, what?" Carson asked. Nobody had said anything about that.

"You didn't know?" the man asked. Once again, he seemed genuine. He sat back and ran a hand over his face. "Christ, son. You've had a rough go if it, haven't you?"

Carson wasn't sure if the man's approach was meant to put him at ease or to throw him off. He sure *seemed* genuine. "I guess so."

The man leaned forward, and his expression hardened. "So many people around you seem to be meeting a horrible end."

The change in demeanor rocked Carson. He had not been prepared for the shift.

"First your father, then your sister attempts suicide," the man continued. "Lucky for her, it wasn't successful. Then there's the security officer near your kids' elementary school."

Carson's heart began to pound, making his already intense headache worsen immensely. The man had briefly closed the folder and was dramatically counting on his fingers.

All the guilt that Carson had been burying rose quickly to the surface. He already blamed himself for the deaths of those innocent people but hearing it from someone else made him intensely sick to his stomach. He wished, in that moment, that the man would pull a gun and put a bullet between Carson's eyes.

"Then there's Paul Booker, his wife- "

"What the fuck are you talking about?" Carson interrupted. Paul had been fine when Carson had seen him last. Now this asshole was counting him amongst the dead? He had to be mistaken.

The man didn't react. Instead, he carried on as though Carson hadn't spoken. "Allison, and their two boys, Kevin and Andy."

"Seriously! The fuck?" Carson yelled. He had been feeling guilt, but it had quickly been replaced with rage.

"After your visit," the man began calmly. "A dozen anomalies swarmed the apartment complex. There were no survivors."

The news made the strength leave Carson's legs. He dropped heavily to the floor.

"No," Carson said quietly as he stared at the floor between his legs. "They can't be dead. They *can't* be."

"I'm afraid they are," the man said.

Carson looked up. Kate, he knew, was very dead. Her family? Probably dead too. Booker, though? They had been safe and there hadn't been anything around. This man said the monsters came shortly after he left, though. He supposed it was possible. Hell, why not? Everyone else around him was dying.

"Okay, what the fuck is going on?" Carson asked furiously with tears in his eyes, determined to divert the conversation and get some answers. He was fed up with what the asshole was insinuating. "Why am I *actually* here? You have no fucking evidence that I had anything to do with any of their deaths! Especially Booker's! You said it yourself, a bunch of 'anomalies' swarmed them. How the fuck do you assume I had anything to do with that?"

The man steepled his fingers in front of his lips, as though trying to determine how to answer. "I'll skip ahead. I'm going to assume, given the state of your vehicle and the number of belongings you had packed, that you are aware of the anomalies that have popped up all over."

"Anomalies?" Carson scoffed. "Is *that* what you fucking call those? Yeah, I am *very* aware of these 'anomalies.'"

The man seemed unphased by Carson's retort. "I suspect, then, that you have noticed that the anomalies have popped up quite a lot. I would also hazard a guess that you initially believed them to be localized to the base that you were stationed at, since you fled almost immediately. Unfortunately, they aren't. Our reports indicate that this is a global occurrence. Major cities seem to have been hit the hardest. We suspect that, if it continues, governments around the world will begin to fall in the coming weeks."

"The fuck does this have to do with me?" Carson snapped. "Shouldn't you guys be out there trying to get this shit under control?"

"Well, that's part of the problem," the man continued. "We don't know when or where these things will pop up. It seems random. Or it did. Until recently, we had no leads. Fortunately, our organization has some of the brightest people employed, and some of the most advanced technology on the planet."

The man went quiet for a moment; his gaze fixed firmly on Carson. His stare was making Carson increasingly uncomfortable.

"Okay…" Carson said slowly. "And?"

"First, let me introduce myself," the man said. The change in subject was infuriating. It had felt as though the mysterious bastard had been about to provide a grand reveal. "My name is David Andrews. I am the head of our research department. I also happen to work directly with our head of security. I had to call in a favor to have you picked up."

"That answers *so* many questions," Carson said sarcastically. "Thank you. You still didn't tell me why *I'm* here, though. And where are my fucking kids?!"

"I'm getting to that, son," the man who had identified himself as David said.

"Don't call me that," Carson snapped.

"As I was saying," the man who identified himself as David continued. "I had to call in a favor to bring you here. We suspect that you, or one of your children, may be connected to the anomalies that have been occurring. We suspected your wife, too, but recent developments have obviously ruled her out."

Carson let out a disbelieving laugh, once again refusing to let the man continue talking about his recently deceased wife. "Are you serious? How the fuck are *we* connected?"

David smirked. "I thought you might ask."

He flipped several pages in the envelope before coming to a glossy printout. He turned the folder and held it up for Carson to see. As much as he wanted to get away from the man, and his goons, Carson couldn't help but to move closer. He stared at the image before him. It showed a red grid on a black background with a pixelated shape like a colorful storm cloud in the middle.

"What you see here is something one of our sensors picked up. Without going into the science behind it, our sensors detect changes in matter, particularly *dark* matter. Think of it as a seismic reading of sorts, but instead of earthquakes this picks up shifts in our dimension."

Now Carson really laughed. "Seriously? This has got to be a joke. Dimensional sensors?"

David's smirk didn't falter. "Oh, trust me, Sergeant Tanner, I know how it sounds."

Carson stopped laughing. "You're serious."

"I am," David replied with a solemn nod. "I wish this was a joke, Sergeant Tanner. But the truth is, this is all very real.

Our technological arsenal is more advanced than any other organization on earth. We are dedicated to monitoring what we perceive as reality for anomalies. Some are of little consequence. Small dimensional rifts that shift object from one location to another, like your car keys, aren't anything to worry about. However, there are other things that are far worse. You see, Sergeant Tanner, what you know of the 'real world' is a carefully curated perception."

"That's funny," Carson said after a moment. "I mean, sure, it makes sense. Teleporting car keys. Honestly, I thought something *was* odd. There've been times I *knew* I put something somewhere, only for it to be somewhere else. I just thought it was typical forgetfulness. But teleporting objects makes more sense at this point."

David nodded, the smirk reappearing. "Well, what I'm about to tell you isn't so funny. The things that people consider myths and folklore are not entirely incorrect. Mind you, not *every* mythological creature or cryptid is real. Some are pure fiction. But unfortunately, others are not. The folklore about bigfoot is somewhat accurate. Now, bigfoot is not a big ape like people think. It is actually part of a divergent race of hominids that evolved to be subterranean. They come out occasionally, which is why some have been spotted, but they usually keep to themselves."

Carson started shaking his head. "No way. No fucking way is *bigfoot* real. Even after all the shit I've seen that one is hard to take seriously."

David's expression didn't change. "It *is* real. So are a great many other things. We don't have time right now to get into all of that, though. The reason you're here, Sergeant Tanner, is because these readings originate from where you've been." He pointed at the printout. "This one came from your address twelve hours ago."

David slid the printout from the folder and presented another, followed by several more that appeared almost identical to the first. "These ones *also* originate from your last know positions on your way to your in-law's house."

He pointed at another, though the image was significantly larger than the others. "This reading is particularly distressing. You see, all the other readings are fairly small. But *this* one? Something truly gargantuan was trying to come through. We don't know what stopped it, but we suspect that we may not be so lucky next time. Which is why we need to determine who is causing the anomalies and how to stop them. That's where you and your kids come in."

Carson stared, his mouth agape. Upon closer inspection he could make out faint roadways. Each was labeled. To his dismay, David was telling the truth. He *had* been at each location. And, from the timestamps on the printouts, he had been there when the readings had been taken.

"How?" he asked.

David sat back again. "Now *that* is the million-dollar question. Which is another reason why you're here. Not only do we monitor changes like you see in the pictures, but we do our best to remove or isolate the worst offenders. Some, like I said, are potentially world ending."

Carson stared at the pictures, his mind struggling to digest everything he was hearing. David flipped the envelope closed and Carson noticed an insignia on the cover. It was circular, with three arrows pointing inward. David stood and gestured to one of the soldiers. The soldier nodded, stepped out of sight for a moment, before returning with a bundle of orange fabric folded in his hands. David slid open a slot in the heavy door and pushed the clothing through.

Carson tentatively picked up the clothing and held it up. It was an orange jumper, just like he'd seen inmates wear on TV.

Across the chest was a barcode and a number designator. He looked up to see David staring at him, a small smile on his lips.

"Get comfortable subject Alpha Six Six Two Eight Nine," David said as he departed.

"Welcome to the SCP Foundation."

Case File 1

Subject: A-66289

Name: Carson Andrew Tanner

Age: 29

Subject appears physically healthy. A laceration was discovered on his torso that he claims he received from what he calls, Death Hoppers. Medical examination shows that no infection is present in his system and minor surgery was sufficient. The subject's mind is questionable. Subject rants about portals and monsters and is often seen curled up in the corner of his cell. He refuses to eat or speak, unless his children are brought to see him. This seems to have a calming effect on the subject for a short period of time.

When questioned about the events that took place at Beale AFB, California, on 23 February, 2019, the subject becomes aggravated. Initial interviews were unsuccessful.

Dr. [Redacted} suggested that the subject be provided with drawing materials and to be asked to draw the anomalies he had encountered. Surprisingly, this approach worked. After the initial retelling of the subject's encounters, the subject was asked to draw the anomalies. Several of these requests were met with no objection. However, two of the anomalies, when mentioned, caused the patient to experience a panic attack and the subject refuses to even try.

It is clear that the patient suffers from PTSD. Mention of the subject's wife is often met with anger or despair, though neither are consistent. The subject frequently demands to see his children. Dr. [Redacted] has stated that allowing visitation is allowed under heavy supervision.

Moreover, initial testing has shown a possible connection to the rifts when subject is unconscious. Further testing is needed.

Current classification: Euclid

Included in the following pages are copies of the drawings completed by the subject.

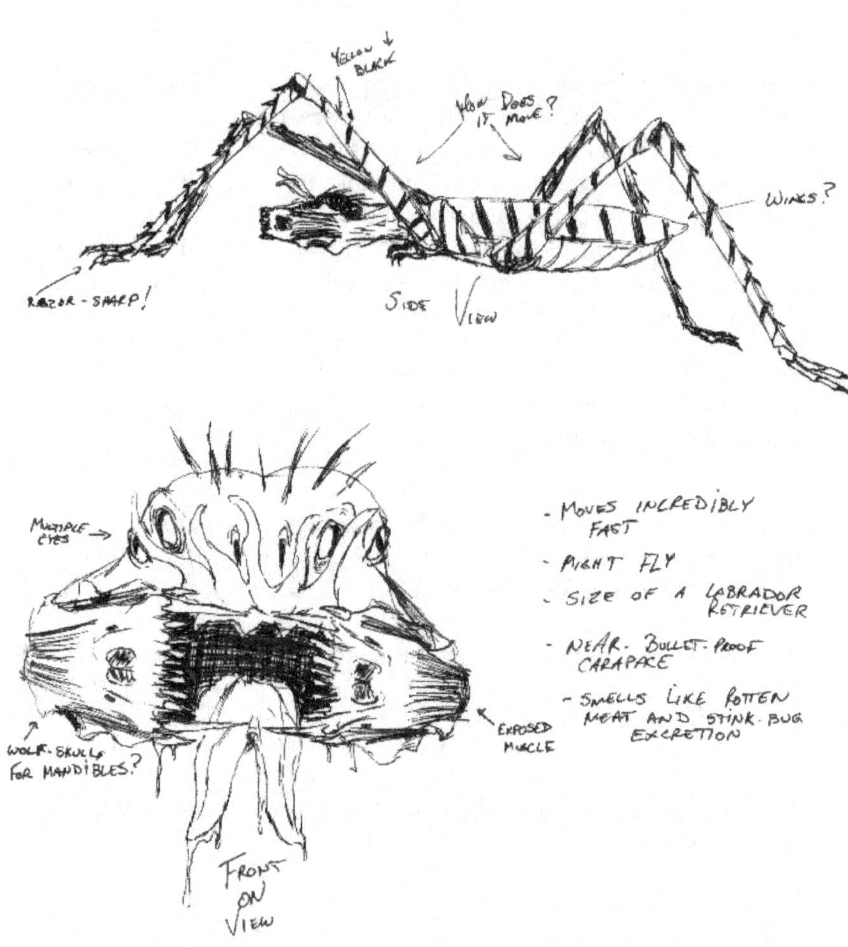

DEATH HOPPER
(I KNOW, SILLY NAME)
YELLOW & BLACK
HOW DOES IT MOVE?
WINGS?
RAZOR-SHARP!
SIDE VIEW
MULTIPLE EYES
WOLF-SKULLS FOR MANDIBLES?
EXPOSED MUSCLE
FRONT ON VIEW
- MOVES INCREDIBLY FAST
- MIGHT FLY
- SIZE OF A LABRADOR RETRIEVER
- NEAR-BULLET-PROOF CARAPACE
- SMELLS LIKE ROTTEN MEAT AND STINK-BUG EXCRETION
Carson Tassar

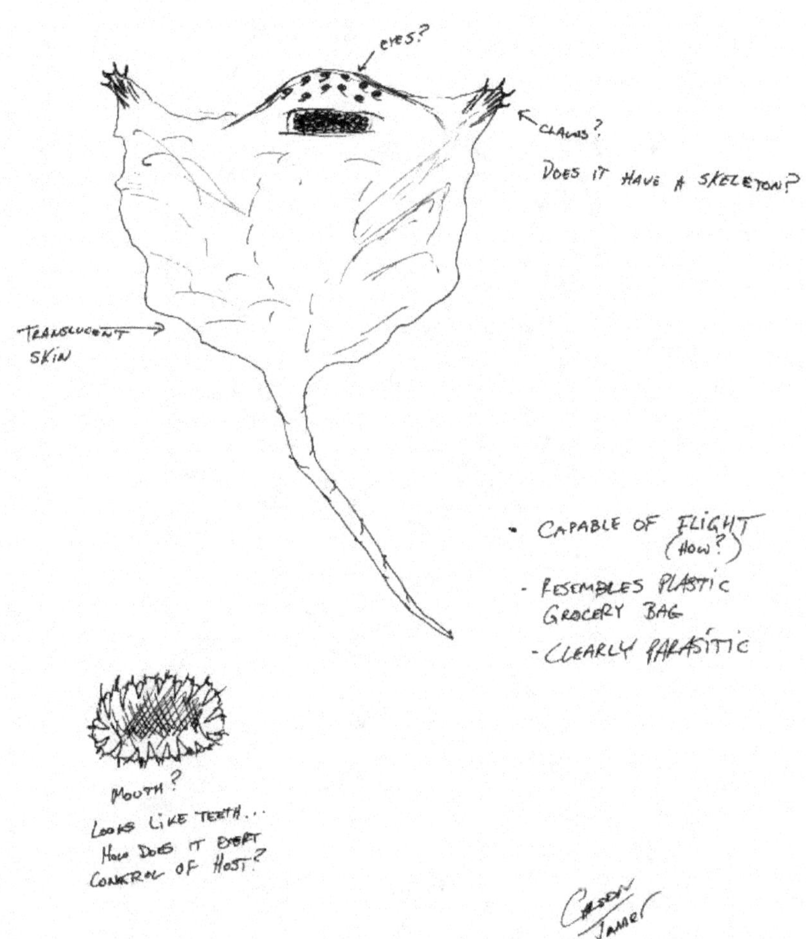

BAG MEN
(WHAT THE HELL ELSE
DO I CALL THIS?)
EYES?
CLAWS?
DOES IT HAVE A SKELETON?
TRANSLUCENT SKIN
- CAPABLE OF FLIGHT
(HOW?)
- RESEMBLES PLASTIC
GROCERY BAG
- CLEARLY PARASITIC
MOUTH?
LOOKS LIKE TEETH...
HOW DOES IT EXERT
CONTROL OF HOST?
CARSON JAMES

FUCK-NO SPIDER
(NOT 8 LEGS, BUT I COUNT IT ANYWAY)

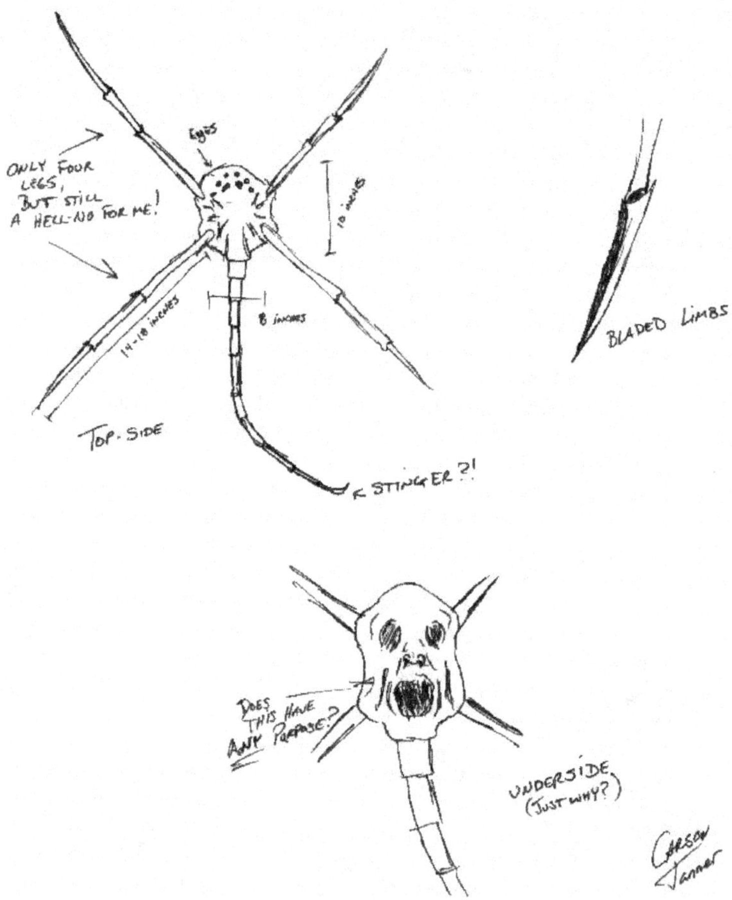

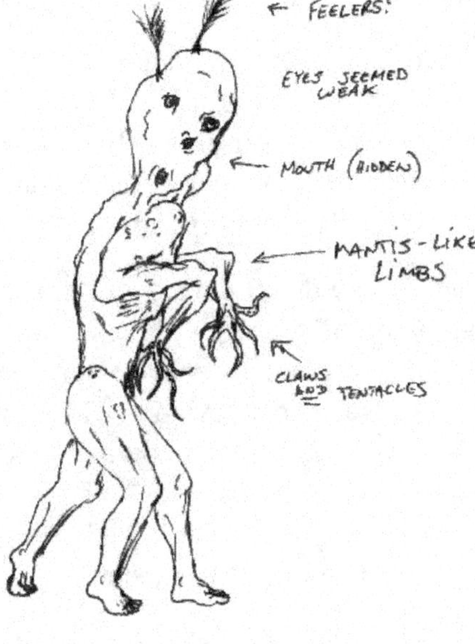

SPUDDY
(NO IDEA WHAT ELSE
TO CALL THIS)
← FEELERS?
EYES SEEMED WEAK
← MOUTH (HIDDEN)
← MANTIS-LIKE LIMBS
CLAWS AND TENTACLES
ONLY SAW ONCE...
SEEMED FRAGILE,
BUT FAST AND DEADLY.
OVER 8 FEET TALL
GREENISH-GREY

Afterword

A lot of time (eight years) has passed since I published my first novel, <u>Phoenix One</u>, a lot has happened. I suffered a terrible loss, was medically retired from the United States Air Force, moved to another state, bought a house, got divorced, sold that house, moved three times and got remarried (NOT to the same woman). A lot can happen in eight years.

I have found that rejoining the civilian world was a big adjustment. Then, almost right after, the world was hit with the COVID-19 pandemic. Everything shut down for a while. I had hoped that, after finishing my degree, I would be able to jump back in to writing. This, unfortunately, did not happen. Life did.

Having said that, I never fully stopped writing. This novel, along with the sequel to <u>Phoenix One</u> (I haven't forgotten) have been in the works. I also have a couple of others in the pipeline as well, so keep an eye out. This novel was something I started several years ago and put on the back burner when I dove full force into getting my bachelor's degree in English. Then, like I said, I ended up getting divorced. That took up far more time and energy than I naively expected.

Anyway, I jumped back into writing in the last year and was happy to finish writing this book in (for me) record time. None of this would have been possible without the support of my wife, Karina MacLeod, and my daughter, Iris.

I have been asked where I draw my inspiration from. For this novel, the idea came all the way back when I was nine years old (seriously!), and I was walking home from school. Off to my left were rows and rows of grape vines and I remember imagining a monster with grasshopper-like legs. This thing would eventually become the Death Hoppers in this novel. Very little of the creature's description has changed in all that time. From there, I began creating more and more nightmarish monsters. My plan: to come up with things that were as original as possible.

Horror has always been my favorite genre, and I was excited to jump in to writing a horror novel of my own. I hope that I can carve out my own place in the horror pantheon. Will I be successful? Who knows? What it all comes down to in the end is that I was able to fulfill a dream. That's what really matters. So, I hope you enjoyed my foray into horror. If so, I ask that you please leave a review. It really does go a long way for independent authors.

Acknowledgements

Special thanks to my wife, Karina, for the never-ending support. Without your support none of this would have been possible. Your love of all things horror helps encourage me to explore my darker side. The nightmarish things would have stayed locked in my imagination. Next, thank you to my daughter, Iris. I hope that you continue pursuing your dreams and it makes me happy that you have begun discovering a passion for writing as well. I would also like to thank my sisters, Kori and Bailey, my brother, Morgan, and my mom. Lastly, I want to thank Joshua Farestveit and Josh Vicenzi for taking the time to read the manuscript of this novel and providing your feedback.

About the Author

Chase MacLeod is an American author of both Science Fiction and Horror, as well as potentially other genres because he can't decide on any one thing. He graduated from the University of Arizona Global Campus with bachelor's degree in English. He retired from the US Air Force in 2019 and currently lives in Colorado Springs with his wife, Karina, and two kids; as well as three cats, two dogs, a snake, and eight frogs.